The Acting Duke

BOOK ONE IN THE BOUQUET SERIES

Cathy Duke

He had caught her by surprise...

"Relax. Do not move. Promise you will not scream and I will remove my hand."

She did not move for a moment, but then nodded her head affirmatively. He slowly removed his hand and turned her body to face him. And then she looked up into the familiar face of...Sebastian James Stainton, eighth Duke of Ashford.

Her mouth hung open as she gaped at the last person she expected to see just now.

"Now, close your mouth you little fool. Do you realize what a dangerous position you are in at this moment?"

His voice was soft, but deep, serious and strong. The timbre of his voice sent vibrations through her body. His hands were on her shoulders holding her so tight that she knew bruises were forming along with his verbal reprimand.

"You lying Ker...," she nearly shouted.

He placed his gloved hand back over her mouth to silence her, looking toward the street left and right to see if anyone had heard her.

"Control yourself my love, or you will alert every demon in the vicinity," he whispered in a voice not subject to debate. There was authority in his demeanor. He was not used to being disobeyed. "Behave or I will have to muzzle you."

"How dare you!" Hallie whispered back. "I did not ask for your help, Sebastian James Stainton, eighth Duke of Ashford," she spat.

A sly grin lit his face. "Ah. So you discovered that I am indeed a Duke."

Other titles by Cathy Duke

Marriage by Proxy

I would like to dedicate this book to my husband whom I met in 1968 and upon seeing him for the first time decided I would someday marry him. Love, at first sight? Almost. He has been my soul mate, my anchor, and my chief supporter in all things. He made it his life goal seeing to my happiness and, oh, Lordy, he has done that.

I give a very special dedication to my Daddy, who passed before I finished this book. He forever inspired me and showed his love for me every day. He gave me positive feedback and encouragement and always made me feel good about myself. I was very close to him, especially the last two years of his life, but when he passed, I realized how much each moment with him meant to me.

Acknowledgements

Family and friends were instrumental in making my books successful. I am forever grateful especially to Bonnie Reichle, who is my constant cheerleader. Also Bruce and Leslie McClung, Tiffany Anderson, Pam Boutsaboualoy, Brandi and Sandra Daniels, Vi Aranda, Judy Hale, Carol Sims, Debbie Ganley, Lynn Heltmann, Sandi Buehner, Mani Ryan, and Travis and Cindy Anderson for their special support. A special thanks to my editor Jennifer Whitelaw and to my cover artist Patricia "Trish" Schmitt, Pickme. Also unique in my life are those special people who keep me inspired -- my grandchildren, Brittany, Austin, Hunter and Ryder. A great grandson, Tristan, has just joined the family.

Chapter 1

Drury Lane, London, January, 1870

Sebastian James Stainton, eighth Duke of Ashford, stretched his long, muscled legs out and crossed them at the ankle. His black Hessian boots were finely polished, and his tan breeches were tight, showing off finely muscled legs. Something on his left boot caught his attention, and he retracted his legs so he could reach down and flick a small speck of lint from his boot. He was meticulous, which was evident in this single gesture. He put his arms behind his head and sighed, tipping the chair back as he did so. Deep rich, chocolate brown eyes closed, his black lashes the envy of many women. He enjoyed the outdoors and rode his favorite horse daily, his skin tone and physique a testimony to his avid horsemanship. A dark shadow of a beard denied the fact that he shaved each morning without fail. He was ruggedly handsome, not as effeminate as was the style among the ton, also known as the social elite. His rugged boyish good looks weren't unnoticed by the ladies of the English ton. His obliviousness to the attention did nothing to temper his appeal. Sebastian was known as a rebel, not caring what the social-elite thought and didn't hide his distaste for the negative energy the ton pulsed toward those they disfavored. He was careful, however, with his reputation for the sake of his family and especially his mother, whom he adored. He walked a fine line between acceptable and trouble maker, nearly a scoundrel, but not quite.

He stared at his brother who was attentively applying stage make-up to his face. Sebastian was fascinated.

Pure entertainment.

Sebastian never rushed to conclusions, and he liked to study his subject before forming judgment. He was a good and thoughtful judge of character. He practiced being solemn for practical reasons. It never benefited to display one's emotions. His training to the title was thorough in that regard. He continued to stoically study his brother.

"You are much too serious, brother," Alex said between brush strokes to his forehead. "Any idiot can tell us apart just by your sullen mood. You must not take life so seriously," Alex muttered between chuckles. He was inspecting his make-up and peering into a mirror, which dwarfed the small dressing room allotted actors. His eyes narrowed on his artistry. His brother, Sebastian, watched with casual indifference.

"I am the eldest and the one to set an example. You can afford to be jolly and fare-thee-well, as the spare. What worries have you, besides when to rehearse your next part or what actress to dilly-dally with next?"

"I have worries, just as you do. It is how you deal with your troubles that counts, brother. I don't allow my problems to get the better of me. Besides, you are just five minutes older and not so much wiser, I think," Alex laughed at his identical twin.

Very few, if any, could tell them apart but five-minute lead makes all the difference to inheriting a title. Nevertheless, even their mother struggled at times when they were dressed out of character. For the most part, Sebastian always dressed the part of a Duke, and there was no mistaking him from Alex. His dark hair was streaked with several shades of auburn that glittered red in the sun and slicked back in a neat queue. Alex ran his hands through hair streaked with white powder.

"I have offered to do a switch if you are bored," Alex teased mischievously. His dimples were pronounced as he allowed his grin to widen, begging his brother to take the challenge.

Sebastian had dimples too, but since he nearly never smiled, they were a mystery characteristic not many had seen. He often cracked a sardonic grin, but not the honest, heartfelt grin that unleashed the dimples he so disliked. He didn't fancy himself whimsical.

"We are far past our Eton university days and those stunts we orchestrated for amusement. It was too easy to fool our teachers by switching places. What sport is there in that? Besides I doubt you would last a day at overseeing tenants, managing estates, writing reports, and putting up with she-nanigans in business, not to mention disputes between the hired help."

"It would be acting, which I excel at, if I do say so myself, dear brother. Besides I bobbled around beside you and Father as you were being groomed. I am not a total idiot, after all. I do, however, have you to thank for my dream come true, Sebastian. Do not think I shall ever forget your generosity." Alex gazed at Sebastian with affection, waiting to see if Sebastian received the message.

Sebastian waved an arm in denial at his brother. While their father was alive Alex would never have brought out in the open his love of the theatre. Second sons were expected to buy a commission in the military or serve as a vicar. Alex knew his father had a heart condition and respected his father enough to hold silent on his unusual priorities. He went to university as did Sebastian, and behaved in a suitable manner to please his father. His desire to grace the professional stage might have caused an apoplexy to his beloved father. Only his twin understood. So, he buried his dreams for the time being.

Only when his father, the seventh Duke of Ashford, died of a heart attack two years ago did Alex approach the new Duke, his brother, about his desire to pursue the theatre in earnest. It was important to Alex to get his brother's approval, although not necessary. He did not regret being five minutes younger and thus the second son. Their personalities were perfectly suited as they were. And well they both knew it. Besides, there were no jealousies between them thanks to the loving attention of Sebastian, who valued his family.

Sebastian had convinced their mother to support Alex in his career on Drury Lane. Without her husband, Sebastian could influence her thinking just as their father had once done. Only in this case he was taking a more liberal view than his father would have. Sebastian had taken to being the head of the family with vigor, and creating peace and well-being among all of them was paramount to him. He bought his mother a townhouse in London. He could have set her up in the dowager house in Kent, but she preferred the busy life style of London. He did not want her under foot in his own townhouse entertaining her various charities and matchmaking mamas, which was the official family residence. It would have disrupted his peace and focus.

Sebastian's generosity was not limited to his mother. He bought Alex a residence of his own as well as their younger brother, Derrick, who was a detective for CID (Criminal Investigation Department) on a limited income. The Duke was not expected to share his wealth with his family, but he did. He wanted them all close at hand and made certain they had the means to do so. His honesty, integrity, and support of family were paramount to him.

"Mother is in the Stainton box with her cronies tonight. She would not miss an opening night, you know. Nice touch, by the way, throwing her a kiss upon your last bow." Sebastian gave his brother one of his rare smiles. "You do that every performance she attends?"

Alex nodded as he turned in his chair to regard his brother. "When I saw the joy in her expression the first time I did that, I could not resist doing it each time. It was quite well received in my last production, as you mentioned, so I will not disappoint tonight." He chuckled in remembrance. "You know, she never disappoints me. She grins like a Cheshire cat and makes certain her friends are witness to it. But changing the subject since you avoid my question…, if you could be me for a few hours, what would you do?"

"Well, I would not put my arse on the Drury Lane stage, of that I am certain." He gave Alex an affectionate smile and then shook his head slowly in denial. After a moment of silence, Sebastian grew thoughtful. "Truly, Alex, you amaze me. You see the good in everyone, and nothing ever seems to challenge your constant sense of humor. Troubles seem to bring you joy, as if you look forward to solving them. You depress me with all the glee you wring out of each day. How long does it take you to memorize all those blasted lines? I am lucky to retain a poem or two. You go about it as if it were easy to learn so much for one part. I can remember a quote or two of Shakespeare, but you memorize the entire play!"

"I get into character, and the lines make sense to what is going to happen…it really is quite reasonable, actually." He smiled and shrugged.

"I remember in university you could not retain facts to save your soul…and now this." He stretched his arms to encompass the room.

Alex stopped his task and turned to stare at Sebastian. "You concern me. You seem to be in a dark place. I rarely see you laugh. Are you that unhappy? You are actually morose most of the time in point of fact. What about Marlene…does she not bring you satisfaction, at least? She is quite the beauty, with all sorts of men drooling over her. They all envy you her attention."

"That's over." When Alex looked surprised, Sebastian sighed and shrugged his shoulders with discontentment. "She was getting too possessive. It happens if the relationship lasts too long. They see wedding bells and babies and their bloody internal clocks ticking away. They natter on and on until one must give up or go mad. If that is not bad enough, there are all the matchmaking mamas chasing me around, hoping I will notice their eligible daughters who are barely out of the school room. It is all quite exhausting."

"But Sebastian, you take the title seriously. Surely you see the need to marry. You aren't getting any younger. Why not marry? Why not fill the nursery now while you are young enough to bounce a son on your knee?"

Sebastian laughed. "I am *still* just five minutes older than you. I am not decrepit. Besides, I cannot imagine a single woman I know that I could tolerate in marriage."

Sebastian looked around the small dressing room with interest. Costumes hung on hooks, feathered hats sat stacked up on top of the only dresser. The room smelled of grease paint and flowers. A vase of roses adorned the dressing table where Alex sat.

"Who sent you the roses? A fan? That Viscount's daughter who attends your performances and stares at you in adoration? What is her name? Cicely?"

Alex sent his brother an amused smile. "Her name is Cicely Prescott, and she is only interested in Shakespeare, not me. But the roses are not from her. Those roses are from our beloved mother. Thanks to you, she has gotten into the role of supportive mother. I would never have believed she would give me her blessing in this career choice."

"And here I thought an admirer was hot on your heels."

Alex laughed. "I am too serious about the theatre to draw interest from a marriage- minded-minx. Flirtations…perhaps. They amuse me. An actress or two has warmed my bed without promises of marriage. That suits me well. Are you staying for the performance?"

Sebastian sighed. "I have a prior commitment. The Home Office has asked me to attend the Bickford ball."

The Secretary, who ran the Home Office for Internal Affairs sometimes, asked for assistance from the aristocracy they could trust. These titled individuals were in a prime position to collect information.

Since the Home Office did policing for England as well as Wales, they were especially concerned about national security and took that responsibility seriously. Sebastian knew the Secretary well, and they shared the same values and concerns for the country.

Oliver Danders would show up at social events and nod at Sebastian, which was a sign they needed to talk…soon. It was always subtle, but clearly understood…one of the many silent signals Sebastian recognized.

"Who are you after now? Need I warn any of my friends?" Alex responded smirking at his brother, who seemed deep in thought.

"Alas, your friends are safe from me. It seems an American assassin has landed on our shores. They think he is after a fellow American businessman here visiting relatives. I am to locate him and see what I can find out about his mission. Perhaps prevent it. Everyone will be at the Bickford ball, and it is a perfect atmosphere for gathering information. Guests will be drinking and, with entertainment and dancing, the information will be flowing freely."

"Who is the lucky bastard being hunted?"

"A man named Martin who brought his four daughters and wife to stay with English relatives. Probably looking for titled husbands, as all rich Americans tend to do. Harriet and Joseph Pritchard are the relatives...and well-respected....The wife, Harriet Pritchard, is a cousin to Alice Martin. I believe Harriet Pritchard is on the literary committee with Mother."

"I wonder what Martin did to draw an assassin on his tail. Americans are obnoxious, but that's not a crime after all."

"Well, as you can speculate, there is a lot to find out, and need I remind you that all this is confidential."

"Of course. I do not leak secrets about any of your missions. But as usual, I offer any help...."

Sebastian nodded. He knew his brother was good at keeping secrets. He also was an excellent source of information. Many people crossed his path at the theatre and more than once he had plucked some information out of a theatre patron.

Sebastian was very secretive about his relationship with the Home Office. If it got out what he was doing for Oliver Danders, his cover was compromised and therefore he would be deemed useless. He trusted his brother, and his brother had the ability to think through things as Sebastian did and sometimes together they could solve problems faster. Sebastian enjoyed talking to Alex and sharing information. It was like an extension of himself. Their minds could lock onto something with tremendous fortitude.

Just then, a soft knock sounded at the door, and it opened to reveal an old weathered seaman turned staged manager. "Sorry to bother ye mate, but we have a situation. Maria is stewed on whisky again, and I don't know if I can get her sober before the performance. She listens to you...."

Elmore was not as old as he looked. The sun and sea-faring days had taken their toll on his weathered face. His hair was streaked five shades of blonde by the sun, cut by Elmore himself to save the money. He limped from a long- ago injury during his sailing days and found himself well suited in the colorful setting of the theatre. His craggy face was a mass of wrinkles and crevices worn by a life in the sun.

The actresses adored Elmore, and he was protective of them and gave them advice whether they requested it or not. It was good, sound advice, and he was well-respected for it. He had kicked out many an unwanted fan on behalf of his little darlings, as he called them. He was their agent, their priest for confessions, and their chief problem solver.

"Seems I am needed to save a damsel in distress." Alex winked at his brother. "Wait for me to return. I will just be but a few minutes. She has done this before...." Alex rose out of his chair and started for the door. "Do you have strong coffee ready, Elmore?"

"Aye, sir. All ready as well as a cold tub of water waiting in her dressing room." Just then, the sound of pottery smashing followed by a shriek. Elmore sighed. "She has taken to smashing things. Worse than I thought. I better get me broom."

Sebastian looked bemused as he watched his brother disappear out the door. Alex led an interesting life. It suited him. None of his brothers were a problem. No gambling, no debts. He was indeed fortunate. He sat on a fortune his father had protected, and he had increased the family holdings and assets by nearly double. He used his money to invest in shipping and other promising ventures that had paid handsomely.

Another knock on the door.

It did not open so Sebastian responded. "Come."

He watched the door as it opened, and a vivacious face peeked in. She was obviously a lady, come to give her blessings to Alex, but before he could say anything, she floated gracefully into the small room, her flashing green eyes on his face. She smiled at him, and he was suddenly stricken by her uncommon natural beauty.

She was wearing an emerald green velvet gown in the latest fashion, her flaming red hair in an artfully- designed swirl of shiny curls on her head. Two thick curls hung on her shoulder, bouncing with every movement she made. A saucy hat with ostrich feathers was perched on the side of her head. Her mouth was pink and a little fuller than fashionable, but when she smiled, Sebastian was awe struck and speechless. Her beauty radiated in all directions of the room. It was as if she threw sunshine everywhere she stepped.

As she circled the room, in graceful strikes, her eyes on Sebastian the entire time, a subtle scent of roses tickled his nose. Familiar. Yes, his mother wore it, and he liked it. But now the scent was arousing. Somehow different on her.

"Oh, please Mr. Stainton, do not throw me out. I can see you are not dressed yet for the performance, but I must talk to you, and I only have a moment before I am missed. You just do not know how nervous I am to be here."

She looked around and gestured her hands to encompass the dressing room. Again she looked at Sebastian and smiled, her eyes sparkling like emeralds. She seemed to be an observant woman, taking in the details of the room with intelligent eyes and yet never losing her focus on the man sitting before her.

"You see, my business is urgent, or I would not be here. Of course, a lady would never…well, I mean I just need a moment of your time and then I shall get back to my box. Surely you can spare a moment of your time for me."

Another smile shot to her face, which was meant to convince him to listen to her request. She seemed a flirt, but it came so naturally that he gaged it to be her normal persona. It seemed an innocent gesture.

Sebastian was mesmerized by her chatter. She was remarkable. Delightful.

"You are an American," he stated without thought. He wanted to roll his eyes at that intelligent remark. Of course she was American…just to listen to her would validate that fact.

Her flamboyant gestures were pure American, and what the ton detested most. He smiled at the thought. The ton was a reference to high society, the fashionable elite that had incredibility rigid rules governing them with double standards that made Sebastian crazy. But no matter. One had to adhere to the constraints of hierarchy or suffer the social consequences. She was a contradiction to his usual tastes in women. But, watching her made him wonder and question his tastes in women.

"I know." She was laughing at him. "I am afraid it is true. Fresh from the boat. American since birth. Cannot help it." Her lips came together in a near pout.

Again, her eyes sparkled with mirth. She was teasing him. It was impossible not to smile when in her presence. She was simply delightful. She carried joy with her like a bouquet of spring flowers. She was like a magnet drawing him to her as if she had some magical power over him. He could not wipe the silly grin from his face. He must look like a fool grinning like a baboon. Time to take some caution and control of his reactions.

And yet, he found himself staring at her succulent lips, and they were most certainly succulent and luscious and in constant movement. He thought about sucking on her bottom lip and then thrusting his tongue in her mouth for a taste...Bloody hell, he needed to get control of his thoughts. She was talking like a magpie, and he had no idea what she was saying. She was animated, vivacious, and operating with tremendous energy that left him breathless.

Remembering his manners, Sebastian belatedly stood up as was customary in the presence of a lady standing in the room. He gestured toward the chair vacated by Alex just moments before in front of the mirror.

"Please, be seated," he announced.

"Oh, you mean in your chair...I couldn't..."

"Please be seated there in the actor's chair. The chair of honor. Why not introduce yourself?"

Sebastian was not eager to disappoint her in revealing that he was not Alex as yet. He was enjoying himself far too much and had no plans to stop the charade so soon and spoil this moment with this lovely creature. She was a breath of fresh air. She was spirited beyond any stuffy aristocrat. He was used to being bored to tears around most ladies, but this woman made him feel alive for the first time in ages. He could not stop what got his hormones stirring and exciting his mind with interest.

"Why, yes. That would be an excellent idea. I am Hallie Martin. And I already know who you are. I am very excited to see the performance tonight. I have not been to Drury Lane before. And after all, everyone is talking about your talent."

Martin. Martin? Not the Martins he was to investigate? How many Martins from America were there? "Well, Miss Martin. I am pleased to meet you."

He leaned over and took her out stretched gloved hand and kissed the air above her knuckles. He looked up from his bow and met her twinkling eyes.

"I am honored, Mr. Stainton."

She eased back into the chair and took a breath of air. She was obviously preparing for some great moment. He also sat back down in his chair across from her.

"I would like to hire your services, Mr. Stainton." A moment of uncomfortable silence followed. Then she blushed crimson and corrected herself at his amusement. "I mean as an actor, of course." She quickly broke open her fan hanging on her wrist and fanned herself. The breeze from the fan did nothing to erase her reddened face. The damage was done.

He had to contain himself from bursting with laughter. He had not been entertained so thoroughly in ages.

"I am curious, Miss Martin. Why would you need an actor?" He smiled his amusement making her even more uncomfortable. The vivacious energy was still in her, but she was slowed down by the task of asking for his assistance. She grew serious with focus. Such a change in attitude. The energy was still there, but subdued and totally under control. How curious.

"My father is hell bent...ah, excuse my language sir. My father wants me to marry a Duke or Viscount...a title. I do not want to marry at this time, but I thought if I could distract him with perhaps the thought that I was being courted by a Duke, well, that he would turn his attention elsewhere."

She seemed pleased with herself and a satisfied smile graced her face. Her face was a perfect oval, her eyes heavily lashed, but she was not batting her eye lashes in flirtation as so many debutantes were known to do. In fact, she was unpretentious and seemed oblivious of her natural beauty. Her vibrant personality filled the room and made Sebastian uneasy. His pulse was beating a mile a minute.

Sebastian was actually aroused, he realized. She was not his usual type, he kept thinking, as if that would ease the tension in his head. He stayed away from innocent debutantes. There was nothing except marriage on their minds. There was a huge risk for "compromise," which would land him in the parson's mousetrap. Many had tried and failed at trapping him.

He must keep his wits about him, an internal voice urged him. And the red hair. Different from his usual tastes...blonde, brunette...but not red.

"I see. Did you know it is a serious offense to impersonate a Duke?"

She seemed surprised by his comment. "But you are an excellent actor. I assure you, this would be between you and me. I would never reveal this...er... plot to anyone. I just want a little time to enjoy London and not have my father planning my life for me. I simply want to distract him temporarily."

"You see no flaws in this plan of yours?"

"I do not." Her chin came up a notch with her comment. A stubborn trait. Perhaps her red hair meant a temper too.

"What happens when he finds out about your little deception, hum?"

Sebastian looked intently into her eyes which seemed to have turned dark green, blending with her gown perfectly. Her cheeks were flushed a pretty pink. She didn't seem to be accustomed to deception, which was a point in her favor. But there was a moment of silence while she seemed to gather her thoughts. Sebastian had to suppress his physical attraction to this woman and now.

Yes, suppress the attraction before his breeches give him away which seemed rather imminent.

"Well, I thought we would decide we were not suited and go our separate ways." She seemed a little doubtful, but smiled tentatively.

"You think your father would accept that story?"

"And why would he not? It happens. People find they are not compatible and ..."

"You think perhaps your father might put a gun to my head and force me to the alter? That happens too."

"Absolutely not. Father is not a violent man. He wants me to be happy, of course."

"Then why the deception? Just tell him you want to select your own husband." Women. Such a hair-brained scheme. Utterly ridiculous. Simple communication would solve her issue with her father.

Anger crossed her face, her eyes glittered fire and her mouth moved but no words came out. She was enraged, and he had to give her credit. She was magnificent. Fireworks!

"You do not have to accept my offer for employment. I am prepared to offer you more than you make here to do this small acting job. I did not come here to argue with you or to find fault with my plan."

She stood up as if to leave. Her eyes had turned so dark, they seemed nearly black. Redheads were known for their tempers, and she did not disappoint. What drama. The play was here, not on the stage.

Sebastian held up a hand to stop her and stood before her, blocking her path to the door. Actually, this was a perfect situation to study her father for the Home Office. He just questioned the intelligence of such a scheme. So typically female. It seemed like a spider's web that might trap him in an uncomfortable situation. His gut told him to back off...but he suddenly found himself impulsive. A new trait for him and certainly unfamiliar.

"Miss Martin. I accept your offer. Now how do you presume we get started?"

Chapter 2

Two weeks earlier

*H*allie sat on the large canopied bed beside her younger sister Violet. They were sharing this beautiful guest bedroom in the house of their Aunt Harriet Pritchard. Technically not their aunt, since Harriet was a cousin to their mother, however, it was easier to refer to them as Aunt and Uncle, than cousins once removed.

Soft blue velvet drapes hung on the tall windows that faced a colorful, spacious garden. Wallpaper enhanced the blue theme with bouquets of spring flowers in blue and yellow. The furniture was French and delicate, all upholstered in rich satins and brocades of various flower prints using blue of all shades with an accent of yellow. The room was spacious, allowing two guests ample room, including a seating area, as well as a cushioned window seat overlooking the garden that was a favorite of Violet's. The little alcove was perfect as a hiding place for reading, but should she venture a peek out the window....a colorful garden greeted her. Perfect.

Poppy and Iris shared the room next door and were properly paired since Hallie was closest to Violet in age and sisterly devotion. Rose, the eldest of the Martin daughters, was happily married to their father's assistant in business and presently residing in America. Rose's husband, Daniel Stewart, was home in Ohio taking care of the Martin business during the absence of Benjamin Martin. The Martins came to visit their Aunt and Uncle every other year in London. Hallie's mother, Alice, was affectionately close to her cousin Harriet.

This year was different, however. Hallie was of an age to enjoy the adult attractions in London. She was looking forward to going to the theatre and some of the grand balls of the aristocracy, not to mention shopping in London's finest stores.

This was the grand season in London. Parliament had just finished its sessions and it was time to hold public festivities and capture some of the members of Parliament before they retired to their country estates. Her father, Benjamin Martin, was here from America just for that purpose. He was a proud American aristocrat, successful in business, and there was quiet interest from many English aristocrats to do business privately with him. After all, the titled would not publicly show they were interested in such a common pursuit as business, as that would be unacceptable and uncouth in their culture. It was common knowledge that many of the titled were lacking funds to manage their entailed properties, and their estates were in poor decline. They frowned, however, on the idea of actually working.

Instead, many would look for brides with funds to put back into their estates and Benjamin Martin was rich. For his part, Benjamin knew he could buy a title for his daughters. Cits," as they were known, were unacceptable and yet tolerated for their wealth and opportunity. A rich heiress was very much in demand, and the cash-strapped titled were prepared to ignore the stigma against people who worked for a living, sometimes even the dreaded Americans.

Hallie sighed and looked at her sister, who was reading a Jane Austin novel she had snatched from her uncle's library this morning before she was caught under her mother's watchful eye. Her mother thought Violet read too much and wanted her to enjoy a social life.

"You are in love with love, Violet. We are in London. You must put your reading aside and live in this magnificent city while there is time."

Was Violet even listening? She wore spectacles just for reading. It did not distract from her simple beauty. Violet had red-blonde hair, not as dark and rich as Hallie's hair. But she did have the purest white complexion and pale pink lips, which were moving with the words she read so intently.

Their mother was forever telling Violet to remove her spectacles or she would never attract the interest of a suitor. Violet had learned to ignore that vital piece of advice since it held no importance to her. There was a sprinkling of pale freckles across her nose, on which her mother was forever trying to place a little sprinkle of rice powder. It seemed her freckles too would most certainly discourage a suitor. That suited her just fine.

"The city is dirty and smelly. You cannot even see the sky at night. I feel sorry for the stars that are lost in the dung of the sky. Fog, rain, soot, mildew…miserable. I do not see the attraction you do," Violet mumbled as she marked the page she was reading with her finger and glanced up at her sister. "I will put down my books when there is something worthwhile to capture my attention."

"Perhaps you will meet your true Darcy right here in London and he will sweep you off your feet."

Violet rolled her eyes and sighed in defeat. That was an unlikely occurrence if there ever was one!

Hallie smiled at the thought. Her sister was not moved by the sentiment. She was a realist after all, not a dreamer. She loved the world of imagination in books, but did not confuse that with real life.

"I admit there is abundant culture in London, and I do love culture. But I deplore the crowds, the ton…people who are too eager to judge and find one lacking. It is all too pretentious for me." Violet sighed. "If I could visit a grand library, or see theatre with no other in attendance, that I would do. I dislike the snobbery and false conversations one must practice in society."

Violet smiled shyly at having shared her unusual feelings with her sister. But she trusted Hallie. She did not have friends, and her sister understood her and was patient with her oddities. Although Violet did not think she, herself, was odd. As long as there were books yet to read and quiet places to meditate, Violet was content. She loved the world of imagination she found in books. She could lose herself in her books and escape some of the harsh realities of life.

"Perhaps, if you were royalty, Violet...all that could happen for you. You could reserve all the sights just for you alone to enjoy."

Hallie giggled at the thought. There was a brief silence while they both reflected for a moment.

"I abhor the idea of a loveless marriage, not to mention a man having complete control over you as a woman. Imagine...a husband could take a punch at your face, and basically he has the right to do so. A woman is the property of her husband, for goodness sakes. You are fortunate that Mama does not needle you to seek a husband yet." Hallie turned to see what her sister thought of that reality. Although as an after-thought she had to give her mother some much deserved credit. "Perhaps she's more sensible than we give her credit for."

"You mean the same mother who named us all after flowers? We are fortunate indeed to have decent flower names. What if you were Daffodil instead of Hyacinth? At least Hallie is a decent nickname. Your nickname could have been "Daffy," for heaven sakes. Why would Father allow her to name us as callously as if we were a bouquet of flowers?" Violet asked with some degree of earnest insistence. "It's a good thing she stopped at five daughters, for goodness sakes. I only dread what names would come next. Perhaps Peculiar."

"Petunia," Hallie offered. Hallie looked at her sister and frowned in thought. "Father wanted sons. Can you imagine what she might have named them? Instead he was presented a bouquet of flowers."

"Does he care so little for daughters that he sat silent when she named us all after flowers?" Violet looked at Hallie for her thoughts.

"He loves Mama so. He could not break her heart to even mention that she has lost a button or two." Violet laughed at Hallie's words and then Hallie too burst into laughter.

"I can live with it, if you can." Violet retorted. "Have you talked to Poppy lately?"

"No. I mean only of her shopping escapades…What is going on with her now?" Hallie asked.

Poppy was their younger, seventeen-year-old sister. Not so long ago, she had wanted to be a nun…even though they were not Catholic. She was searching for her purpose in life; although their mother would constantly tell her she had no more purpose than simply being Poppy her beloved daughter. Was that not enough? They were all relieved when she stopped talking about the convent. To say Poppy was impressionable was a vast understatement. She could easily get caught up in any bit of conversation and be completely gullible to any story. Iris, the youngest of the Martin daughters at twelve years of age, once bragged that she was able to convince Poppy there was a breed of dog in Wales that could fly, not very high in the sky, mind you, and was very desirable for catching birds…such as ducks.

"She now thinks she is a reincarnation of a woman who lived a hundred years ago." At the surprised expression from Hallie, she continued. "She read a book about reincarnation… something to do with the Hindu religion. She is certain that she feels the soul of this woman within her. She has experienced deja vu...like she has been places and done things before. Mother is nearly mindless with worry. Poppy is very certain of her beliefs this time, if you care to listen to her. Someone needs to get that book away from her. Perhaps find a more proper book of ideas to influence her."

Hallie was speechless and then she slowly smiled. "This too will pass." She laid down on the bed, her legs dangling over the edge. She stretched her arms over her head and groaned. "Everything would be perfect if Father was not so motivated to marry me off to a titled English gentleman. I am not ready to marry, and I definitely do not want an arranged marriage."

"Father is very set on this thought, I know. He thinks our money will buy this for you, and it is one thing he does not have, and wants. Now it is an obsession with him." Violet muttered as she turned a page. "Do you really think Father would force you into a loveless marriage?"

"I do not honestly know. But I have so much to do, so many places to see, and I cannot imagine anyone I would want to spend the rest of my days with."

"Mama says none of that is of importance. The only purpose a woman has is to be a wife and mother."

Hallie sat up and looked at Violet with disgust. "Now look who you are quoting. The same mama you ignore most of the time. It is important to me, I tell you. I need to find a way to get Father off this quest of his. I want some freedom to do as I please, as we all do, I might add. It is all so much poppycock."

"Please don't turn him on me, Hallie. I am quite content at the moment. I am ill prepared for a battle with Father on this subject."

"But that is exactly my point. I am content as I am also. I want to see London. I want to attend the theatre, go to balls, concerts, and museums. I do not want to be tied to a courtship to please Father and his need to gain more."

"Maybe you ought to play his game and simply find a title tolerable to spend some time with sightseeing. It sounds like all those places you want to see can be accomplished with courting."

Hallie tilted her head in thought. "That is not a bad idea. But I do not know of someone I could trust enough to..."

"You must hire someone so that you can control, sister." Violet muttered so softly she was hardly heard.

"Ahhh. But I still do not know of someone to hire that I could trust."

"An actor would suffice, I would think. They are in the trade of pretending, are they not?"

Hallie smiled and nodded. "As always, you have brilliant ideas, Violet. I am to attend the theatre in two weeks. I shall approach that talented actor everyone speaks of...what is his name?"

"But will he not be recognized as that talented actor?"

"He is always in face paint. If he was dressed as a Duke..."

"This is complex Hallie. The aristocracy knows its Dukes. Why not hire him for the country activities in Kent? That way he could perhaps pull it off."

Hallie was pacing the floor, tapping her finger on her chin trying to figure this out. It had to be planned carefully. She did not want to get caught. But this ruse could distract her Father just a little to give her time to have some freedom and perhaps meet someone to her liking.

"Just do not involve me in this plot. I want to remain invisible for the time being. I do not relish being caught in the center of a drama."

Hallie stopped pacing and frowned. "I will approach Alex Stainton, yes, that is the one... before the performance when we attend the theatre. I will excuse myself from the Pritchard box to powder my nose and none will be the wiser."

"Do you have a plan how long this masquerade will last and just when you will launch it?" Violet asked as she closed her book realizing she was not going to be allowed a moment of peace to read.

Violet liked to get into her stories, allow them to swallow her whole and divorce her from reality for a short time. She so loved to read. But alas, once Hallie got going with one of her-hair-brained schemes, she was not in a position to concentrate. Never mind that she actually conceived this scheme. She removed her spectacles and folded them neatly and put them in her pocket. She had pockets designed in all her gowns specifically for her spectacles. Her mother gave her a pound of trouble for that, but she refused to wear a gown without someplace to keep her spectacles. She turned to Hallie to give her full attention.

"I hope you are prepared for this, for it is quite complex and could cause you a great amount of grief."

"I know. It might be the grandest, most complex of all my schemes to date. I do not know how much to offer him in payment."

Violet rubbed her temples as she often did when she was perplexed.

"What exactly are the expectations? An event or two? A walk in the park? Then you must determine the value. Not too much, but enough to get his attention and keep him on the task. And do not pay him until he has accomplished the task successfully."

Hallie looked at Violet with respect and gratitude. Violet was just two years younger than Hallie and yet her eighteen years seemed so mature. Hallie always thought Violet an old soul.

"Yes, you are right to see all the pit-falls and crevices of this scheme. A great deal of thought and planning will save me some trouble, to be certain. I think it best to hire him for one event, to be safe. I can always ask for another event, however I might be able to keep the illusion I am seeing him without really having him at more than one event. And so that he is not subject to suspect, I will ask him to attend the country event in Kent where so many of the attendees are American business people and neighbors of Aunt and Uncle."

Violet nodded her approval. "Yes, that just might work."

"I have it!" Hallie turned with glee to see Violet's face fall. Violet has seen this look before and it means she is somehow involved in the plan. "We will go to Gunter's for ice and I will meet him there first. He is so enamored with me that he wants to attend the Kent country event to see me again! Is that not brilliant? One event, two meetings in all."

"Not the part where I am with you. I was hoping to not participate in this, Hallie."

But she could see that she was not going to be able to get out of this. She sighed a deep, soul-wrenching sigh.

"Oh, blast it, Hallie." Violet loved to curse in Hallie's presence for the right effect. But it made no difference other than to give Violet a small amount of satisfaction.

"That is it, just the one visit for ice and you buy. I do so love the maple flavor." Violet would negotiate what she could, again for some little satisfaction.

When Hallie nodded, Violet opened her book again and turned to the last page. Her finger scanned several lines and her lips were moving as she read intently as if she had excused Hallie from her mind and thoughts. A slow smile curved her lips.

"Tell me you have not skipped to the end of the book and to read the ending." Hallie said as if she were scandalized.

Violet looked up and rolled her eyes at Hallie.

"Of course I read the end. I want to know in advance if the heroine gets the hero or not. I want to be prepared to cry or sleep better at night. On the other hand, if I read an ending I do not think I can tolerate, I quit the book altogether." She smiled in satisfaction at her answer, and then gave a look at Hallie daring her to oppose her views.

"But that is a form of cheating, is it not? I would say even dishonest. Why would you read the middle if you already know what happens? That is just ridiculous."

"Because I care about the characters, Hallie. I just want to know what to expect. I assure you it does not spoil anything. Besides, I have read this book before."

Hallie looked astonished and threw up her hands. When Hallie turned away, Violet grinned mischievously. Oh, how she loved to torture her sister, who she loved dearly.

Chapter 3

Pritchard townhouse, London, two weeks later, hours prior to the Bickford ball

Alice Martin still turned heads even though she was over four decades in age. Her vibrant red hair was perfectly styled showing very few white hairs. Her eyes were still a brilliant green and her rounded figure only added to her allure. She was not vain and dismissed her physical beauty as not important or of interest to her. Alice was a firm believer in beauty coming from the soul.

She sat in her sitting room, which adjoined the guest bedroom she and her husband shared in her cousin Harriet's home, working on her needlepoint with an eye on her husband who was pacing in front of her. She would look up now and again as though to make certain he had not changed course. Also to let him know that she could do two things at once.

"Benny, you must relax and think of your health. This cannot be good for you. You take your business far too seriously. We are rich. We need no more. I would like to see you relax and enjoy life as is your due. How important could this be? Certainly not worth a heart seizure."

Alice had a soft alluring voice and never raised it even in anger. She was his anchor, his salvation. She was always there for him, supporting him, although she made no qualms that she would prefer he give up his business and lead the life of a lazy nobody. She only had kind words for most all things and declared that negative energy was of no use to anyone. She hated gossip which was in fact a negative thought in reality. But she even made every effort to control that negative dislike. So many people thrived on gossip though. Finding good in all things was sometimes very difficult, even a challenge. One of her most challenging projects was her husband who became easily agitated.

"Alice. Alice. You do not understand. I am frustrated and angry. It does not feel good and I must find a solution. And the solution, I can guarantee is not to quit my business life." He stared at her a moment as if to make his point, and then turned to continue his pacing.

Benjamin Martin was nearly all gray now. His rich auburn brown hair was nearly invisible. Although his face was finely wrinkled, showing signs of laugh crinkles around his eyes and mouth, it did not distract from his otherwise handsome face. The laugh lines were a hint at his once prominent sense of humor, which now seemed rare. He had character in his face. Each line was well earned and Alice fantasized a story for each crease. But it was the humor that Alice was searching for again…what she so loved about him.

They had been a love match. He had once been care free and made her laugh. They used to find humor in so many little things. His business had not always been the focus of his life, robbing him of the happiness Alice so wanted to see again.

"Harriet and Joe are going to the Bickford ball, and I would like to attend and meet some of the dignitaries attending," Benjamin said, stopping for a moment to admire his wife.

She was as beautiful today as she was twenty-six years ago when he married her. He never tired of looking at her. He believed it was her goodness inside that kept her beautiful outside, and no one would disagree with that. Her goodness was admired by many. What could the gossipmongers even fabricate about his beloved Alice?

"But Benny, you and I are escorting Hallie to the theatre that same night. You cannot disappoint her. She has been talking of nothing else. She is wearing that green velvet gown you admired," Alice remarked as if the subject was closed.

Her voice was as smooth as velvet and never irritated him as some other women did, no matter what she said. She could irritate him, that was certain, but the methods she used were like gliding on a road of slick chocolate pudding. It was not always distasteful. Her techniques of handling him were brilliant and many times he did not recognize her strategy until it was too late and he was nearly asleep. Then it would occur to him that he had been "had." But he did not mind. Sometimes he would laugh to himself over her ability to bamboozl him.

"I know. I know. Harriet's married daughter and husband will be in the box to chaperone. Hallie likes Isabelle and will have a mountain to say since she has not seen her recently. Our Hallie is full of conversation and will not have any trouble finding company with Isabelle. And Hallie will not mind since she is so taken with Drury Lane. She will not notice our absence. We can send Daisy if you would like."

Daisy was the maid who cared for his bouquet and traveled with them from Ohio. How Alice found a maid with the name "Daisy," he did not know. He was certain that her name had something to do with being hired, although Benjamin would not put it past his wife to actually ask the maid to change her name to suit the family flower theme.

Alice sighed. "You know I do not like this, but if you must, Benny. I do not like leaving Hallie on her own. But, as you say, she does have Isabelle."

Benjamin smiled at his wife. She always did as he wanted. She may object, but she never made much fuss when he wanted his way. He was fortunate in his choice of wife. His happiness was important to her. He did a great deal to make her happy too, but where business was concerned, his sanity was at risk and Alice understood that much. She made concessions for that. He was a driven man.

"Why do you not sell the refinery to this Mr. Rockefeller and then this struggle would stop and give us all peace of mind. Mercy, he has caused you to nearly have a stroke."

Alice had mentioned this before, and the answer was always the same. But she had to try again. This was eating Benny up, and she wanted him to let it go. She knew his stubbornness well and understood that she must not only carefully select her battles, but wear down his hard exterior little by little. Patience was something she had, and patience would win in the end.

"Because he already forced me to sell my share of the railroad, and I already regret that. He is very persuasive in his dealings. I owned it but a short time, but I had plans, and the investment was sound for me to hang on to it."

"I understand he is ruthless, Benny. He will not stop until he has what he wants. And he wants your refinery. Does he offer a fair price? Perhaps it would not be such a bad thing to sell."

"Damnation, Alice. I do not want to sell. He offers a fair... minimum price, as a start, but I want to keep my refinery." Benjamin's face had reddened as it often did when he was angry and frustrated.

"His people are bullies, Benny, and they scare me. I do not think they plan to allow you to keep your refinery. I think you should hire a hefty bodyguard to protect yourself. It would not be a bad idea to carry a firearm." Benjamin looked surprised and his eyebrows rose in question as he stopped pacing.

"My, my, Alice. You do surprise me. I do not think things are that desperate, love. How ridiculous. Me walking around with some great big gorilla ready to trip over. I think your imagination is getting ahead of you, my love. Imagine me carrying around a firearm. I am more liable to shoot my toe off. Besides, I will not allow them to force me into such measures."

"I remember that odious man who came to see you about the railroad. He did not seem to be a nice man." Alice stopped her needlepoint and looked at Benjamin, shaking her head. "I could tell he was not your usual nice family man."

"He was not a nice man. He is a rough shot for Rockefeller. His job is to make certain Rockefeller gets want he wants. Frankly, I was glad to get him out of our house, Alice."

"You do own other businesses that don't cause you so much stress and bother. I wish they were enough to make you happy."

Benjamin had tired of this subject. It was easy to turn Alice around to something else, and he was a master of it. Twenty-six glorious years of experience made him top notch at shifting her mind. He imagined she, too, stressed over his business dealings, so he was as determined as she was to keep her placated.

"Why not take Violet to the Bickford ball? She needs some socializing. I see her reading books and doing nothing else." There, he had changed the subject nicely. He smiled at his cleverness.

"My dear Violet. She would go if you asked it of her. She would not like it and would sit in the corner like a wallflower."

"Ali, Ali. Did you not just make a flower joke?"

Alice looked up and waved her hand in denial. "I cannot help if that word has flower in it. But I am serious." She put down her needlepoint and gazed a moment at Benjamin. "Our Violet will have her time, when she is ready. We can ask her… but we must not force her into society. There will be a special time for her."

"How will she meet people? She has sequestered herself into her room with books as her companions. We must not wait until it is too late." He stood behind his wife and put a hand on her shoulder. She covered his hand with her own and then patted it.

"You worry too much about such things, Benny."

She looked up at him in question. Oh, no. Now what, he thought. Her mind worked liked a jigsaw puzzle. So many pieces, with no clear idea what one piece was…until it fit neatly alongside another. He frowned as if trying to guess what was next and then shook his head in denial. No use. No one could follow a woman's thinking.

"I am thinking of Poppy, Benny." She breathed a deep sigh and then continued. "She thinks she was someone else a long time ago."

Benjamin snapped his head up suddenly. "What? What are you babbling about, Alice?"

"I am babbling about our Poppy, Benny. She thinks she was once someone else. It is quite disturbing. Do we not go to heaven, Benny? It makes me wonder who I once was. Mercy. I could have been a murderer."

Benjamin was steadily angering, like a teapot about to blow its lid. His face was red and blotchy, his fists clenched as he tried to get control of his temper. He clenched his teeth, another symptom of his rage boiling over.

"Damnation, Alice. Where did this come from? Have we no control over this rubbish she comes across? Where on earth does she get these ideas?"

He looked out the window now as Alice went back to her needlepoint with a sigh. She knew best to stay quiet a moment and allow his temper to cool down before saying something that would set him off again. He was taking deep breaths as she always told him to do when he was angry. A few more and he would be right again.

"What nonsense. Poppycock. When will this ever stop? She is flypaper to lunatics and their ideas. We should marry her off soon and let some young lad take on our job," he muttered the last part under his breath.

"You do not mean that. This drama keeps us centered and alive. At times I have to say this to myself over and over just to stay focused." Benjamin looked at Alice with admiration.

"What patience you have. I admit I am challenged with daughters. I am fortunate to have you, Alice, to guide this circus."

As Benjamin stared out of the window, he spotted his daughter Hallie wandering through the garden. He smiled. She was truly a lovely girl.

"There is our Hallie among the garden flowers. It is cold out there…but she does not seem to think anything of it. You know there will be Dukes, Viscounts and a Baron or two at the Bickford ball. I shall do a little shopping for Hallie. Would that not be grand to have our Hallie a Duchess?" Benjamin stood taller with that thought.

"I think you should allow Hallie to do her own husband shopping. You are driving her to near insanity with this talk of snagging her a title. She is old enough and smart enough to know what she wants."

"Surely you jest. It was my interference that resulted in Rose snagging my assistant Daniel Stewart, which I will point out proudly, is a love match, my love." Benjamin smiled and rocked on his feet, which he loved to do when he made a point he felt confident would ride on its on merit.

"You know perfectly well, Rose loved Daniel on first sight with no help from you. I do appreciate that you supported that union, but we did nothing to light the match to that fire. Which makes the point, I think, that our daughters are fully capable of deciding themselves whom they want to marry. Mercy, Benny, if we should muck up their lives for heaven sakes, I would feel terrible."

"Could not Hallie fall in love with a Duke or Viscount at first sight? But we need to make the introductions do we not? In fact, is it not Hallie we should take to the Bickford ball?"

"Hallie is going to the theatre, which has been planned some time ago, and you purchased a gown especially for this occasion. I will not agree to disappoint her, Benny. You go ahead and shop for a Duke if you like. But, beware that you do not get too driven on this subject. All we need is to overstep and then regret what we have done."

Alice stood up and turned to face her husband. She looked into his eyes with the love and support she always had for him. She put her arms on his shoulder and looked him in the face with her most charming beguiling smile. This was the look he adored.

"You know I love you. Just be cautious when you are dealing with the hearts of our daughters," Alice whispered as tears threatened her eyes. Their daughters were a sentimental subject.

Sebastian sat at his massive, finely-designed walnut desk reviewing bills for seeds, lumber, and mortar for his tenants. His father had laid the groundwork in taking care of properties and tenants with careful thought and insight. He had instilled the importance of gaining trust, respect, and appreciation from their tenants and in so doing gaining more profits and harmony in the long run. Sebastian had been successful in assuming the same quality of work his father was respected for doing. He had also expanded into other business, such as shipping and investing in other promising enterprise, gaining him even more wealth and respect among his peers. Although not popular among the aristocrats, the reality was clear...it was necessary to do something other than sit on one's laurels to maintain the estates that were entailed by the titled. That or marry money, which was not an option Sebastian wanted to entertain.

The desk was well used and had been his father's, along with the throne-like, upholstered chair with dark green stripes that matched the desk. It was considered Renaissance Revival. The walnut desk sported rosewood high relief carving of a generous nature. Sebastian, as a child, loved to touch and admire these animated animal faces of each fox appearing at the corners of the desk. Sebastian spent a great deal of time in this very library with his father learning about his future responsibilities. Alex would tag along and watch with some interest, although Sebastian felt it was more about feeling included. Their father was generous in including both boys when preparing Sebastian for the responsibility of the title. After all, Alex was the spare.

The desk was covered with neatly stacked papers. One stack held unanswered inquiries, one stack contained matters already sorted and one stack was full of issues that required more thought and research. Another stack, for shipping issues, containing contracts, schedules, cargos, and articles on profitable destinations. One stack was reserved for his favorite issues at Parliament. Another stack concerned his tenants. There were bills for new roofs, seeds, and even for sheep to breed with his small herd. He also had articles on the changing agricultural science of farming. A paperweight lay on the center of each stack. Sebastian was very well organized in all things, and he had nightmares of a big surge of undirected wind sweeping through the library, carrying all his carefully-organized work with it to land in a heap on the ancient Persian rug. He would adjust the paper weights from time to time to assure himself all was safe. In fact, he collected paper weights, because he dared not be without one when in need. He would not gaze long at the stacks for fear of being overwhelmed. He had a secretary who was invisible for the most part, but ready to take on more tasks if Sebastian required it.

Alex, in contrast, was creative and unorganized, sensitive and thoughtful. They were identical, and yet they were different in so many ways. Alex looked to Sebastian for business advice. He put money in investments, but still wanted Sebastian to manage them. Alex did not have the business instincts that Sebastian had as a natural talent.

The room still smelled of his father, or maybe his father smelled like the room he loved so well and had spent so much of his time in doing what Sebastian was doing now. Lemon oil permeated the air. A leaded glass decanter filled with his favorite brandy and several glasses were arranged on a table behind his desk. He never drank too much, as he always liked to be in control of himself, but he did like his occasional glass of brandy.

A light tap on the door interrupted Sebastian from his thoughts on tenant farming and how to incorporate some new ideas on drainage and crops that were more productive. The door opened, and his butler Holland stood at attention. He was a proper butler who had worked for the Stainton family for more than twenty-five years, Sebastian guessed.

Holland was a stuffy fellow, which made his state of dress more comical. Sebastian suspected Holland was color blind, and that the tailor who provided livery for the Stainton household was having a bit of sport. His dark suit and trousers were proper enough, grays and blacks, but his cravat, usually black or white for service, was a rainbow of colors every day, without exception. Sebastian certainly was not going to mention it, and besides, it was a source of amusement for Sebastian. It literally brightened his day to see that contradiction. His lips quirked at seeing a rose-colored cravat today. Most unusual. However, he was well respected by the male staff he managed, rose cravat and all.

"Your Grace. Sorry for the interruption. Viscount Montjoy here to see you." Holland practically clicked his heels when he announced guests. His eyes stared straight ahead, awaiting his direction.

"Thank you, Holland. Show him in." Sebastian carefully placed the paper he was reading on the appropriate stack, secured a paper weight on top, and turned to the door to greet his friend.

Garrett Montjoy had attended university with Alex and Sebastian. He was of a similar age and came into his title recently. He was tall, sporting short blond hair and was sought after by every marriageable woman in London. His blue eyes and fast smile made him seem mischievous and ready for some fun. The crinkles by his eyes laid testament that he was not a stranger to laughter.

"Garrett, good of you to come on such short notice."

"I am curious…what could cause you to send for me with such an urgent message? That curiosity got me dressed and out and about sooner than usual." Garrett came into the room and flopped down unceremoniously in a chair in front of the desk, as if he had done so a thousand times. Although protocol would dictate a bow, these men had lived like brothers and were beyond formality, at least in private. Garrett stretched his long legs in front of him crossing his ankles. He smiled at Sebastian as he folded his hands on his lap and then waited in anticipation.

"Nothing serious. I would like to take you for ices at Gunter's, Wednesday next at three." Sebastian did not look Garrett in the eye as was his usual habit, but was looking down at something on his desk. Perhaps a nervous trait.

A bark of laughter over took Garrett before he could catch himself. After he gained control, he looked at his friend and realized that Sebastian was serious. A moment of silence where both men studied each other.

"Are we courting, Sebastian?" He could not help the smirk that followed his question. He could see that Sebastian did not appreciate his humor. The man was serious.

A frown marred Sebastian's brow. "I crave a lavender ice, is all. I know how you like the pistachio ice and thought we might indulge. We have not been there in an age."

Garrett looked doubtful. He was speechless. He just stared at his friend in confusion. "Of course, if you need a chaperone for an ice, I am your man. Wednesday next at three."

Chapter 4

The Bickford Ball, Mayfair, January, 1870

*E*dmund and Agnes Bickford stood at attention greeting their guests as they paraded into the large impressive hallway. Guests greet their hosts and continue up the wide marble staircase toward the second story ballroom. Portraits of ancestors hung the length of the staircase.. Footmen stood directing the crowds by taking their coats and wraps, guiding them up the stairs and to the ballroom where chandeliers with leaded glass prisms lit the massive room with a romantic glow. Chatter could be heard from the circular drive where carriages lined up to deposit finely dressed aristocrats. The carriages backed up for nearly a mile awaiting their turn to follow the procession into the Mayfair residence.

Viscount Edmund Bickford and Viscountess Agnes Bickford were well-respected among the ton. They hosted one of the first events of the season and their guests anxiously awaited the annual invitation to what was known to be the biggest crush and best attended event of the season.

Agnes Bickford wore as many jewels as she could squeeze on her short, wrinkled frame. Her silver curls were stacked on top of her head with jeweled hair pins of all colors. She wore several bracelets over her long white gloves, and her neck was too short for the heavy ruby necklace that she wore proudly. Her husband once joked about his wife being so heavily equipped with jewels that he would have her stand at his door so he could not only admire his gifts over the many years they were married, but because she also made an excellent door stop.

The procession took nearly an hour while the guests drank punch and listened to the orchestra tune up for the first dance. A card room attracted many of the men who liked to gamble, smoke, drink hard liquor, and tell stories.

It was Edmund Bickford's job to rattle a few men out of the card room ever so often to dance. Agnes Bickford prided herself on making certain every wallflower danced at least once. She also was noted for pairing and introducing couples and taking credit for matches that eventually transpired to marriage through her efforts.

Debutantes were eager to enjoy their first balls, where they were introduced into society. They were easily detected in their white gowns, slippers, and conservative hair styles and gown design. It was not proper to show too much skin, and they were usually attached to their protective mamas. Some were barely out of the schoolroom. They would cluster together and share their insecurities and their hopes for a dance partner.

Sebastian strolled in late and greeted his hostess. She was ever so happy to have another Duke at her humble event, she told him. She immediately wanted to introduce him to some of her special guests. It was appreciated by the mamas when the hostess would drag a Duke around to introduce him to their marriageable daughters. Sebastian never saw so many fluttering eye lashes, fake smiles, and fan waving in his life. He was able to finally extract himself to check out the card room without promising any dances. He considered himself lucky. He wanted to see who of importance was there, and the card room would hold the answer.

Just before he could escape the ballroom, a fan tapped his shoulder. He turned to see the tall blonde dressed in crimson, her breasts over-flowing her neckline by just enough to cover her nipples. A daring rogue could extract them with hardly a touch. She was a widow, beautiful and well sought after. He had enjoyed her company for several months until she thought to marry him.

"Good evening Marlene. You look ravishing tonight. I trust you are exhausted already from beating off the attentions of…"

"Stop patronizing me Sebastian. The bracelet was… thoughtful. But not as generous as I would think…I am worth. Do you think you can throw me away like yesterday's newspaper?"

She was controlling her temper, but Sebastian knew her well enough to know that she was angry at his action to finish their relationship. She obviously was counting on being a Duchess and thought she had his favor.

"I know how to run a house, how to be a hostess…I am perfect to be your Duchess and I do think you have not thought this through properly." She placed her gloved hand on his sleeve.

"This is neither the time nor place for such a discussion… something a Duchess would know. I think I was clear when we last spoke."

He removed her hand from his sleeve and turned toward the card room, leaving her gaping at him. Unfortunately, she was probably only getting started with her goal to get him back. He sighed his frustration as he opened the door to a smoke-filled room. This was the disadvantage of keeping a mistress. Some accepted the gifts and moved on. In this case, Marlene expected more. He was confident she would find a new protector in no time. She had the attention of many men, and now the gossips had already learned of their falling out. Her offers would soon be coming in, and she would be wise to put him behind her. She had gotten emotionally involved, unfortunately.

Sebastian scanned the room. He saw Garrett engrossed in a card game across the room. He must be winning. The slow smile on his face as he studied his cards was an indication that he was doing well at the tables. Sebastian strolled toward the table where Garrett was playing and spotted Joseph Pritchard at the same table with someone he did not recognize. Perhaps it was Martin. He stood behind his friend and saw the winnings in front of him. When they were finished playing the hand, Sebastian took that opportunity to be introduced.

"Garrett, I do not think I know your comrades here." Garrett looked up at Sebastian and smiled.

"Ah. Well, I think you know Joseph Prichard already. Benjamin Martin is a relative of Pritchard's from America.

Benjamin, may I introduce to you the Duke of Ashford, his Grace is also recognized as Sebastian Stainton."

Benjamin stood and gave a slight bow.

"I am pleased to meet you. A Duke, you say. Well, well. I hope to get better acquainted with you, Your Grace."

Benjamin had a huge grin on his face that seemed odd to Sebastian, but perhaps he had been drinking. Looking down on the table he saw the cut glass filled with amber liquid. Martin's face was red, either from the overly warm room or perhaps the liquor.

"Is your Duchess here? I would like my wife to meet her... if that can be arranged." Benjamin asked with interest.

Sebastian hid a smile. "I have no Duchess, Mr. Martin."

It seemed that Martin's grin got bigger, if that were possible. Sebastian immediately thought about how predictable Americans were.

"Please join the game, Your Grace." Martin actually pulled out a chair to offer Sebastian. Sebastian took his place at the card table, and the dealer dealt the first set of cards as the men settled into their game.

In the ballroom, the orchestra was in full swing. Colorful couples danced around the ballroom framed by clusters of people admiring the dancing and catching up on the latest gossip. Several debutantes were gathered around the punch bowl, not far from their doting mamas. One debutant spoke in a whispered voice to the others.

"You must try and avoid Baron Battencourt. He is the one dancing now with the widow Sanders.

"Why ever not," another debutant asked.

"He is wearing gray gloves that are dyed. You should see poor Clara's white gown in the back where he placed his hands when they were dancing. It has made a terrible stain and she is now hiding in the ladies retiring room," the first one responded.

"But to be holding her in the back of the waist means she was waltzing!" The second debutante said with shock. All the girls gasped.

"I imagine she was caught red-handed, was she not?" Their third debutante offered.

"To be caught and waste the rage of your mama on an elderly man...well, it would be worth the trouble if he were handsome and titled."

The girls were entertained for quite some time at Clara's expense. Most all the gentlemen wore the traditional white gloves. Once in a while, one creative man would dye his gloves to set himself apart.

Across the ballroom, Viscount Garrett Montjoy stood watching the dancers twirl around the floor. He had collected his winnings and was recruited to dance with the wallflowers.

Garrett was tall, over six feet, matching his friends Alex and Sebastian in height. His blond hair was swept back, leaving one strand loose to fall just opposite his side-parted hair. His vivid blue eyes stopped on a colorful figure seated near a palm. She should not be a wallflower. She was beautiful, although not in the traditional way of English women. Her hair was not quite red, but not blonde either. It looked like a summer sunset. She was young, but not dressed as a debutant. Her gown was soft mint green voile, not as low cut as the English women preferred. She was looking down, perhaps reading a book. Who would stick a lovely creature like that in the corner next to a palm?

She looked up, as if she knew someone was watching her. Her eyes settled on him. She was wearing speckles, but they did not distract from her unusual beauty. She blushed and looked back down to her book as if to hide beneath the pages.

He was used to women flirting with him. After all, he was considered a catch of sorts. He was a Viscount. Attractive, was he not? Marriageable. Wealthy. To have a woman ignore him was new to him and, frankly, had him at a loss. What was she about? He had never seen her before, but he often avoided ton events. He was fair game to the marriage minded mamas and would have a miserable time running from determined women who wanted to entrap him.

Violet wondered for the hundredth time how she managed to get herself trapped into attending this ball. For that matter, she could have gone to the theatre with Hallie and not be in this predicament. All she wanted was to stay away from crowds of people and social events where she had to watch her manners and beware of her determined father trying to marry off his remaining daughters. Iris was safe for now, of course. She was only twelve after all. In preparation of the ball, Violet had hidden a book of Shakespeare sonnets in her pocket with her spectacles.

Mama had insisted she attend, and she was certain her father was behind it all. Rather than cause a fuss, because she believed in choosing her battles, she decided to go and hide with a good book to keep her occupied. That would make everyone happy.

When she felt as if someone was watching her, she looked up and wondered if her spectacles were dusty. Seeing the tall, handsome, blond gentleman watching her was her undoing. She had the notion to look behind her to see who he was focused on, except she was sitting against a wall with no one behind her.

She felt herself heat up from her toes to her face. What on earth was he doing starring at her? Was she that unseemly? She could not see a word on the page of her book, but stared at it anyway and pretended to read. After a few moments, she could not stand it any longer. She had to look and see if he was still there and still looking her way. She cautiously glanced up slowly trying to be nonchalant. Dratted man. He was still looking at her. Seeing her look at him, he smiled slowly at first and then his smile grew to be nearly a laugh. Did he find her amusing? A joke, perhaps? Damn his hide.

Sebastian took a sip of his brandy and studied Martin across the table. It was a friendly game, and thus Sebastian felt comfortable with his hand, but then he was wealthy and could afford any losses. He never played deep anyway. But it was a good way to casually pick up information. Martin liked to talk. His cousin-in-law Pritchard was quiet and kept his thoughts to himself. Sebastian was not capable of better judging the American. Nothing like a game of cards, liquor, and smoke to loosen tongues. There was a trusting attitude among men at the gaming table if they were not too serious about their cards.

Neil Piedmont was dressed as a gentleman. His clothes were expensive and black, as he preferred. Black leather gloves, black greatcoat, black trousers, black boots, and black cravat. A wide-brimmed black wool hat was pulled down low on his head, nearly covering his eyes. Only a small portion of his face showed. He wanted to blend into the background and into the crowds of people he liked to use as cover. He was a nondescript man of average height and build. He had dark hair, and his face was expressionless. He always kept to himself and did not trust anyone.

Piedmont liked to work alone rather than trusting others. He was always heavily armed and trained with knives, guns, and even walking stick swords. He avoided confrontations because he did not want to attract attention to himself unnecessarily. His goal was to walk around like anyone else and not have a soul remember him. Brilliant. He was arrogant, confident, and deadly.

He hated London. It smelled, was foggy most of the time, and rainy when the fog lifted. Miserable place. People piss in the streets and dump their garbage in the alleys. In the places he frequented, a man was mugged, beaten, bloodied, and left for dead, for whatever was on his person. He did not want to converse with the people, or as little as possible, because they might detect his American accent. He did his best to cover it. Just listening to the chatter in the streets created a learning experience for him.

Disgusting, all of it. Part of being a chameleon.

Then there was the ton. Disgustingly powerful group of people that could destroy a person, their family, and their means of income. The ton looked down their noses at almost anything and everything. They all thought they were better than anyone else. He preferred America. At least people had a fighting chance at survival. Their reputations were not at risk for each and every little thing they did.

His dark brown eyes scanned the landscape. He never wanted to be ignorant of what was behind him or if a cluster of men were to gather near him. Danger was everywhere. He had to stay smart and alert. He never drank much, because his survival depended on his wits and skills.

He slithered into a pub, glanced around, and then sat at a table in the back where no one seemed to notice. A maid came by to serve him. She was a friendly sort and eyed him with some interest. He was richly dressed and might tip her fairly. She smiled broadly and fluttered her lashes at him.

"What ye have, mate?" She was buxom and waved her hips at him.

Piedmont frowned and muttered, "Ale, and nothing else," he said glaring at her directly to see if she got the message he was not interested in her offer. It was obvious he was not good with conversation, so after a moment she turned to go.

"Ale, tis, mate." She responded as she went to get his drink.

He drank his ale, wasting no time. It was time to go.

Piedmont worked his way down alleys and under traveled streets until he found the residence he sought. Now he would wait and watch.

Violet folded her spectacles and placed them in her pocket with her book of sonnets. The pocket was strategically hidden between the pleats of her gown. She knew her mother would soon remember that she had a daughter to chaperone and would seek her whereabouts. Violet could almost feel the disappointment her mother would experience if she caught Violet reading a book while hidden by a palm at the ball.

Violet glanced around and sighed in relief when she saw that the man who had been watching her was nowhere in sight. He was tall and would be easily detected if he were on the dance floor. She looked down at her clasped hands and said a prayer to herself that this evening would soon draw to a close. To be home in the solitude of her room would take the butterflies from her stomach.

Violet looked up to see Lady Bickford coming her way with what seemed to be an urgent agenda. Violet realized in that moment that **she** was apparently the destination. With no one else within ten feet of her, sadly the host was destined to seek her. Behind Lady Bickford was the tall man, following in her wake.

No one in her path was able to way lay her. What would be Lady Bickford's purpose in coming to address her? Seeing the determination on Lady Bickford's face caused Violet to stand with uncertainty and concern. For goodness sake, what was this all about, Violet thought with dread. Perhaps she was caught reading a book. Drat.

Lady Bickford stood before Violet and smiled and then turned to see if she still had the man behind her. Violet performed a curtsy for Lady Bickford. The man took his cue and stood beside Lady Bickford. He bowed his head and smiled at Violet with the most charming grin and warmth she had ever experienced. It was truly a charismatic experience.

"Miss Martin, may I present to you Viscount Garrett Montjoy." Garrett stepped forward and took her gloved hand and kissed the air just above.

"I am honored to make your acquaintance, Miss Martin." He looked up then and captured her eyes. She was speechless and her mouth opened, but nothing came out.

"Miss Martin is an American. She and her family are visiting the Pritchard's," Lady Bickford said as she nodded to Garrett and then took her leave. Her job had been a complete success.

"Perhaps you have saved the next waltz for me, Miss Martin."

"I...I was, that is..."

"She would be delighted Lord Montjoy." Alice Martin replied as she slipped in next to her daughter and put her arm around her waist. "Violet is a little shy, My Lord, until you get to know her," she added, smiling. Luckily, Alice had spotted Lady Bickford's efforts and made herself available to help.

The music sang out the first notes of a waltz. Garrett gently took Violet's hand to lead her onto the dance floor and turned back to smile his appreciation to Alice Martin, who nodded and smiled her approval.

"My Lord, I do not waltz very well, I am afraid…perhaps you…"

"I am exceptionally good at leading Miss Martin. I will not allow you to stumble, I promise." He put his hand on her lower back and took her other hand as they started to circle the dance floor in graceful strides. "Ahh. You are humble, I see. You dance beautifully, Miss Martin."

"I think it tis you, My Lord. You are a good partner."

After staring anywhere, but at him, she finally turned her head up to see his face. He was looking at her with bemusement. He had been watching her intently, it seemed. She was frazzled.

"What…Am I funny, My Lord?" She asked with some trepidation.

"I apologize if it seems that way. It is just that you are so enchanting. I cannot believe my fortunate to have this dance and you in my arms."

He seemed sincere, but my or my, he was a charmer. Could she trust him, or was he an outrageous rogue?

"I do not know what to say, My Lord."

"You must tell me I am enchanting too." At her nervousness, he chuckled. "Forgive me, if I make you uneasy. It is not my intention, I assure you."

Oddly, his waistcoat was the same shade of pale green. She stared at the coat with surprise. "Perhaps my gown and your coat came from the same bolt of fabric," she whispered in awe.

Garrett gave a bark of laughter. "It would seem so. We must share the same taste in colors." There was a twinkle in his blue eyes that made her smile despite herself. She suddenly felt comfortable in his arms.

"That is much better. Your smile is like sunshine. You must smile more often. Are you staying long in London?"

"We visit London every couple of years for the season. We will return to America when the season is over."

"How do you find London, Miss Martin?"

"I do not particularly like it. I prefer the country. I am not fond of all the social occasions, or the weather, soot and smell..." She suddenly realized her blunder. "Oh, I am sorry...." A blush reddened he face at her mistake in etiquette.

"Not at all. I happen to agree with your point of view. I admire your honesty." He smiled then, and she lost all sense of where she was.

She felt as though her feet were flying off the floor. His firm grasp kept her centered. Those butterflies were causing havoc in her stomach. She tipped her head back and laughed. She was having fun...actual fun. He laughed too.

As the music was dying down, he squeezed her hand and asked, "Would you like to go to Gunter's next Wednesday at three for ices? I crave pistachio…" Garrett wanted to kick himself at the impulsive gesture.

He did not know her nor her family…was he courting? Not a wise offer to an innocent. But it was too late. It had fallen out of his mouth without thought. Obviously without thought. He wanted to groan at his poor judgement. What must she think of him? It simply was not done like this. He could not pick her up because he would be going with Sebastian…Bloody hell. How the bloody hell did he get in this predicament?

Violet was surprised by the offer from Viscount Montjoy. She was to be at Gunter's at three with Hallie. How odd. It must be fate.

"As it turns out, I will be at Gunter's for ice with my sister that day, so I will be there to greet you a 'hello,' if you should be there at that time," she responded with a shy smile.

A little frown marred her face as she considered this new development. Hallie did not even know she had decided to attend the Bickford ball and now this. What had just happened?

Garrett was stuck speechless. She would be there. That is what one would expect from an American. Straight forward, look-in-the-eye honesty. He smiled.

"That is brilliant." Then he laughed.

She was interesting, that was for certain. He was entertained by this new adventure that he had not planned or expected. The music came to an end, and Garrett laid her hand on his arm as he escorted her back to her mother who was waiting. Alice Martin was smiling like she had just eaten a wonderful new sweet cake. It was then that Garrett recognized where Violet had inherited her beauty. Garrett bowed and took Violet's gloved hand in his and kissed the air above it and repeated the gesture with Alice Martin who squirmed with glee. Garrett nodded and retreated to the other side of the room, knowing better than to mention the appointment at Gunter's. Mothers tended to read too much in such an innocent outing.

Garrett's gesture in dancing with Violet stirred up some interest in the other young men attending the Bickford ball. Before Violet could retreat to the palm once again, three young men had rushed to her side and wanted introductions to the lady who had won the favor of Viscount Montjoy. Violet was stunned, and her mother was delighted. Garrett watched the drama from across the room and smiled. The lovely wallflower was a wallflower no longer.

Sebastian walked out of the smoked-filled card room. He took a deep breath of fresh air. The women's card room was filled with ladies and old men.... and no smoke. They played for small amounts of money and ate cakes and drank tea. Sebastian had to smile at the dissimilarities. There was a lot of cackling going on, giving credit to the kind of entertainment favored by the older women.

He had learned some things about Martin with nearly no effort whatsoever. Between Pritchard and Martin, there was quite a bit of information shared between sips of brandy. Martin was being pursued by Rockefeller, the American millionaire who was dispassionately buying up railroads and refineries all over his country. Martin was none too happy about it. He had come to London, in part, to escape the man.

Sebastian had gambled just enough to be acceptable and shared just enough to be trustworthy. Martin seemed more impressed with his title and the fact that he was not attached than anything else. Of course, there were his four daughters and the marriage market to consider. It was tricky and a slippery slope to escape that trap.

He gazed around the ballroom. He spotted Sir Oliver Danders on the other side of the room who nodded and would expect a nod back to acknowledge their cause. Sebastian nodded and then sighed.

But he did not see the colorful gowns swirling around the dance floor, nor did he hear the music. All he could think about was the red-headed vixen in the dark green velvet gown at Drury Lane. She captivated him. Her green eyes flashing sparks, her innocent vitality. Her so- American personality and charisma were not far from his mind, even in the cardroom. She must be a witch, he decided. At no time before had a woman dominated so much of his thinking before.

He would see her again. Wednesday next at three at Gunter's. She was a distraction to what he was directed to do. He did need to stay focused, and it would be difficult with her swimming around in his mind. The room was over-heated with sweating bodies, too much perfume, and over-zealous mamas exercising their duties. He needed fresh air and a moment to think. Then he must send a note to his younger brother Derrick.

Chapter 5

Berkeley Square, Gunter's Tea Shop, Wednesday, 1870

"How are you going to invite him to the Kent house party, Hallie? The invite should come from Aunt. Aunt Harriet would want to know where you met this Duke... and then where would the invitation go? To Drury Lane? Addressed to the actor playing the part of a Duke?" Violet asked as she sipped her tea.

They were dressed and enjoying their tea in their private sitting room before going to Gunter's. Poppy and Iris had wanted to go upon learning of the destination. It had been pure luck that their mother had other designs on their time. Poppy and Iris were going for a fitting for their new gowns on Bond Street.

"I was able to locate Aunt's secretary alone in the kitchen having tea. I told her there was an important Duke that Aunt had forgotten and simply asked for an invitation. I personally wrote the name on her list and said I could personally deliver the invite on my excursion today."

Hallie smiled after taking another sip of her tea.

"I admit I was a little concerned about this detail." Hallie admitted.

"This lie is growing tentacles and will be the size of a whale in no time, Hallie. I hope you can control it," Violet added as she put more sugar and lemon in her tea, stirring in concentration.

Hallie frowned. "I know. I am a little concerned about that. One thing leads to another, and it is running at a pace I can hardly keep up with. Even Mother wanted to know if I could not go earlier and then join them on Bond Street and, thus, another lie. It makes me sick to lie and then lie more to cover the lie."

She looked at Violet, who was pouring them another cup of tea. She frowned and then thought a moment about her meeting with Alex Stainton.

"He annoyed me."

Violet looked up and did not pretend to misunderstand the train of thought. She was used to her sister changing the subject with no notice.

"Heaven forbid." Violet smiled with amusement.

"Actually, it was irritating."

"Men can be irritating I admit," Violet responded.

"He questioned my plan. He suggested there were flaws."

"He must be an idiot to doubt you."

"When the plan comes to a reasonable conclusion, he suggested that Father might put a gun to his head and force a marriage. I wanted to slap him."

"Because he does not want to marry you?"

"No. Of course not. Because he questions my brilliance in this plan."

"I see."

"But it will be worth the irritation. I have put too much energy into these lies. I have to wonder if the freedom I gain is worth it. I do not intend to turn around on this adventure now, however I am in too deep to stop. I feel so deceptive and crafty. Not qualities I want to nurture. I certainly am not proud of these traits. The fact is I am rather good at it, which is another blunder of sorts."

Violet felt deceptive herself and looked down into her tea cup to cover her nervousness. She had told Hallie she went to the Bickford ball, but did not tell her about the Viscount that she had met. He probably won't show up at Gunter's anyway. He would think about the American girl he met at the ball and see reason. He would not come, she decided. She did not want to share the disappointment when it happened. It would feel like a failure, and she could not bear that. She had learned that the British ton was not very impressed with Americans. They were snubbed many times.

Hallie did some woolgathering of her own. She thought about the meeting she had with Alex Stainton in his dressing room. He was more aggressive and forceful than she expected. He filled the small room with his size and presence. She was intimidated, and that did not happen often. Perhaps he was trying to get into character before the performance. She understood some actors went through such a process. But then she thought about how he smelled. Bay rum...maybe a little sandalwood. It was a rich strong smell that was purely male and intoxicating. Yes, she liked his male scent.

His voice was baritone. Rich. Smooth. Captivating. She understood his choice of vocation. It made sense. He *should* make a living from his voice. He should also read books aloud. His voice was smooth like spreading butter on toast. Except when she started to listen to what he was actually saying, he made her angry...furious actually. How dare he question whether her father would cause a problem. She was hiring him to do a job. Simply that and nothing else. The trouble was she wanted him to buy into her plan, and he obviously found flaws. She hated the fact that he brought up some good points. It made her feel like an idiot. Dratted man. She wanted admiration from him. Respect. Was that too much to ask or expect?

She did want to hear his voice again. She admitted that much to herself. To be truthful with herself, she enjoyed the sparring. It rather put some life into her boredom. He made her stomach flutter. There was a discomfort she experienced thinking about him, as well as being in the same room with him, but she never felt more alive.

"Hallie, please come back to earth. You look like you are sleeping with your eyes open. It makes me want to smack you," Violet muttered over another sip of tea.

Hallie blinked twice and smiled. Violet nodded her approval.

"I am sorry Violet. I admit I was woolgathering. It was a wonderful day dream." Her face was flushed and she had a dreamy look about her.

Back to earth, however, she must change the subject. This she would not discuss, even with Violet.

"What if it rains?" Hallie looked at Violet wanting her response. "Then my plans will fail, will they not?"

Violet smiled and reassured her sister. "Your plans are on track, Hallie. The skies are not predicting rain and the sun has appeared. There are no excuses. We shall leave in an hour, unless…of course you have changed your mind."

"No. I have not changed my mind."

Holland tapped on Sebastian's library door. He had been assessing his neat piles of papers and deciding which stack to attack next when Holland opened the door to announce his younger brother Derrick.

Derrick was six and twenty and carried all the Stainton distinctive traits. He was tall, over six feet, had the dark hair and rich brown eyes with thick dark lashes that drove women wild. Because he was out of doors a great deal, he sported sun streaks in his hair and a healthy tan from what sun there was in London. He was muscular and of a sturdy nature, which would be expected of a Police Detective. He was skillful at his job, finding and apprehending criminals, and he loved his work. Many times, he wore plain clothes and found himself in precarious positions where he needed his skills physically as well as strategically. He practiced his skills boxing and fencing. Sebastian would request his services now and again, and they loved to work together. The brothers were a tight knit family.

Derrick plopped down on a chair in front of the desk facing his brother. He grinned at the serious expression on Sebastian's face. "Got your note, brother. You captured my curiosity. What's cooking?"

"There's an American visiting relatives in London... the London relatives are Harriet and Joseph Pritchard. The American is a man named Martin. Benjamin Martin. It seems he has attracted an undesirable...also from America. I met Martin at the Bickford ball, and he seems a nice enough fellow. Hardly the type to attract an assassin. He is rich...owns a refinery in Ohio. It is definitely troublesome, to say the least."

"The Home Office, you say? Oliver got wind of an assassin, did he?"

Sebastian nodded his head and sighed.

"Do you want me to take action or..."

"At this point, gather information. If we do not find the 'why' of it, another assassin will be contracted to take over. I want some answers." Sebastian gave a stern look at his brother. "I know you will be able to help me solve this mystery."

Holland tapped on the door and entered carrying a tray with tea, sandwiches, and little lemon cakes that were Derrek's favorite. He laid it down on a table and waited for direction from Sebastian.

"That will be all Holland." Holland bowed and retreated out the door. "I see you have influence on the staff still...your favorite is awaiting you," Sebastian said as he saw the assortment on the tray. Derrick grinned and took a ham and cheese sandwich.

"This is one regret I have from moving out. I so love Cook's food."

"I never kicked you out, Derrick. You are always welcome if you want to share my company again."

Derrick laughed. "I love my townhouse...thanks to you. I also love my solitude. My cook is not quite so talented or sensitive to my likes."

"Then get a new cook to your liking, Derrick. The trick is in the hiring." Sebastian stood up and walked to the table to collect a sandwich for himself.

"No, cannot do that, I'm afraid. This cook is in need of work. She is the widow of a criminal I...well, I feel responsible. She has two children."

"You took down her husband and feel badly for her. Something called guilt. You have a heart, brother. Of course, it is not your problem...but I think I understand your sentiment. Is she a good cook? That would count for something."

"No. She knows only a few dishes, and they are not that good. She promises to learn how to cook better. One can hope. I eat out a lot. Maybe I can take a sandwich with me."

"You are a good man, Derrick. Why not bring her over to work with my cook occasionally to learn, as well as help out my cook? I am certain Mrs. Wentworth would not mind."

"That is a generous offer. I might take you up on it." At that he poured himself some tea and toasted his brother.

Hallie and Violet sat at the little round table across the street from Gunter's Tea Shop. When the tea shop was crowded, many people chose to sit beneath the maple trees across the street, where waiters appeared to take an order. The shop was located in Berkeley Square, Mayfair, a fashionable location for business. It was so well accepted as a location for the much-desired ices and tea, that ladies could be seen with gentlemen, unchaperoned at no expense to their reputations. Popular flavors included maple, bergamot, pineapple, pistachio, jasmine, white coffee, chocolate, vanilla, Parmesan, elderflower and lavender. Ices were also served in decorative molds such as flowers and fruit. Adults and children alike found this establishment the height of fashion and the best source for a special treat.

Both ladies, clad in their finest day dresses and bonnets, watched the people enjoy their ices. Hallie's yellow periwinkle gown complimented her red hair and straw hat adorned with flowers. Violet wore blue merino with darker blue trim. Neither lady seemed bothered that they had not ordered, but chose to watch the people come and go. They were early, after all, so it was not odd that Alex Stainton had not yet appeared.

Violet saw the duo first and waved, bringing a look of confusion from her sister. She followed her sister's gaze and saw the pair of men advancing on them. Hallie wondered for a moment how Violet recognized Alex Stainton. Both men were dressed as aristocrats. They both preferred black instead of colorful waist coats that were popular. Hallie noticed the other gentleman with Alex and wondered who he was.

As Garrett approached, he reached out for Violet's hand and bowed, kissing her gloved knuckles. "Miss Martin. Such a pleasure to see you again. I am still thinking about our dance from the Bickford ball." He looked at Sebastian. "Ah. May I introduce the Duke of Ashford to you, Miss Martin?" Violet stood and curtsied. She then looked at her sister.

"Hallie is my sister. May I introduce Viscount Montjoy and the Duke of Ashford to you, Hallie?" Sebastian took Hallie's outstretched hand and kissed her gloved knuckles.

Hallie was having trouble following. How did Violet come to know this Viscount and how did they know each other? Why did they come together? What was going on? Her jaw must have been hanging, because everyone was staring at her. She finally found her voice.

"It is a pleasure to meet you, My Lords," she finally choked out.

Hallie looked at Sebastian and thought that he got into the part with comfort. No one would suspect that he was not a Duke...and this Viscount. Was he an actor too, she wondered?

"Will you not join us? Violet and I are thinking of ordering ices. They are the rage, you know."

Garrett jumped in to take charge.

"I think Gunter's is crowded, and it may be awhile before we are served. I will take Miss Martin across the street to put in an order for us." Violet smiled her approval and after taking orders, they left Sebastian with Hallie.

"You play the Duke well. Very convincing," Hallie said, as Sebastian joined her at the table.

"Thank you." He smiled at her and watched as her face blushed.

"Who is Viscount Montjoy, and is he an actor too?"

Sebastian laughed. It was a rich deep baritone laugh. He was handsome when he laughed. Dimples automatically appeared out of nowhere and made him look years younger.

"Garrett is a good friend, and he is not an actor by trade. We grew up together."

"He met my sister at the Bickford ball?" Hallie asked with interest.

"So it seems, Miss Martin. It was as much a surprise to me as it obviously was to you," Sebastian admitted.

Hallie pulled out the invitation from her reticule.

"Here is the invitation for the Kent house party." Sebastian took it from her and slipped it into his coat pocket.

"Perhaps we should discuss what kind of courting you expect, Miss Martin. Being American, you must have specific expectations." Sebastian said looking at her directly in the eyes.

"What do you mean...being American...I have certain expectations?" Hallie asked, not certain if this was perhaps an insult of sorts.

"Well, do you have a beau in America? Maybe there is an expectation of some subtle liberties...like some touching." He whispered close to her ear as if it were confidential.

Hallie looked surprised and then anger crossed her face, creating a sparkle in her eyes he had learned to recognize and admire.

"Why that is scandalous, Alex...er Mr. Stainton..er...My Lord."

He chuckled at her discomfort.

"Good to remember my title. One slip and the charade is over. A little touching is harmless depending on where the touching is, of course. It would definitely add to the pretense." He quirked a wry smile her way.

"I do not think touching is necessary. It can only lead to trouble, I can assure you."

"Can you? It sounds like you may be experienced in that kind of trouble, Miss Martin. I mean the fact that you can assure me and all." He suppressed another smile.

"Why that is despicable, My Lord. What do you take me for? I am a lady...er not in your country. I am nobody, but in my country, I am of a good reputation and considered a lady of the highest standing." Her face was flushed and she was rattled.

"I do not mean to offend you, Miss Martin. It is rumored Americans offer certain liberties..."

"Not those kind of liberties, My Lord. Why, that is outrageous…" she huffed.

"What is it in your country…the pursuit of happiness? Yes, that is it, the pursuit of happiness."

He was in his element. He had not experienced this much fun in ages. In fact, since he was in knee highs teasing his twin.

"Not that kind of pursuit of happiness. You must think us barbarians."

"I suppose we got off the subject. I believe I would like to know your expectations of our courting. Perhaps I should take you for a drive in Hyde Park where everyone would see us. Tomorrow. Say two?"

"You have a carriage?"

"I think I can get my hands on one, yes."

"I would tell my father we met here at Gunter's." Hallie added as if rehearsing.

A tiny frown marred her expression as she thought through this story for flaws.

"Not to mention, Viscount Montjoy introduced us. Your sister has already had introductions to the Viscount at the Bickford ball." Sebastian added.

"He may not be a Viscount."

"Oh, he is a Viscount."

"Really? Why is he socializing with an actor?"

"Are you a snob, Miss Martin?"

"Of course not."

"I already explained that he is a childhood friend, and we went to university together."

"You went to university?"

"You are indeed a snob, Miss Martin." He laughed.

"Blast it, I am not. Er...sorry. You just strike me the wrong way. You are quite good at it, I might add. It just seemed so unlikely that...oh, never mind. I am just digging myself a deep hole."

"Maybe some practice would not be out of line. To make you more comfortable. Remember you want to convince people we are courting."

"What do you mean...practice? That sounds suspicious to me."

"And that is why you need practice. Take off one glove, Miss Martin."

"Pardon? Why?" Hallie looked uncertain now. Maybe this entire thing was a bad idea.

"Just take off the glove and trust me."

He held out his hand for the glove. She started to unbutton the pearl button at the wrist and he took her hand in his and deftly unbuttoned the pearl button and eased the glove slowly off her hand watching her facial expression the entire time. Then when he had the glove off, he bent his head over her wrist and kissed her pulse there ever so gently...and then the palm of her hand.

Mercy.

She could feel his warm breath fanning her wrist. Hallie tried to take her hand back, but he held it firmly in his and again touched his lips softly over her skin like a whisper of breath.

Hallie heard a sound and realized it came from her own mouth. Was it a groan? How humiliating. He was watching her face for her reaction. She closed her eyes a moment to catch her breath. Could he hear her heart beating? It was pounding so hard, it felt like it would take flight. It seemed an eternity before he was working her glove back over her fingers and buttoning the wrist once again.

"I could do that. It's a nice touch to convincing people we are courting," he said casually.

She looked at him like he was crazy. He wanted to laugh but took control of his humor.

"Are you out of your mind? Who taught you that? What kind of fancy trick...you scoundrel! Do you do that with all your..."

"Careful, my love."

"And do not call me 'your love.'" Hallie retorted, gaining some control over her condition, such as it was.

"Do not dismiss it out of mind. I think it a nice touch, my love. See?"

"I see nothing. You are irritating at best. I would never court with you."

"But you are. Remember, hummm?"

"I remember that I hired you. That means you do as I want, not the other way around, My Lord. Oh, lud."

"You are quite dramatic. You must be high strung."

"What if I fire you? I am losing what little patience I have."

"I think they are coming back. Take a deep breath and relax."

She looked at him with daggers.

Hallie looked across the street as the Viscount and her sister were coming across. Violet was laughing at something he said. They were each carrying the ices as they made their way to the table. The Viscount and Violet obviously were enjoying themselves, adding to the fuel Hallie had coursing through her veins. Hallie wished she had thought to bring her fan. Her face must be ten shades of red.

Sebastian stood and reached to help Violet with her two ices she was carrying.

Oh, you should have seen the crowds. We had quite a time getting our ices, did we not, My Lord?" Violet looked to Garrett for confirmation.

"I have never seen so many people wanting ices all at once. But Miss Martin was very aggressive and squeezed her way to the front." Garrett laughed.

"Well, we were next, but that little girl just shoved her way to the front and expected everyone to just let her in. We had waited patiently. I was not going to let her steal our turn!"

Garrett broke into a contagious laugh.

"She was magnificent. The Queen's army could use her."

They all sat and started in on their ices.

"They have every flavor imaginable, I dare say," Garrett said, as he swallowed a large bite.

"No. They do not have strawberry. It is not my favorite flavor, but I do like strawberries," Violet said.

"For that matter, they do not have my favorite flavor," Garrett added.

"What flavor would that be, My Lord? "Hallie asked with interest.

"Brandy. They do not have brandy. I would come here daily if they had that flavor." Garrett said with a mischievous smile.

"Maybe that is why they do not have it, my friend." Sebastian smiled wryly.

Violet looked at Sebastian. "My sister tells me your play is wonderful. I am sorry I missed it. Although if I had not been at the Bickford ball, I would not have been introduced to the Viscount Montjoy." She gave a coy smile to Garrett.

Garrett raised his eye brows at Sebastian in confusion. Sebastian ignored the look he got from Garrett.

"You have plenty of time to see the play Miss Martin. It runs for two more months. The Bickford ball is the event of the year."

Violet smiled. "I am certain you are right, My Lord." Violet returned with a chuckle and looked to Hallie.

Now, Garrett looked positively flummoxed. He looked again at Sebastian, waiting for an explanation that did not come. There were secrets here, and he was not in on it. He wondered what Sebastian was pulling. Some odd deception.

"Oh, he was quite believable, I dare say," Hallie added, as she ate another bite of her ice with relish. "I loved the part where you swept the character Kate off her feet. It was very unexpected and so funny."

Sebastian nodded and Garrett bumped his shoulder in hopes of clarity.

"You are doing a tremendous job. No one would question that you are a Duke. Your performance is absolutely flawless. You are arrogant, confident, smug, and cocky...all the qualities that make a title real, "Hallie added.

"I would not think those are qualities anyone would want." Sebastian muttered and then sighed.

"Just the same, you have them, and they are believable. You have known him, what do you think Lord Montjoy?" Hallie asked as she licked a drop of ice before it ran off her spoon.

Garrett grinned and nearly laughed. "Yes, I would agree. He pulls it off well. Very realistic, I would say."

"You should look down on people like they are inferior." Violet added and looked for approval from the others.

They all nodded, except Sebastian who scowled. Sebastian realized they were making sport of him, and he was not certain he liked it. Garrett knew something was adrift and wanted answers Sebastian realized, but now was not the time. Garrett had no problem joining in the fun, however.

"You could dress a little more colorfully too. Your black is tasteful, but not typical of most titles, do you not agree, Lord Montjoy?" Hallie suggested as she inspected Sebastian's apparel.

"The entertainment is over. You have spoiled my ice, quite frankly." Before he could say more, a waiter appeared to remove the empty dishes. Sebastian stood. "I apologize to you ladies, but I must be off." Garrett also stood and bowed to the ladies.

"I forgot you have a performance tonight." Hallie said.

"Yes, well, I will see you...say two tomorrow for our ride in the Park, Miss Martin." Sebastian nodded once to Hallie who smiled in return. They all said their good-bye greetings.

After the men left, Violet looked at Hallie with concern. "What has you at odds, Hallie? He is perfect for the job."

"He is just difficult. He is supposed to be working for me, but he seems in control. I feel like he is getting the best of me somehow."

Hallie looked bewildered and frustrated at the same time.

"I am not happy. It's as if there is some private competition I am not aware of." Hallie muttered.

"I think you are over-thinking this, Hallie. You already put this in motion. You are not thinking of quitting your plan, are you?"

Hallie was silent a moment.

"I just do not know. He makes me uncomfortable. My stomach is upset every time I am around him. Lud. He is hand-some, I will give him that."

"You are not falling for him, are you?" Violet asked as she straightened her hat in place.

"Heavens no. He is not what I want in a husband. He demands too much control. I would wear myself out trying to be independent." Hallie cringed at the very idea.

Violet leaned in close.

"Perhaps you feel lust for him." Violet whispered in Hallie's ear.

Hallie cringed. "You think I want to have bed sport with him? I am not insane."

"Just a little 'touched' is all, I would say," Violet said standing.

Hallie frowned and looked up to her sister.

"Please sit down, sister, and tell me why you did not share the fact that you met a Viscount at the Bickford ball...and that he met you here. Was that planned? Do you not trust me? I am hurt beyond repair," Hallie admitted sighing.

Violet sat down and put her hand over her sister's.

"Please do not be hurt Hallie. I just did not think it would come to anything and just wanted to protect myself from disappointment. I was actually surprised to see him here. He did say he was coming, but seemed uncertain...I did not think he would follow through."

"Does Mother know?" Hallie asked.

Violet nodded. "Of course, she was over-joyed. I thought she would faint when Lord Montjoy took me from the wall-flower shelf to dance. She answered for me, before I could turn him down."

"You would turn him down a dance?" Hallie asked, stunned.

Violet nodded.

"I thought I would disappoint him. There were so many beautiful women there. I was afraid my dancing skills would not be good enough. But he is quite the dancer. He makes even me look good."

"Violet, you must have confidence in yourself. You are beautiful and accomplished. Do not let Father hear you say this about your dancing after what he spent on dancing lessons for us!" Hallie responded. "Viscount Montjoy is quite the catch. He is handsome. I wonder if he is rich or looking for a rich wife."

"You are not serious, are you? The man just had an ice with us," Violet muttered wide-eyed. "You are sounding like Father now. You are practically planning a wedding."

Violet looked at Hallie with disappointment.

"I have not betrayed you. I just pointed out the obvious, that is all. With this brewing, I may have Father off my tail. Does Father know?"

"If Mother knows, and she does, then Father knows. They keep no secrets. You are virtually talking of one person." Violet was starting to show her frustration with her sister. "You are not using me to get Father off your case. You must stop this now, or I will stop sharing anything with you!"

"I am sorry. It just seemed too good to be true. I will not speak of it again. I don't want to lose what we have. I promise to support you." Hallie drew Violet into a hug.

As Sebastian left Gunter's with Garrett, he knew Garrett would demand an explanation. Just how much to tell him… that was the question.

"What is going on, Sebastian? It sounds like…well, the lady thinks you are not a Duke, but acting like one. I am intrigued, I must say. It does sound complex. I was certain I might give it away...because my *friend* did not trust me enough to tell me what the bollocks is going on!"

"She thinks I am Alex."

Garrett looked astounded. "Now, why would she think that?"

"I went to see Alex the night of the Bickford ball to wish him luck. I was in his dressing room when Alex left for a moment. Miss Martin came in and said she wanted to hire me to play the part of a Duke. Obviously, she thought me Alex."

"Why did you not tell her you *are* a Duke, for God's sake?"

"Actually, I don't know. Perhaps I was afraid she would not hire me...and I wanted to see her again." Sebastian frowned in thought. "She is interesting." Why was he making excuses? He was a decisive man. He was showing how rattled he was.

"Why does she want an 'acting Duke,' and not a real Duke?" Garrett was feeling even more confused and frustrated.

"She wants to fool her father into thinking she is being courted by a Duke so that he will stop setting her up with future husbands."

"Bloody hell, Sebastian. Do you know how dangerous that is? You could end up actually married. Have you thought of that, pray tell? It could very well be a trap."

Sebastian glared at Garrett. Of course he thought of that. He was not a total buffoon. "Suffice to say, I am bent on this course, so how about supporting me, friend?"

Chapter 6

Hyde Park, February, 1870

Sebastian drove his phaeton toward the resident townhouse of Joseph Pritchard. He stopped for some cross traffic and pulled the piece of paper from his coat pocket and read it again as he waited. Derrick had sent him the note, and he had to smile at the caution Derrick always took. No names, no dates, no seal, and the paper was torn as if it were a scrap of unimportant paper. It was a simple message but said what it needed to say. No one would guess who it came from or what it meant. Derrick did his job well. Of course, survival depended on such measures for Derrick.

He is being watched.

It was not surprising that Martin was being watched. There was still a great deal to be learned, and time was not in his favor. A life was at stake. He pulled in front of the townhouse and looked around. There were many places a person could stay hidden to watch this townhouse and not be easily seen. He jumped down and walked toward the front door.

A butler answered the door and invited him inside to wait for Miss Martin. He was told that he was expected. He looked up the stairs to the first landing and saw her. Her hair was magnificent. She did nothing to hide it. The shiny red curls bounced to the rhythm of her steps. She looked saucy. Her muslin gown was simple, but nothing to tame her spirit and energy. The light green color showed off her eyes, and the bonnet she carried matched her gown exactly. She stopped a moment and stood on the next step as she met his eyes with her own sparkling gaze. She smiled directly at him and continued on. It was not rehearsed, but she was good at it.

Flirting, that is.

She seemed innocent of that pretense, but she had natural ability. Oh, he was smitten, that was certain. He could not help but smile at her. That is what she did to him. Kept him off balance and guessing. There was nothing common about her.

"My Lord. I hope that I did not keep you waiting. I do hate to be tardy," she said as she put the bonnet on her head.

Most women used a mirror to adjust their bonnet just so... to get the most out of their appearance. Not Miss Martin. She was oblivious of her appearance and even her charm for that matter. She tied the ribbons beneath her chin capably and without concern. But how could a mirror improve her appearance anyhow, he thought?

"I am early. Also a sin to some. I also hate to be late and thus end up most places with time to spare."

He escorted her to his phaeton. She gazed at it with surprise. "You can drive one of these...?"

He laughed. "Yes. I can drive this phaeton, although I would much rather race it."

He was teasing her. But still she had never ridden in a phaeton. Her father thought them dangerous. Well, Alex did admit to racing them.

"Are you planning on racing this afternoon, My Lord?"

"I would not dream of endangering your life by racing, Miss Martin."

He put his hands on her waist and lifted her easily to the seat. He walked around to the other side and jumped onto the bench. He scooted next to her as he grabbed the reins from the footman holding them.

There were four beautiful, matching gray horses that led them down the street toward the park.

"I am surprised you did not have your father lined up to meet me. You are trying to impress him that you are being courted a Duke, are you not?"

She turned her head to look at him only to see his profile.

"Well, it seems he has already met you at the Bickford ball. He is quite pleased that we are going for a ride in the park. You recklessly took an existing Duke's identity, Mr. Stainton. This poses a serious problem. You said yourself that posing as a title is a serious offense. This seems a bit reckless."

Sebastian quirked a sly smile at her. "You hired me to act the Duke and I will. Allow me to take care of this small issue. I assure you it is not a problem."

"How can it not be a problem? He has met the Duke of Ashford. He will see you as an impostor. It will give credibility that I do not have any sense."

Sebastian gave a bark of laughter.

"There is nothing funny about this. What are we to do now?"

"For now, enjoy the park Miss Martin. There are nearly four hundred acres of lush vegetation, trails, and water features to attract your interest." He was smiling now and seemed unconcerned with the issue at hand.

Once again, she had to question her judgment.

"Humph..." she muttered as she sat up taller on the bench and watched the traffic promenade in the park.

This was a social occasion where people dressed up to be seen. They traveled in their best carriages, using their best horses. Those who walked carried umbrellas to protect them from the sun. It was the place to be.

But she could not enjoy her ride, because he did not understand the problems they faced. She would have to do all the planning and thinking now. He was obviously not capable. He was frustrating and stubborn. How could he attend the house party now? Her father was forgetful, but not so much that he would accept Mr. Stainton for the Duke of Ashford, whom he actually met...and liked.

"How did your family fare in the war, Miss Martin?"

"What?" She had not been paying attention. Caught woolgathering.

"The Civil War, Miss Martin. What state do you come from?"

He was changing the subject. She took a breath and sighed. "Ohio," she muttered.

Hallie hated talking about the war. She had been young, but not so young that she did not understand how horrific things were back then.

"We lived down the street from a house that was part of the underground railroad. My mother would take food and clothing…sometimes money to give to Samuel and Sally Wilson. It was their house and efforts that helped escaped slaves get to Canada or just keep them hidden for a time until it was safe."

"Your state was Union. It was dangerous, was it not?"

Hallie nodded. "Mother asked my father to take a young girl home who was injured and needed quite a bit of nursing. Father brought her home at night wrapped in a blanket. We all helped. We knit caps and socks. Mother made blankets out of rags, and we made packages for the people to take with them to Canada."

"What happened to the girl?"

"She was so young that Mother worried how she would survive on her own without anyone to care for her. Mother nursed her to health and offered her a job working for our family, although she would have to stay hidden until after the war. It was still dangerous."

"Did she stay?"

"We all loved her by then, and she began to trust us. Yes. She stayed. She helps my mother with sewing and mending. We girls taught her to read and write, and she now reads books from our home library. Her name is Missy."

Sebastian listened and filed away anything Benjamin got up to during the war that might have attracted trouble for him. He nodded at people as they passed.

"Was your father in business during the war?" Sebastian asked as he tipped his hat at a group of walkers standing to the side of the path.

"Yes. He has a shipyard where he built gunboats and Union vessels that carried supplies to the troops during the war. He thought that after the war, there would still be a need for vessels of some sort. And he does build vessels...just not as many."

Sebastian gave this all some thought. He could have created enemies. He certainly dabbled in a lot of different things.

"He sounds like a shrewd business man. I admire that in Americans. Titles in our country are not admired when they pursue business. And yet, so many estates are in financial ruin and could use some good sound business sense."

Hallie smiled. "Perhaps you are fortunate to not be a Duke."

Sebastian laughed. He enjoyed her company. The Civil War had affected many other countries that depended on cotton. Some had supported the Southern states just to obtain cotton. He personally could not support slavery. He had met a man from Virginia and disliked his arrogance and his pride in owning other human beings. There was a cruelty in that man's eyes.

"I am fortunate, that is true." He avoided the truth. He could have corrected her and deliberately avoided doing so. He would feel guilty for that later.

Benjamin Martin watched his wife negotiate with the seamstress. He was proud of her. She was beautiful and resourceful. They had money, but she was cautious with his money just the same. She treated money with respect, as he did. They shared knowledge about business, and she was smart and capable of giving him good advice. He would tell her so. Yes, as he watched her, his love for her always grew. Iris and Poppy were learning from her, too, as they watched their mother discuss her purchases. They would soon be going on to Gunter's to celebrate their purchases. He needed to leave them to their errands. He was off to meet Joseph Pritchard. They were going to an auction for farm equipment. Joe wanted to see the latest equipment, and he was always interested in business of any sort.

"Alice, I am going to have to leave you women to your business. I am going to meet Joe."

"Oh, Benny, I wanted you to have ices with us. Gunter's is such a wonderful place and the ices..."

"I know, I know, Love. Another time. There is an auction..."

"Of course. Business. How will you get there? Will you take the carriage?" Alice looked at him with admiration. He always took care of her even when business called him. She knew he would take care of things even though his heart was being tugged to an auction.

"No. I will get a public carriage. I will see you at dinner. You will need a large carriage to take home all your purchases," he said with a smile.

"Did I spend too much, Benny? I just wa[nt] compare with the English beauties."

"My bouquet does not need any gowns or lace to enhance their natural beauty, Alice. Never worry about the money. "

He gave her a kiss on the cheek and left the women to their shopping. He stepped into the street and flagged a public carriage that stopped in front of him. He told the driver his destination and stepped in, sitting on the seat facing the driver.

Before the carriage began moving, however, a man opened the door and jumped into the opposite seat.

"This is my carriage sir." Benjamin said, wondering at the gall of this man. He drew in a breath of frustration at this man's audacity.

"I want just moment of your time, Mr. Martin." Benjamin was surprised that this man intended to accost him. Knew him by name. Which meant he was being followed. His family may even be in danger, Benjamin thought with some dread. Neil Piedmont pulled out some papers from his satchel. He handed them toward Benjamin.

"I offer you a fair price for your refinery. It is nearly double what you paid for it." Neil waited for Benjamin to respond.

Benjamin grew red in the face. He could barely control his anger. "I trust this comes from Rockefeller. I told him my refinery is not for sale. That is final. I do not wish to discuss this further. Tell him that and get out of my carriage. There are other refineries he can buy. He already bought my railroad, and I have nothing else I want to sell to him or anyone else."

Neil reached over and grabbed the lapels to Benjamin's coat and drew him across the space between the seats. They were face to face.

"You must reconsider my generous offer Mr. Martin You will not get another opportunity like this one."

Benjamin tried to swing his fist at Neil who had a firm grip on his coat. He had no momentum. With no warning Neil punched Benjamin in the face so fast that Benjamin had no idea it was coming. Before he could take a breath and recover from the assault, two more punches came in fast succession. He sagged against the seat, defeated with pain over-whelming him.

'Neil tapped on the roof of the carriage. The carriage stopped and Neil opened the door to get out. He turned. "Sign the papers." And then he was gone.

Benjamin was gasping for breath. His nose was bleeding, and he had a cut on his lip that was bleeding profusely. He took out his handkerchief and blotted his face. His handkerchief was soon wet with his blood.

Alice was right. He needed a bodyguard, or a gun. Although a gun meant practice and the mind set to use it when necessary. Perhaps his entire family was endangered. He would speak to Joe about his options. He was astounded that his problems followed him overseas. He could not believe his tiny refinery would merit so much violence. It was only a small business, just getting started. What difference could this small fledging operation make to a man rich beyond comprehension? There was something else. There had to be. His pride was injured. How could he hide this from Alice? She would worry herself speechless...he actually chuckled at the thought. God in heaven, it hurt to laugh.

Neil walked quickly and efficiently to his hotel room. His knuckles hurt. God, how he hated to injure himself. But it had all been necessary. The stubborn fool. Rockefeller did not ask him to injure anyone. Someone else did, and he did not get paid to fail. He was persuasive. It usually got him what he wanted. He did not have much time now. Once he got physical with someone, the time was short if he wanted to succeed and not get caught. A crucial detail, but very important...to not get caught.

He poured himself a small glass of brandy. He never wanted to drink too much as to risk his survival. A tap to the door. He swallowed the last drop in his glass. As he opened the door, a man shoved his way into the room.

He was a short man, dressed inconspicuously as to draw no attention to himself. Yet, his clothing was expensive. "Well,...?"

Neil watched the man with narrowed eyes. He did not trust him, and why should he?

"I have given him the papers and warned him to sign them. Martin will be a tough one. He does not want to sell for any amount, and he is stubborn."

"Did you try to persuade him?" The man said mockingly.

Neil found the man offensive. "I did. And gave him an opportunity to reconsider."

"Martin still believes it is Rockefeller?"

"He does," Neil muttered under his breath.

"Perhaps if a member of his family were to disappear...You do know that the Standard Oil deal has happened? I will not have much more time to prove my value as a partner. I need that refinery under my belt."

"And you shall have it. I am a professional. I do not like to be rushed. You do your job, and I will do mine."

"Rockefeller is not one to cross. He is ruthless when necessary," the man snapped.

"I, too, can be ruthless. I do not appreciate interference or impatience. Mistakes can be made when one is too anxious. Go back to America and leave this to me." Neil said in no uncertain terms. "You are a liability to me."

The man pulled an envelope out of his coat and laid it on a nearby table. He stood a moment and stared at Neil as if there was more to say. But there was not, so he turned and quietly shut the door behind him.

The man drove Neil crazy. His impatience was going to cost him. Sometimes in this treacherous business, one had to deal with the witless fools like this one. Neil sighed. He might take exception to his own rules and pour himself another brandy. He looked at the envelope on the table. It was only half the money he was promised. He could walk away now and let the bloody bastard do his own dirty work. But, that would be reckless. He already had his touch on this, and it had to be done right. He had his reputation to consider, after all.

Sebastian turned to Hallie and smiled. "You are a strong, opinionated woman. Do you have brothers?"

Hallie laughed. The sound was musical and contagious. He couldn't help but laugh in unison with her. "My father wanted sons. He allows his five daughters a mind of their own. As close to sons as a father can have. Did you know my mother named all his daughters after flowers? Father calls us his bouquet. My name is actually Hyacinth."

"I like your nick name, Hallie. He is proud of his daughters. That much is clear. Your fifth sister is not here."

"Rose is married, and her husband is helping father with his business ventures in Ohio. Daniel had been his assistant prior to marrying my sister."

Sebastian allowed a silence where a frown marred his otherwise gentle expression. "You know, I think I like your mother very much."

Hallie looked at him confused. "Why would you say that? You have not met her."

"To name her daughters after flowers…she is very loving, is she not?"

"Why, yes. She is."

"Let me guess. There is Rose, of course. And Hyacinth. Let us not forget Violet. Ummm. Let's see…Daisy?"

Hallie laughed. "That is our maid. And please do not ask. We all are suspicious of that."

"Then Pansy, perhaps. Or Crocus, Foxglove, Cowslip? Let us not forget Daffodil."

Hallie snickered. "No. All your guesses are good. If we were to have more sisters…"

"You must tell me."

"Poppy and the youngest is Iris."

Sebastian laughed. "They are good names. Thank the stars she did not name you after trees. Oak, Magnolia, Poplar, Spruce…" They both laughed. Sebastian found himself laughing more easily and naturally with Hallie.

He gazed at her a moment as they stopped for cross traffic. "I am curious, Hallie. You are beautiful, intelligent…why not court? You would have many desirable men at your heels."

"I thank you for the kind compliments. You make the fatal mistake all men seem to believe. That is, that women…all women wish to be married and have a family."

"And you do not?" One eyebrow quirked at her in question.

"I do not. I want to travel…try things on for size…live and experience things. Once married, a woman belongs to a man. He can beat her, tell her what to do and run her life to his fullest. Keep everything that was hers for himself and deny her property of her own. Women have no say in their lives. They are basically belongings. Titles see their wife as a brood mare."

"I see…Perhaps men wish to protect their wives."

"Ha. That's the common answer. In courting, one see's the best of the other. Then once they take their vows, it is over and one see's the true character of the other."

"So cynical for one so young. What has caused this path you are pursuing?"

"Observation. Simple observation, Mr. Stainton. One only needs to look around to see that I am not just a blathering fool."

Sebastian smiled and worked to keep from outright laughing. She was very opinionated. He found himself entertained by her company and intrigued by her beauty.

"Besides, men are not instantly taken with me here in London. Being American comes with some draw-backs. Titles here are only interested in an American bride if she has money to get them out of financial trouble with their estates. I do not admire the belief the titles have that they should not work for a living. Of course, that is the American coming out of me."

"What you say is true, however, your beauty and…"

"Oh, hog-wash."

Sebastian's belly laugh rumbled the bench. She surprised him over and over again. Courting her would not be a chore whatsoever. In fact, he was having the time of his life.

Chapter 7

Ashford townhouse, February, 1870

Hyacinth Martin, his bride-to-be.

He didn't know when that thought came to root in his brain. But it was a comfortable decision and not one that gave him a bit of grief or even a second thought. Sebastian sat behind his desk in deep thought. He was thinking about the lively conversation he had with Miss Martin. Yes, she would be his Duchess, not a bit of doubt in his mind. His family had been nagging him to marry, and he had always resisted. He certainly understood his responsibility as a title. No question. He had just never met one woman he would consider marriageable. But Hyacinth Martin was just what he wanted and needed. She did not know it as yet, but he would have her as his wife.

An American, no less.

This would prove somewhat a challenge, however, someone of his status set the standard, did they not? His standard. Yes, she would do quite nicely. His mother would have her work cut out for her. Preparing Miss Martin for the ton. He smiled at the thought.

Sebastian understood his responsibility well. He was not eager to take marriage vows until he met this vivacious minx. She challenged him. His solemn demeanor usually gave people pause. Not Hallie. She stood her ground. She would make a fine Duchess. One with spunk, and he did admire spunk. Until now he faced his daily rituals in solemn boredom. And now, he smiled, he even laughed. Things were not so grave. He quirked a wry smile as he thought about her passion for her family and their Americanism. He had to think of the next outing. She thought it to be the Pritchard house party in Kent. But he could not wait for that, and why should he? She wanted to see London and the sights...what better person than himself to show them to her? He discovered that he missed her when he was separated from her company and looked forward to their next confrontation. When he was not with her, he thought about her. How he liked to ruffle her feathers and how easily done it was. Her green eyes would become dark, nearly black with rage, and her hair...well, it was like a fire with flames all shades of red. Her need for independence attracted him too. It was pure American and showed courage and spirit. Their children would be a perfect mix of independence and intelligence.

Holland broke his train of thought with a tap on the door. Holland stepped into the room to announce his brother Derrick. Sebastian leaked a grin at the lavender cravat prestigiously tied to perfection around Holland's neck. The lavender was new. Holland was ever the professional and stood at attention, seemingly unaware of the entertainment he provided his employer.

"Your brother, Your Grace. Master Derrick Stainton to see you."

Sebastian grinned, but had no opportunity for further direction to the butler. Derrick passed the butler into the room and flopped in his usual manner into a comfortable chair in front of the desk. He had the Stainton good looks, and his eyes were the same rich chocolate brown. He wore his hair short, and it was neatly combed. He possessed the Stainton dimples that were displayed frequently by Derrick's easy going casual manner and humor.

Holland bowed. "I will send some lemon cakes and tea in shortly." He left the room and closed the door quietly behind him.

"I like the lavender. Holland has not changed a bit. If he were married, I would accuse his wife of some humor." Derrick smiled at his brother and then grew solemn. "Martin had an unwanted visitor in his carriage this afternoon. I don't think it was friendly. I had the man followed to a hotel, but he has since checked out."

"What makes you think the visitor was unwanted?" Sebastian asked, clearing a table nearby for the tea tray.

"The visitor jumped into the carriage and when he got out several blocks later, he was nursing his bruised knuckles. I need to put another man on this."

Sebastian was frowning as he thought through what he knew. "Martin owns several small businesses and has been of interest to that rich American Rockefeller."

"He is the one who has been busy collecting railroads and refineries."

Sebastian nodded his head. "He just recently announced a new company by the name of Standard Oil. He is powerful and connected. Some say ruthless in his dealings."

Holland knocked and immediately came in with the tea tray. He set it down on the cleared table and politely bowed before leaving. Derrick leaned forward and poured the tea for both of them. He took a lemon tart and bit into it with relish.

"How is your cook coming along?"

Derrick finished chewing his tart and reached for another. "I think she is better suited at something else. She did spend a day with Mrs. Wentworth and can now make a decent scone. I suppose there is hope."

Sebastian took his cup of tea and drained it in nearly one swallow. "I think Martin needs a bodyguard."

"Will he agree to that?"

"I don't know. I will have to talk to him." Sebastian leaned in to get a small cucumber sandwich.

Derrick nodded his agreement. "Perhaps you should have an in-depth conversation about his enemies."

"I agree."

Hallie walked briskly through the front door and started toward the stairs for her room. She heard low voices coming from the library. She normally would not have even been distracted by the voices, however, they seemed to be nearly whispering, and there were several people talking. The voices seemed concerned about something, and it was too much for her curiosity. She tip-toed close to the door and peeked ever so slowly through the crack. Luckily, she was at an angle where no one could see her.

Harriet and Joseph Pritchard and her parents were huddled together talking in low voices. Her father's face was a mess, and she had to swallow her gasp. Stitches and bandages. Abrasions that looked sore. What had happened to him? She caught herself from walking in on them to ask questions since experience taught her that she might be turned right back around and sent to her room with no explanation. Somehow, she would never be an adult to her parents worthy of adult privileges. Unfair as that was, her options were simple and singular. She would eavesdrop. The only sensible thing to do to gather the information needed.

"Benny, you could have been killed. These people are serious and a menace." Alice's voice was strong and assertive.

Alice sat on the arm of the chair her husband occupied. She bent over and touched his wounds ever so gently. She had been crying from the look of her face. Her face was reddened, puffy, and tear stained.

"Was the man American?" Joseph asked with his arms folded across his chest.

"Yes. Most definitely." Benjamin admitted through swollen lips that were cut with dried blood as testament. He pressed a cloth to his lips and winced at the effort.

"Joe, we must alert the authorities, "Harriet whispered with obvious concern.

"I do not know who the man is, and he is so average look-ing...there are hundreds that match my vague description," Benjamin muttered. "I don't see how they will get the man. He could be anywhere."

"There are people I can call for help, Ben. You are under my roof and in my country when this happened. I must insist on some help," Joseph said in a stronger voice.

"Listen to him, my dear man. I cannot tolerate this any longer. You must protect yourself from these bullies. They cannot get away with this brutal behavior. What next? Will they not be happy until they kill you?" Alice stated emotionally dabbing a handkerchief to her eyes.

"They will not kill me, dear. They simply want my signa-ture. Only then will they be happy and leave us alone. I do not want to sell, but I do not want to risk safety ...I just don't know how desperate they could become," Benjamin responded, groaning as his face caused him sharp pain.

"But you should not be bullied into selling if you do not want to do so...," Harriet added reluctantly. "That would give them the upper hand. What next? Do they want all you have?"

Hallie eased away from the door and frowned at the new development. Her father was in trouble and she wanted to help. Uncle Joseph would get him a bodyguard she was cer-tain, but they needed to actually find out who this man was and why exactly he needed her father's refinery. She knew about the very well-respected CID detectives in London. They were known for keeping peace and tracking down criminals. She would ask them to track down this criminal. With that in mind, she quietly walked up the stairs to her room.

Derrick Stainton had just finished apprehending a thug that was wanted for murder and a number of petty crimes in the surrounding community. He had just washed his hands and face from some bloody scratches and abrasions he had gotten for his efforts. He loved the investigations and research involved in his job. His bulk from physical activity as well as his normal body height and weight gave him advantage over most of the criminals. Many knew him on sight and did not want to pick a fight with him. He learned and employed many of what some called "dirty tricks" but all was fair when you were up against criminals. No criminal played fair, and so Derrick learned in order to survive, and his reputation grew. One that served him well.

In 1844, Sir James Graham gave sergeants the right to work in plain clothes, which proved integral to successful investigative work. The emphasis shifted from prevention to detection, which gained respect because it was providing results. That and the telegraph being used to share records, descriptions, and other elements of crime needed to solve mysterious unsolved crimes. Crime was now being reported in records with statistics which could be used to increase police power and specific talents. The National Criminal Record was established and police work became even more dedicated to the science of facts-findings.

Derrick was considered one of their best. He was perceptive and observant. He paid attention to details and had a remarkable memory, making him unique. He put his feet up on his desk, leaned back in his chair, and sighed as he closed his eyes a moment. He got very little sleep, but his work was never dull. There was a cup on his desk waiting for him. It was strong coffee to keep him awake. But closing his eyes for a few minutes was just the thing to keep focused.

Derrick must have fallen asleep. His mouth was dry from hanging open, and he caught a sound just loud enough to jolt him awake and take him off balance.

"Aahummm."

There it was again. He took his legs down from the desk and looked around him. And then he saw her. She was sitting in his office in front of his desk. Staring at him. He adjusted his legs under the desk and looked at her in confusion. How did she get there? Did she even knock? She was a beauty and had the look of a lady. Her red hair was eye-catching, but it was her expressive green eyes that caught his attention first. She appeared to be disgusted with him by her demeanor. And he was disgusted with himself. He was better than this. She had caught him unaware, and that could have been deadly.

"Excuse me sir."

"I did not hear the knock," he said under his breath, hating that he had been caught sleeping.

"Because I did not knock. I saw through the window you were indisposed. I thought I would wait for you to acknowledge me."

"I see." Bloody damn, he thought. It was like rubbing salt in the wound.

She studied him almost rudely. Was his shirt unbuttoned? Was he wearing the scone he ate a short time ago? "What can I do for you?" he finally asked her.

"Have we met? You look so familiar...ah, I know. You appear to be related to the actor at Drury Lane...Alex Stainton." She seemed pleased with herself for solving her own mystery.

He gave a broad smile with a dimple that appeared giving credit to her observation. "Alex Stainton is my brother." He admitted proudly.

She smiled and he witnessed a rare beauty in action. The smile lit her face, making it difficult not to smile in return. "There is definitely a family resemblance. I very much enjoyed his performance. He truly has a talent for acting."

"Indeed, he does."

"Actually, I came to ask for your help."

"First tell me who you are."

Her face reddened. "Oh, my. I do apologize. My name is Hallie Martin." She folded her hands in her lap and waited to explain her need of his service.

When Derrick heard her name, he covered his surprise. Could this be the daughter of the man he was having tailed? She was American. There was no doubt of that. He did not believe in coincidences. He studied her a moment before he commented. "How can I be of service Miss Martin?"

"My father has been assaulted, and I would like you to track the man down and arrest him."

"Why has he not come with you to make a formal complaint?"

Derrick watched her intently. He had an uncanny ability to read people. He could tell she was nervous. She could not keep her hands still in her lap, although she gave it every effort. One eyebrow quirked up in question awaiting her answer. Derrick was a boyish representation of his older brothers. He had the features reminiscent of the Stainton men, but he also had a more youthful appearance. Awaiting her answer, he gathered papers and stacked them neatly. In so doing, he unearthed his name plate facing Hallie.

It read, "Derrick Stainton, Detective."

Hallie groaned when she read the name and then formed her answer. She did not realize there was a "Stainton" brother. A coincidence?

"I think he will get a bodyguard to protect himself, but he feels he does not have enough information to make a formal complaint."

"And you do?" Derrick was confident in his work. His job was dependent on his ability to ferret information out of people. If one made too many assumptions, it could be a determent to finding out the truth. He kept his face blank and watched her body language.

"No. I do not have any more information than my father. I just thought it important to have the incident reported, and since I assume you have more expertise than we do in this field, the next steps would be left to your discretion."

She glanced at the undecorated walls and then the mountains of files on the floor and in file cabinets.

"I would like to talk to your father. Do you think he would see me if I paid him a visit?" Derrick took a sip of his already cold coffee. "Would you like a cup of coffee Miss Martin? I cannot recommend it, however." He smiled at her.

"I know he would see you Detective Martin. And no, I will not require coffee. We are staying with Joseph Pritchard..."

"I know the residence, Miss Martin. Does he know you have come here to acquire assistance?"

"No. He does not."

"I take it that he would not approve."

"You are correct. He would not."

"I will do my best to keep your name out of it, however, I do not lie Miss Martin."

"I would not ask that of you," she responded softly looking down into her lap.

"Tell me what you know about the assault, Miss Martin." Derrick began to take notes as Hallie began to relax in her chair and tell him all she knew.

Got a call from daughter. Now, officially,
I must call on her father with questions.

Sebastian slipped the note from Derrick into his pocket. It could be one of four Martin daughters, but he suspected it was his spirited Hallie deciding to involve herself in this mystery. He decided to wait and see what Derrick was able to ascertain from his interview with Martin. He might not have to interfere. His brother was talented at his craft, and he found no fault in leaving his chore to the qualified. He was on his way to have lunch with his mother at her town house. Ellen Stainton, Dowager Duchess of Ashford, was beloved by all three of her sons. She had been an attentive mother, always taking delight in her children and their activities.

When they were young, she was known to sit on the floor with their toy soldiers and create war strategies with them. They would laugh and find issue with her woman's strategy. However, they always found delight in her visits and attention. She was no different now. She insisted they all take a day to have lunch with her and share their lives, stories, and grievances with her. Ellen was quite well read and connected and found great joy in assisting in some way. The sons were most challenged in finding some element of their lives to share and allow her to partake. They had made an agreement among themselves to do this.

Sebastian pulled up his curricle in front of her fashionable townhouse. He climbed the front steps, and her butler, Jackson, opened the door. Sebastian nodded his greeting.

"Jackson."

Jackson bowed and took Sebastian's coat, gloves, and hat. "Her Grace is awaiting you in her parlor."

Sebastian walked up the stairs, taking two at a time, gathering his thoughts for his visit. He usually did not have to create a problem for her to solve because there were so many things in his everyday life that were perfectly acceptable to share with her for her thoughts. She was intelligent and needed to participate in something worthwhile.

Their father had always discussed his dealings with her, and she missed that the most. Keeping her life interesting was paramount with Sebastian as head of the family. Although both his brothers did not find sharing time with their mother on a regular basis unmanageable, he had told them he expected that much of them.

Sebastian entered the parlor his mother so loved. It was blue. Bouquets of blue flowers of all types decorated the walls in silk wallpaper. Blue was her favorite color, no argument. A Persian rug in beiges and blue set off the furniture, which was feminine and covered in brocades of stripes in light blue and lapis. Vases held arrangements of flowers including white roses, irises, and crocuses. She always wore the scent of roses, and the parlor held onto that scent, even in her absence. He remembered her kiss good night as a child and how the smell of roses would bring comfort and a calm that never failed to put him to sleep. She always murmured, "Sweet dreams, my little darling," before leaving.

She sat in her favorite stuffed chair before the hearth. She wore black, as usual, in honor of her beloved husband, although it was far past time for formal mourning. Her hair was nearly all still dark chestnut with only gray at the temples. She was still beautiful, her dark brown eyes missing nothing as she gave him her head to foot examination. She smiled, and her entire face lit up as if she hadn't seen her son in ages. She stretched out her hands in greeting, and Sebastian took them in his and brought them to his lips for a kiss. He then reached down and kissed her cheek.

"Sebastian. How delightful to see you."

"Mother." He took the matching chair across from her. "You look beautiful as ever."

She laughed at that. "You are a rogue. I will give you that."

She studied him for a moment, her usual inspection, but it was never without careful observation.

"You look…happier…more relaxed. Tell me what has happened since the last visit."

She waited patiently and was not to be denied. She could ferret anything out of anyone. Derrick gave her credit for his talents with the CID.

A slow smile formed on his mother's face. "You think something has happened?"

"I would like to meet her."

Sebastian hid his surprise. "What makes you think it is a woman?"

"Is it not, my dear son? Do I not know you like the back of my hand?"

Jackson tapped on the door and entered with their lunch on trays. His mother liked to eat casually in her parlor with fewer interruptions. Jackson brought two small tables, which he arranged before them and then placed their trays on the tables. Jackson lifted the silver lids and revealed roast beef, carrots, potatoes, and bread.

"Have you seen Alex's performance yet? I was very proud of him. I have been twice now and plan another visit to the theatre."

"I have not as yet gone, but I do plan to shortly."

"Be certain that you do."

Sebastian knew he must go to support his brother. He caught himself before he could laugh, thinking about taking Hallie. A natural thought since he liked her company, but an interesting way to inform her of who he really was. His lips barely twitched.

"What do you find amusing?"

Sebastian realized his mother caught everything. Any nuance would certainly be detected. She should work for the CID.

"I seldom see you display your attitude. You are so good at hiding your feelings," she remarked.

"I am very happy to be here with you, seeing you look so ravishing," Sebastian said with a hint of a smile. He took a bite of roast beef.

"Poppycock. You are hiding something, and I want to know what it is."

"I have something to discuss with you. Do you recall our tenants by the name of Dorsey?"

"Yes, of course. Wilbert Dorsey is a farmer. You talked him into alternating his crops, which turned out to be brilliant, if I recall."

Ellen poured herself more tea and looked to Sebastian..

"You have an excellent memory." Sebastian paused in his story as he took a bite of his carrots. "Several weeks ago, I made it trip to Kent to check on some of the tenants. I paid a visit to Dorsey at his farm. His eldest daughter was there. She is enceinte."

Ellen looked up and paused before putting her bite of potatoes in her mouth. Sebastian, too, had paused. "She was violated by a traveling salesman."

Ellen's eyes widened at that, and she was stunned for a moment as she processed the information. "He is gone, I take it."

Sebastian nodded his head and waited for his mother's wisdom. He had already formulated some ideas, but always allowed his mother the courtesy of coming up with a solution. Nearly always, it was close to his own solution. Sometimes she even offered to do more than just suggest ideas. She would get personally involved.

"They must be heartbroken. They are good people."

Sebastian nodded.

"They must be worried for the scandal, but I cannot see Wilbert sending her away," she added.

"He will not do that. She is not showing her condition as yet, but soon the entire community will know their secret. She is a lovely girl."

"Find her a husband, Sebastian. I believe if my memory serves me, she is a pretty thing."

"It may be difficult with her already carrying a child."

"Give her a small dowry. That ought to get their attention."

Sebastian smiled. "You are a good woman, mother."

She smiled warmly at her son.

"You are so like your father. I cannot be with you and not think of him. He would have been so very proud of you."

Sebastian took a sip of his tea. "Do you think a small dowry might entice some bad options for her?"

"Send out a letter to some of the appropriate unmarried sons of our tenants, and let them know you are sponsoring her, and interview them. Let her make her choice of the ones that pass your scrutiny. In fact, I will interview them. I would enjoy a trip to our Ashford manor. Yes, count me in."

Sebastian laughed. "I will write the letter when I return to my townhouse. Then the rest is up to you, Mother. In fact, we have a small cottage on four acres that might entice a new family."

"Ahhh. Brilliant idea. They would have their own place and a new start."

Sebastian left following lunch with his mother. He knew she would like the task of finding a husband for the Dorsey girl. He smiled as he got into his curricle. He liked his visits with his mother. She had her charities and lady friends who spent their time having tea and thinking up ways to raise awareness for the unfortunate, but he knew his visits, as well as those visits of his brothers, were the ones she truly treasured. She did not show her age or any sign of slowing down. It was his responsibility to take care of her. Not just put a roof over her head, but to keep her happy and occupied.

Chapter 8

Ashford townhouse, February, 1870

*S*ebastian sat at his desk and composed the letter to the five tenants who had unmarried sons of an age be appropriate for the Dorsey girl. He was offering the potential groom four acres, a cottage and twenty pounds to start their farm. It may seem a bit generous for one daughter of a tenant...but he strongly believed that giving a good start in life produced the best success, and it also created loyalty and trust, which doesn't always come easy. It must be earned. If interested the tenantsy would be interviewed by the Ashford Duchess Dowager. Upon the Dorsey girl's selection of the approved grooms, a marriage ceremony and small reception for the tenants would be arranged.

He knew his mother would handle this matter perfectly. He sealed each communication with wax and used his signet ring to place the Ashford symbol in the center. Now for his courting appointment with Hallie Martin. She was somewhat suspicious of another outing which she herself had not planned or requested as part pf his "job" as the acting Duke. He knew he should tell her, and soon, who he really was, but he was reluctant. He was nervous about her reaction, and it was out of his comfort zone. She might end the charade and not want to see him again.

He simply enjoyed her company too much to end it now. He was worried, too, how she would feel about the deception. Sebastian had never outwardly lied to her, but through omission, she was under the wrong impression of who he was, and he had never corrected her. He sighed, knowing her temper. She might not forgive him. Sebastian was not ready to accept that very real possibility. In business or his actions as a title, he did not give a rat's arse what people thought. In fact, he did not deliberate much over any matter...until now.

Alex and Sebastian had played "swap places" many times during their school days. It not only amused them, but it was practical at times. Alex was not always glued to his books and studies as he should have been, and he feared failing and their father's reaction So, Sebastian would take his tests for him and pass with flying colors. Everyone was happy. Sebastian was happy to protect his brother and was beginning to already play the part of the future head of the family, showing leadership skills and a seriousness in all matters.

It had been years since they had done such things.

As time crept by and he had not faced Hallie Martin with the truth, he began to worry about the damage this deception might have caused. He silently swore. What had he gotten himself into? He did not even feel comfortable talking about it. His best friend, Garrett, was finding this all so amusing and seeing him squirm delighted the idiot.

Sebastian was on time to pick up Hallie Martin. She came downstairs wearing a breathtaking yellow merino gown with puffed sleeves and a matching bonnet tied at the side giving her a sassy appearance. A few red curls were bouncing down her back, and she looked so fetching that he could not take his eyes from her.

She held out her gloved hand for him, and he did not miss a beat from taking that hand and kissing her knuckles. The soft scent of roses permeated the air surrounding her. He inhaled the rose scent so familiar to him and yet now so intoxicating on Hallie. He could never associate the scent with his mother again.

"Miss Martin. You look quite fetching today." Ah. Lame. Did he not have a better compliement? Some piece of respected poetry? Damn.

"Thank you, Your Grace. I feel quite fetching…and I should for what this gown cost my father."

So American, he thought. No English lady would dare say such a thing. He laughed. How could he not? She was a delight. "I have special plans for you today."

"I do so like surprises. Are we going for a walk in the park? The weather is perfect for that."

"Have you ridden on the Metropolitan underground train?"

Her mouth was open in surprise like a child might do in a similar situation. "I have heard of it, but never…"

"This part of the track was laid mostly in shallow cuttings dug along the street. There is a roof covering it. We are going to catch it on Paddington Street. It is quite the spectacle. As more and more sections become available, it has become the rage for transportation. Many people are moving outside the city and can easily return for work in very little time."

They rode his curricle to Paddington Street where they caught the Metropolitan train. Sebastian had already purchased the tickets. He assisted her onto the platform and then into the train where she took a window seat to see the sights. It was a far better way to travel in the city, she decided. It was a nice smooth ride with no bumps.

"This is truly amazing."

He watched joy light her face as the streets passed them by. She was easily entertained and did not pretend boredom as so many aristocrats did. There was an innocent rapture in her face that he enjoyed watching. It inspired him to show her more sights, just to see her expressive face and the delight of her fresh, innocent enthusiasm. She appreciated life and the simple things.

"Just look at all the people here…children, mothers, men on their way to work. This must cut down on the horse traffic in the streets."

Sebastian nodded his head and smiled.

"The streets would be cleaner, would they not?" She offered, and he laughed. Her eyes were bright with excitement.

"A keen observation Miss Martin." She was silent for a time, watching the people and the sights. He liked the fact that she did not feel the need to fill silence with meaningless chatter. She suddenly looked at him with something important on her mind.

"I met your brother yesterday." She watched him for his reaction.

"You did?"

"I did. I asked him to help my father. He was assaulted in his carriage the other day."

"Derrick is very good at his job." Sebastian frowned in concern. "Is your father well?"

"He has a black eye and abrasions on his face. He was a punching bag for some vile villain who is roaming the streets, free to do more harm."

"Does he know who did this or why?"

"He does not, unfortunately. I have walked the perimeter of the house to see if someone is watching…or for a clue…"

"Miss Martin. This villain is dangerous, and you must not place yourself at risk. You must allow qualified individuals to handle this matter," Sebastian shot back, with a strong, authoritative voice that left no room for argument.

"But Mr. Stainton…er Your Grace, I am very capable of taking care of myself. "Hallie opened her reticule, which was sitting on her lap, and allowed him to gaze inside. His eyes widened, and his jaw dropped open in shock.

"What the blazes is that?"

Hallie smiled in satisfaction. "This is a Derringer, Your Grace, and I know how to use it. My father made certain all his daughters were trained. I assure you…I am a crack shot, as they say." The gun had a steel barrel and a pearl handle obviously made for a woman.

"I assume it is loaded, which makes it very dangerous to be bumping around in your reticule."

"Of course it is loaded. What good would an empty gun be for goodness sakes? I am not a fool, "she said, closing her reticule with a snap. She smiled in satisfaction.

"I assume you carry this around with you," he muttered under his breath, disgusted with this new-found knowledge.

"I am surprised you would assume anything else. One cannot predict when one will be assaulted. Point in fact, my Father."

"And yet, your father was unarmed. Why? He approved of you owning a gun."

"I know…maybe he will carry a firearm now. He never wanted to carry a gun around before. Actually, to be honest, he does not know I am carrying around this firearm."

Sebastian turned his head to look at Hallie. "Would he approve of you carrying around this gun?"

"Probably not. But his life is in danger, and I want to be prepared…"

"Prepared for what, Miss Martin? If you carry a gun, you must be prepared to use it."

"I am trained and would be able to use it if I or someone I cared about was at risk."

Sebastian did not understand why he was so disturbed by this admission, but he was. The thought of her at risk, having a loaded gun bouncing around in her reticule…was nearly too much to imagine.

He did not know if he was angry or concerned, or a little of both. If he did not care for her so much, he might even think it was funny. It did seem to be another American trait of independence.

"My father had us all trained in self-defense." Now, she felt she was defending herself. His authoritative manner was starting to wear on her nerve. English men! They were so stuffy. She was not gaining any freedom with this man. He sounded like her father, and she did not go about this scheme to get more of what she already had.

"Your Grace, please rest assured that I am very capable of taking care of myself. You need not concern yourself with this issue. If I had known you would take this so seriously, I would not have shown you my gun."

"Did you have it with you at Gunter's, may I ask?"

"No. When I found out about my father being assaulted, I decided to arm myself."

"I see." Actually, he did not "see" her point of view at all. No surprise there. *She is a woman, and who could follow the logic of a woman?*

"I do not think you understand how very concerned I am for my father and his welfare. I know he has had some other issues that seem to trouble him."

"What kind of issues?"

"I don't know how to describe them. He would get a correspondence that troubled him...and then he would close his office door. It seemed more serious than just his usual business. Once I saw him crumble the note and throw it in the fire. I asked him if he had received bad news...he seemed distressed that I had seen him. He was more careful after that."

"Have you tried to talk to him about your concerns?"

"He would never tell me something like that. I am still his little girl. I don't think he sees me as an adult. You can't imagine how frustrating that is."

They were approaching their stop. Talks like this were important to filling in the gaps of Martin's problems. Derrick had talked to Martin and a body guard was assigned to escort him anywhere he went, much to Martin's distress. Martin was not happy about this arrangement, but was cooperating with Derrick.

When Sebastian got back to his townhouse, Derrick was waiting for him. Sebastian went into his library, his favorite place to think, and there was Derrick, turning the pages of a book. His legs were crossed at the knees, and he was smiling at whatever was in the book to occupy his time.

When he heard his brother enter, he closed the book and stood to greet him.

"I did not know you were courting, brother." He smiled and seated himself once again as Sebastian went around his desk to his chair behind it.

"Want a drink Derrick?" Derrick denied the offer with a shake of his head. "You didn't answer my question."

"It was not a question."

Derrick smiled knowingly. "It must be serious. But I will ignore your evasion. I sent a telegraph message to Rockefeller.

Although he wants every refinery he can get his hands on, including the one Martin owns, he says he already understands it is not for sale. He hired a man to approach Martin with no success and has given up...he says."

"What do you make of that?"

Derrick shrugged his shoulders. "If one accepts that, there is something else at work here."

"Did you ask who he had hired?"

"I did. Neil Piedmont. I had him researched. Piedmont is an assassin for hire, but is also known for being a bully to get what he wants...and he is successful."

"Where is Piedmont now? Do you know?"

"He is in London and matches the description of the man tailing Martin. There is also another American in London who is connected to this mystery. He is a partner of Rockefeller's and is at risk for losing his position with Rockefeller, or so the gossips say. He is also an unsavory character I would not ask home for dinner."

Sebastian leaned back in his chair and stared at Derrick. "So the plot thickens...."

Hallie sat at the breakfast table alone. She was up early before anyone else was stirring except for the servants. She picked at her food, distracted by her thoughts of yesterday. She had experienced the Metropolitan, which was exciting, except when they started talking about her father. Then, the reality had sunk in.

Her father was in trouble, and she felt guilty with this courting scheme and knew it wasn't right to be having fun when she should be helping him. She had doubted her wisdom in this entire idea, and now it was clear what she needed to do. Hallie decided to call off the courting plan and concentrate on helping her father. Besides, she was losing control over the plan. Mr. Stainton was controlling everything. He was making more dates to court than the original plan, and her father already seemed to like the "pretend" Duke of Ashford. So, in some respects, it was already successful. Her father was distracted with his problems and paid her no mind. It was time to call the whole thing off.

Hallie did not know how to reach Mr. Stainton except for visiting Drury Lane. With her mind made up, she began to eat her breakfast with gusto. It was like a huge weight had lifted from her shoulders. Would she miss Mr. Stainton? Absolutely. She could not remember another person she had enjoyed so much and yet challenged her. He did provoke her and antagonize her, but she found that trait invigorating. Even thinking of him created havoc with her breathing. He dominated her thoughts as it was and there seemed to be a problem with her focus. Her focus now needed to be her father.

She did feel some relief to know that Detective Stainton had assigned two very competent bodyguards who watched over her father night and day. They took shifts so that he was always protected, although he grumbled about it being a nuisance. One stood duty outside his door at night so her father was always protected. They were large burly men well-trained and meant to discourage anyone from thinking of harming her father.

Everything was falling into place. Neil Piedmont had registered into still another hotel, and his plans were carefully calculated. He had done this many times before and was a good judge of people and their actions. Martin was not so different from any number of other subjects he had approached.

Piedmont understood the need to move often to stay one step in front of the authorities. He hoped by now that Rockefeller's partner had sailed back to the states. Piedmont did not like having someone else in his business, since there could be a great deal of risk in being caught or detected. The man was not trained in the art of persuasion and might be reckless and clumsy. He refused to have partners or anyone close to him while he was working. There was too much at risk.

What if the idiot had not left? Perhaps he should have put him on a ship personally to make certain he was gone. Piedmont paced his small room in frustration. He did not like the thought that he had made a serious mistake, but perhaps he was overthinking this. He understood well the need to stay focused, and any distraction whatsoever could prove disastrous.

Piedmont glanced at his cold pigeon stew that sat on the table untouched, the grease already separating, the gravy coagulated. He had not been hungry, and seeing the meal now nearly turned his stomach. The bread on the plate looked dry and hard. But then, what did he expect of an establishment like this one? Blending in with the common people had its downsides. But he was not here for the food. American food suited him better anyway.

A soft tapping sounded at his door. He stopped pacing and studied the door a moment, as if doing so would enlighten him of the source. He expected no one and did not like unexpected guests. He dragged the door open with irritation.

"What is it?" he snapped, glaring at the young boy in rags standing at the threshold, bravely standing erect. His face was dirty and he was small for his age. He probably had not eaten a good meal in quite some time. He wore bruises, the proof of survival on the streets. His eyes were intelligent and wise for his age. The boy glanced at the table as if the aroma of the pigeon stew had personally invited him. Then the boy quickly turned his head to face Piedmont. Too late the boy realized he had been caught eyeing the food. A mistake.

"I delivered yer message, sir," the boy said with as much force as he could muster. He looked down at the floor since men like this did not appreciate eye contact.

Piedmont's face reddened with rage. He grabbed the boy by his patched shirt and shook him. Then his right hand came about, slapping the boy across the face, leaving a reddened hand print on his cheek. The boy was not surprised. This was a common occurrence when working for slime like Piedmont. The trick was to show no emotion to cause further harm or anger. He had learned this in the streets. It was one of the many rules of survival.

"I paid you for your task…and now you return…for what? Another payment? My dinner, such as it is? You greedy little bastard. No one cheats me. You understand?"

The boy nodded as his eyes were threatened with tears. Summoning up tears was one of his own little tricks to create sympathy. It was worth a try. Once he got an extra coin for it.

"Now, get out of here. And don't come back unless I ask you to."

With that, he slammed the door. He could hear feet running down the hallway, headed for the stairs. He smiled to himself. That ought to put the little beggar in his place. The boy picked the wrong moment to pester him. He was out of sorts…however, he did not appreciate the boy wanting something more or expecting it. He had paid him and that was the end of things. Little bastard.

Piedmont had no tolerance for the urchins on the street. They would steal a person blind and kill if they had the means and the inclination. It was all part of the London experience that he so disliked. Survival was paramount, and the smartest and most street wise of the varmints found themselves alive for another day. They served a purpose. He used them when he had need.

The ones who were caught ended up on a ship bound for Australia, destined to hard labor, and usually never came back. Depending on the court, they could end up in prison, never to face the light of day. Unless, someone spoke up for prisoner, there was not enough food, water, or blankets to cast off the cold damp climate. Most of the street urchins started their trade to survive, and then it became a way of life. No one had sympathy for a thief, so it was a hopeless occupation. Too many orphans found themselves on the streets, faced with a life of crime or prostitution.

Chapter 9

Ashford Manor, Kent, March, 1870

*E*llen Stainton, Dowager Duchess Ashford, sat behind the large desk that had become Sebastian's desk when her husband, the seventh Duke of Ashford, had died several years ago. She missed her husband. It had not been a love match, but an arranged marriage. They both had been agreeable and they both set out to make their marriage work as best they could under the circumstances. Love had bloomed between them without much effort. Perhaps they were a perfect match.

She could almost smell his scent sitting here in this chair. She rubbed her hands on the smooth walnut carved arms chair and took a deep breath, inhaling the sandalwood, slight scent of brandy with a touch of horse fragrance that lingered from his daily ride of the estate. Sebastian wore sandalwood...but no matter. Ellen preferred to accept the scent as purely Winston's. It was slight...barely detectable. She could feel him in the room. He had a presence, and it was still here. She would close her eyes a moment and reminisce. Such a luxury. She occasionally would fall asleep during this time of pure heaven and then, if she were lucky, she would dream of him.

Yes, it had turned into love because they both were favorable to love over indifference. Winston began to woo her late in their marriage and treated her like he was courting her. A faint smile tugged at the corner of her mouth as she thought of the hat she had admired in London. A hefty price tag had discouraged her from buying it. Ellen was frugal, which Winston found amusing. She did not favor wasting his money. The hat magically appeared on her dressing table. At first, she was stumped and had no idea who would have known she had admired it or how it got there.

Winston was mysterious.

He was friendly with her favorite shopping places and made certain clerks watched for his wife and her attention to things she may favor. The hat was sent to him with a note saying that his wife showed interest in it. He not only paid the outrageous price, but there was a reward for making his wife the duchess happy.

He would tell her that his goal in life was to make her happy. Drat the man for dying. Just when he was perfected to be the best possible husband. It was not easy being married. It was hard work if one wanted to make a doable marriage.

Ellen fell a little in love with him each day. They never told each other that they found love, but it was there just the same. No words were needed. She was fortunate. Marriages were commonly intolerable within the ton. Hers was the rarity. She missed the touching. Hands held, a squeeze of the shoulders, fingers tracing the lines on their faces, spooning in sleep, holding each other in a moment of sadness and even in happiness were all taken for granted. Whoever suspected life could change within seconds?

Then Ellen thought of her three sons. She could not help but smile. Ellen knew what they were up to...each visiting her often with problems they contrived. No, there *were* problems, but problems easily solved by her smart, intelligent, and ever so resourceful sons. But she liked the game they played and enjoyed solving the issues she knew were not really problems. One would think she was a junior detective skilled at assisting Derrick in solving murder mysteries. Or giving her advice about the next part Alex would play at Drury Lane. She was proud of each of them and enjoyed their time together. They were also very good to each other, which made her proud. She could not wait for the next issue to come to her...so creative they were to keep her occupied. How she appreciated their efforts. Her life could have been boring, but thankfully her sons made it interesting. She was truly blessed.

Ellen was just over five decades old and still had some of her beauty. Her sons certainly got their masculinity and stature from Winston. Strong features and tall. They were all muscular and sturdy like her Winston. She saw Winston every day in her sons, and that pleased her.

Imagine having a husband one could barely tolerate and then seeing him every day in one's children? No, that was not the case.

Her slim fingers traced the folds of her black taffeta gown. It was a simple gown. No lace or frills for her. She wore her mother's brooch centered at the throat for her only ornamentation.

Of course, there was her gold wedding ring, which never left her left hand. It was a simple band. When they married neither of them had been overly enthusiastic. Later, Winston gave her a band with rubies set around the entire surface. She loved that ring, but it was not her wedding band.

She smoothed back a strand of dark chestnut hair that was still silky and shiny. The hair at her temples was nearly white and added character, she thought. She did not try to hide her age.

She was proud of it.

It took courage to age and find one's way though the labyrinth of life. There was elegance in her bearing. She was taller than most women and as was taught to women of her breeding, her posture was to be envied. Her back ram rod straight, perched at the front of the chair, chin up…simply her training as a proper lady. She knew nothing else.

To the right of the desk was an ornamental screen. It was strategically placed. A chair was behind it, unbeknownst to anyone else entering the room. There was a tap on the door followed by the butler, who had worked for the family for more than forty years.

"Ah, Davis."

"Your Grace, there is a Miss Dorsey to see you."

"Please send her in Davis. And have a tea tray sent, please." Ellen never forgot to ask politely and thank the help, which was an unusual trait of the aristocrats. But then, Ellen was rewarded with the respect and loyalty of her servants. That alone was an invaluable asset. She always felt that manners showed respect, and she did respect the life of a servant. Another unusual trait, but one she felt strongly about and taught her three boys. Her boys turned out well, she thought. She was proud of them.

Davis ushered in a timid, nervous girl dressed in her best Sunday clothes. She was slight of build with honey colored hair combed back into a neat braid they hung down her back. She had a sprinkling of freckles across the bridge of her nose, and her skin glowed with color from the sun.

She walked into the room and curtsied in an awkward dip holding the edges of her worn hem out as if she would fly. She waited for acknowledgement before looking at the Dowager Ashford, who still sat behind the desk. Davis quietly shut the door behind her.

"What is your name, child?" Irene looked up from her clumsy curtesy and stood tall with her hands folded in front of her.

"I am Irene Dorsey, Your Grace."

"Sit down in that chair in front of me."

Irene sat and smoothed her worn muslin out neatly before her.

"How old are you, Irene?" Ellen asked appraising the girl thoroughly while she waited to be answered.

"Fifteen." She whispered under her breath seemingly ashamed. She could not meet the eyes of the women before her. She had already suffered the embarrassment her father put her through, although she knew she deserved whatever came her way for this grave mistake.

"Fifteen is young. You find yourself in a difficult predicament, do you not agree?"

Irene nodded her head and lowered her face in shame. "I am sorry for it all, Your Grace."

Irene wanted to curl into a small ball and burrow into a dark hole. She had already wished over and over again for another chance to make a better decision, but alas she was stuck with her bad judgment.

"I am certain you are. Did you fancy yourself in love?"

Irene nodded no. "I thought he would take me away for a better life. He talked of all the places he had seen...how grand it all was."

"I see. This is not all your fault, Irene. The scoundrel who misled you was mostly at fault, but he is not here before us to accept his blame or make it right. He is a coward and left without a trace, leaving you to face the music alone. He is the worst coward and reprobate. He probably has done the same to half a dozen young women across the country. I imagine you have been experiencing some unpleasantness with your family as well as grief for your plight."

"My father is very disappointed in me, Your Grace. I wish I could undo this." A tear slipped from her eye, and she swapped it with the back of her hand and sniffed.

A tap sounded at the door and Davis slipped in with a tea tray of small biscuits and cakes decorated with fruit. Davis put the tray on a table near a seating area before the fire, which crackled and snapped with a warm steady flame.

"You may sit in the chair before the fire Irene, and we will have some tea and nourishment before discussing solutions."

Ellen rose from her chair and took a seat before the fire where she poured tea. Irene's eyes widened at the assortment of delicate cakes and biscuits.

"I will put some cream in your tea, Irene...and a little sugar. I trust that will be satisfactory."

Irene smiled and it was the first glimpse of a truly pretty girl. Her faded yellow muslin gown did her no justice.

"Thank you, Your Grace." She held the cup with unsteady hands and sipped the hot brew. "It is very good this way. It is stronger than I am used to, and I have not had sugar or cream in it before."

"Have some cake or a biscuit too. You could use some flesh on your bones, Irene."

Ellen placed some cakes and biscuits on a small plate and handed it to Irene. Irene placed her cup and saucer on the table and ate the cakes with relish, catching a glimpse now and then of the Dowager Ashford for approval.

Ellen smiled. This did her old heart good. She watched Irene's manners and wished she could work on those, but no matter. It would do no good.

"You know Irene, it is a man's world. Women do not have many rights. Husbands can treat their wives like property they own. They can beat a woman, torture her, cheat on her, and worse. It is important to make wise decisions because you will be stuck in the muck you create. You have already learned a little of this."

Irene smiled at that. She had taken several more cakes and had a second cup of tea. All while Her Grace told her about life as a woman. She wiped a crumb from her mouth and sighed with contentment. Never has her belly been so full and with such decadent treats.

"Tomorrow we will go to the village, and I shall buy you some new gowns. One will be a bridal gown, two for when you increase and two for every day."

Irene stared in awe at Ellen, her eyes could not get any larger.

"Some boots and shoes and under things too. A trousseau. But this afternoon, I shall interview some perspective grooms. There are six that I will interview. You shall sit behind this screen, behind us, and not say a word or make a sound. Do you understand?"

Irene nodded her head in wonder. "Will you decide who..."

"*We* will decide Irene. We will make a good decision. One based on good judgement. I will be offering a small dowry for you, but we do not want a groom who is looking at that and not you. What do you think is important in a husband, Irene?"

Irene thought a moment. "I want a husband who takes care of me and our children."

"That is a good start. There is much to consider. A woman should not be abused. She should be respected. You must not fail in this Irene. It will haunt you the rest of your life and that of your children too. You will listen to my interviews, and then we will talk about it."

Irene nodded her head and stared into the fire.

"Why are you doing this, Your Grace? There are many like me...why?"

Irene was emotional, that much was clear. But she was right, too. A good question. She was an intelligent girl, all the more frustrating that this had happened to her.

"Sometimes people just want to help. It makes their heart feel good. Your family has been on Ashford lands for centuries, and your father is a good man. I did not answer your question, I know. I think it is in my power and resources to help you, and it would be a sin for me not to. You must have courage. You and only you can control your own happiness. You are only a victim if you allow it to be so. Come and sit in the chair behind the screen. The potential grooms will be waiting for their interview."

Irene stood up and stared at Ellen with eyes filled with tears.

"I have had no one to help me as you have. I am grateful. I do not know what I can do for you."

"Just select the right young man and live your life to the fullest. Make good decisions because your children will need you to do that." With that she hugged Irene and escorted her to the back of the screen.

Ellen sat behind the desk where Irene could see her. She pulled the rope for Davis who came to answer her call. "Davis, who is our first young man?"

"Daniel Lennison, Your Grace."

"Please show him in, Davis."

A heavy set young man with plenty of arrogance walked proudly into the room. Davis had tutored all the young men waiting on how to address the Dowager Ashford. The young man was clean, and obviously muscular, as he was a laborer. His trousers were too short, his boots well-worn, and his shirt had seen better days. It was worn and too small. He bowed in front of Ellen.

"Your Grace. I am here to apply for the job," he said with confidence.

"The job?"

Davis stood inside the room as Ellen had directed him to do. She looked to Davis in confusion. "Ah. Sit down Mr. Lennison."

She directed him with a sway of an arm, gesturing to a chair in front of the desk.

"So, you would describe this as a job."

"Well, yer paying for the task of marrying this girl who got herself swived, and well, you know. Her Da should have kept her in line. I am just the fellow you need to take her in hand."

Ellen was scowling at his words. "I see. And how would you do that Mr. Lennison?"

He smiled at that. "Well, tis easy. Show her who's boss." He nodded his head in satisfaction.

"What do you do, Mr. Lennison?"

"What do I do?" He asked in confusion. He frowned at that and starred at her for an answer.

"What do you do for a living? How do you support yourself?"

He smiled then in recognition. "Mostly I bet on horses. But with the money I get I would be able to feed another mouth. My father has a little farm, and when he goes...I will get that too. So, I am well prepared you might say."

"What about the child?"

"The child?" Again, he was confused. Then it occurred to him what she was talking about. "Oh, that child. I could feed it too. How much does a babe eat anyway?"

Ellen sighed. "Well, that will be all Mr. Lennison. We will let you know if you are selected." She turned to Davis.

"You can show him out, Davis." Davis stepped forward to escort Daniel Lennison out.

"I will be ready to come get her anytime you say, Your Grace," he said with a cocky smile.

With that, the man was gone and Davis was back. This next young man is Elmer Tanner, Your Grace.

"Show him in, Davis."

A skinny young man walked in and bowed before Ellen. He had red hair and was freckled all over his body. His hair needed cutting, and his clothes were those of a farmer. He was clean and held a wide brimmed straw hat in his hands.

"Be seated Mr. Tanner." Ellen indicated the chair in front of her. The young man sat and nervously turned his hat in his hands.

"What do you do for a living Mr. Tanner?"

"I work on my Da's farm, Your Grace."

"Do you know Miss Dorsey?"

He nodded. "I met her."

"What makes you think you would suit?"

"She seems nice enough. I like her Da. He once helped us raise a barn. I need to marry, and this would suit me."

"I see. She will have another man's child. How do you feel about that?"

"It would be all right. I like children."

"Would you hold that against her? The child being another man's, I mean."

"Naw. My sister had that happen, and it caused a lot of problems. I felt sorry for her."

"Would you continue farming?"

"I would…nothing else I can do."

"Can you read or write Mr. Tanner?"

"Not much. A little. I can sign my name," he admitted proudly.

"Do you have anything you bring to this marriage?"

He thought a moment as if stumped. "Just hard work."

"Thank you, Mr. Tanner. I will let you know if you are selected. Davis has your contact information."

Davis showed the young man out and returned to announce another interview. This young man is Dexter Manville, Your Grace.

Dexter Manville was a tall, well-built young man with dark hair and a smile on his tanned face. He was better dressed than the others, with shiny boots and well-tailored clothing.

He was more formally dressed and had a confident smile. He was handsome in a boyish manner that appealed to women.

He bowed. "Your Grace, a pleasure." He waited for direction and she indicated that he should sit. He sat in front of her, and his eyes scanned the room, noticing the books, the windows over-looking lush gardens, and then back to the Dowager Ashford. He had a keen sense of awareness, intelligent eyes, and a casual confidence that added to his presence.

Ellen perked up at seeing him. "What is your occupation Mr. Manville?" Ellen asked, noting his appearance and studying him shrewdly.

"Unemployed at the moment. I just graduated from University and I plan to be an accountant. I have an offer, but I am waiting for the right position."

"You father is a tenant for Ashford, is he not?"

Dexter smiled. "He is. My father saved to send me to University, and in return I am to assist my sister in selecting a good match. My father always wanted his children to have opportunities. I also was fortunate to have a scholarship that your husband arranged. I owe my father and His Grace much."

"You could have your pick of brides from the village...and elsewhere I imagine. Why come to interview for Miss Dorsey?"

Dexter gave her a measuring glance. He didn't say anything for a moment.

"I like the Dorsey family. They are good people. I met Irene Dorsey once, and I liked her. She was nursing an elderly tenant while I was chopping wood for them. She was sensitive and caring to the old woman. We all try to help where we can. She was giving of her time and kind. Too young to wed, I think... but when I read your correspondence, I thought...well, frankly I was outraged that any man would abuse such an innocent. I started to think about how I could make things better. Then I discovered that I wanted to try."

"So, you responded," Ellen stated staring him in the eye.

"Yes. I am responding."

"How do you feel about her having another man's child?"

"How does she feel about that? My guess is she did not ask for this. If you had not responded, she would be ruined, would she not? She does not deserve that. I imagine she is too young to resolve this issue herself."

"No. She does not deserve this."

"I suppose you want to know what I would do should you decide I am your man... I will secure a job as a secretary or accountant, and I will buy a small house and take care of Irene. I would take care of the child as if it were my own. I would try to make her life better and make her happy. I was thinking of marrying someday soon, so this is not a stretch. I will be taking care of my sister, too, and I think they could be friends."

Ellen smiled with satisfaction. "You are an unusual man Mr. Manville."

"Might I point out that you are an unusual woman to champion Irene Dorsey. I am certain the Dorsey family is grateful for your attention and generosity."

Ellen nodded her head and watched him with interest. He impressed her. She did not think someone of his caliber would respond. Yes, he was certainly unexpected. Irene would be fortunate if she would agree to marry to this man.

"I will be in touch with you Mr. Manville. I assume you have left your contact information with Davis?"

Both Davis and Dexter nodded their heads and Dexter was shown out. There were three other interviews, but none were as apparently right as Dexter Manville. Two others were acceptable, however, Dexter was clearly the best choice. Ellen was tired by the time the last man left. She looked behind the screen and witnessed Irene nodding off.

"Irene. Come out and sit before me."

Irene snapped awake and stood a little wobbly on her legs. It had been over two hours of interviews without a break. Irene sat in front of Ellen and waited to be addressed. Davis looked on with boredom.

"Tell me your thoughts Irene. Remember what I have told you, and think carefully."

Irene looked nervous. Her hands shook in her lap. "I do not like Daniel."

"I agree. He would be a very poor choice, and I would have to stop you if you wanted him for a husband."

Irene nodded her agreement. "I did not like Toby or Vincent."

"Again, I am in agreement. Your judgment is sound Irene. I have hope now that you might have the right of this. Who is your choice Irene?"

Irene looked down at her hands in her lap and whispered something that Ellen could not hear.

"Speak up. Show some spunk Irene!"

"Dexter Manville." Irene nearly shouted.

Ellen dragged in a desperately-needed breath, and then she laughed.

"Well done. Now we plan your wedding, and we shop tomorrow in the village. I will tell your groom the news."

Irene smiled as tears formed in her eyes. She wiped them with her skirt and took a deep breath. "Thank you, Your Grace. I will be forever grateful to you."

"Just stay focused Irene, and that will be thanks enough for me."

Ellen knew her next days would be busy. She would send a correspondence to Sebastian and tell him the problem was resolved and brilliantly, if she did say so herself. These little challenges kept her alive, bless the souls of her three sons.

Irene was a loveable young woman, and nothing gave Ellen more satisfaction than seeing to this happy ending. Perhaps the cottage would do, but Dexter may want a residence in town closer to his work. A nice dowry would be presented to Dexter Manville. A small church wedding and celebration in the village would be easy to arrange. She would sleep well tonight.

She would write brief notes to each of the other young men and thank them for their participation. They were necessary for Irene to see the best solution, and, thank goodness, she did. Ellen did not relish the idea of heavy persuasion, but if need be, she would have done so. After all, Irene was young and perhaps not prepared to use good judgment. Dexter was a mature man at twenty and five and the perfect solution.

Chapter 10

Pritchard Townhouse, London, March, 1870

Hallie watched beautiful Violet brush her long, silky strawberry blonde hair. Hallie paced back and forth in front of the window over-looking the garden, glancing at her sister every so often. Violet could read her most of the time, and it saved discussion. But not this time it seemed. What had her sister in such a stew?

"I have decided to call off my plan with Alex. He is too controlling, and it feels like he is actually courting me," she muttered as her skirts danced back and forth with her agitation. It was quite dramatic, and Violet was fascinated with sound of the fabric in violent waves.

Violet turned from the mirror and smiled at her sister. "But isn't that what you wanted?"

"Not exactly."

Hallie stopped pacing and stood in front of her sister. "I wanted to control the plan. It was to be two meetings. Gunter's and the house party at Kent. I have had walks and rides in the park. And the ride on the Metropolitan! He's monopolizing my time for goodness sakes. He is adding his own plans to my plans. I think he is really courting me!"

Violet laughed. "I have never seen you in such a stew. But are you not seeing the sights you wanted to see? Did you not want to see London in all its glory?" Watching Hallie roll her eyes gave her the answer. "So what will you do?"

"It is quite simple. I will call the whole thing off and thank him for his time…I guess I should pay him something for his time." She bit her bottom lip in thought.

"Were you not going to the British Museum with him this afternoon?"

"That's my point. He is pushing things. I feel like he is seriously courting and controlling me. And he makes me feel like I am coming down with something. My stomach is in knots."

"I thought you liked him," Violet offered, turning back to the mirror to finish styling her hair, her lips twitching with humor. Hallie could create a lot of drama.

"I do like him…but there are too many things that are not quite right. I get an upset stomach every time he gets close. I need him to back off a little and give me room to think."

"So what is your new plan?"

"I will see him this morning and clear things up once and for all. Then I don't have to live with this deception anymore. Besides, with Father having problems, I am distracted, and even Father is distracted and off his game."

"At least Father has a bodyguard with him at all times. There is some comfort in that, I should think," Violet added.

"Father is out of sorts about that and tries to ditch him. He isn't successful, thank goodness. The bodyguard sticks to him like glue."

"So you are going to Drury Lane. Do you want me to accompany you?"

"No. I want to do this myself. It should not take long."

"What do you think his reaction will be?"

"I do not give a rat's arse what he thinks."

Violet laughed at Hallie's language. They liked to discover new and interesting unacceptable language to use on each other for shock value. It had become somewhat a game to them.

"I think he lights a fire in you, Hallie."

"Poppycock. I think he has an illicit business on the side. Actors do not make that much. He drives expensive curricles with matched bays, and he wears very expensive clothes. You should have seen his phaeton! Shiny black with gold trim! And the horses were the most beautiful I have ever seen. Expensive. Maybe he gambles or runs a house of ill repute."

"I can see that we are coming up with a lot of excuses," Violet laughed.

"Violet. You are not taking me seriously. Besides there is another thing. He stares at me and leans in almost as though he was going to kiss me and then does not. It is like he is teasing me."

Violet burst out laughing. "Oh my, but you seem smitten to me."

Hallie gave a disgusted look at Violet, rolling her eyes at the direction the conversation was going. It was her own fault.

She sounded petty and child-like, she knew, but she had a lot on her mind, which meant it would be sensible to get rid of the "plan" and concentrate on helping her father.

"I will see you before noon," Hallie said in a more business-like manner. I shall have everything under control by then. Once I fire him that takes care of the visit to the British Museum." She grabbed her bonnet and headed for the door.

"I eagerly await the story that comes from this adventure, Hallie. I think I might write a novel and you will be the heroine. Your adventures will entertain many a reader!" Violet stood and gave a quick peck to the cheek, wishing Hallie good luck.

Hallie did not want the entire house to know her business, so she did not ask to have the carriage brought around. Instead, she went to the mews behind the townhouse to get a public driver and carriage to take her to Drury Lane. She was known for the trouble she could find, living her life somewhat recklessly.

She wore a blue muslin day gown and a matching blue bonnet with yellow silk flowers, which were placed near the large satin ribbon tied to the side of her face. The saucy of her hat suited her personality.

After ordering the carriage and driver, she waited just outside the stables. It was cloudy and cold but bearable with her warm wool cloak and gloves. She could hear the men settling the horses and the driver talking to the stable hands as they waited for her to approach.

A small urchin of a boy in ragged clothing, not nearly warm enough, came up to her boldly holding onto a note. His face carried a bruise centered on his paper white cheek. She raised her eye brows in question.

"Are ye Miz Martin?"

Hallie slowly nodded wondering what he wanted with her.

"I was told to give this to ye."

He handed her the note and left as fast as his little short legs would carry him. He looked no more than seven or eight... with a life on the street. She stuck the note into her reticule since the carriage was rolling up to her. The stairs were low ered, and the driver helped her step into the carriage. She sat in the seat facing the horses.

The footman told her the urchin had inquired about how to get a message to her, and they had responded that she was to be going out shortly and for him to wait in the mews to give the message to her.

"Will you drive me to Drury Lane, please?" The driver nodded and got up to the driver's bench. As she settled herself on the seat, she opened her reticule and removed the crumbled note. The handwriting was bold and precise but not one she recognized.

I understand you are worried about your father. Come alone to The Red Ox tonight. I can help you. I will know if you bring anyone with you and will retreat and refrain from helping.

Signed A concerned friend.

Poppycock.

Did they think her an idiot? It was probably the very person who had assaulted her father. She would meet him, but leave word where she was, and she would carry her gun. She was not a helpless female.

She was determined to help her father, and, for some reason, she had been singled out by the villain to take action. And she would not disappoint him. It did not occur to her to allow the bodyguard or Detective Stainton to take this on. She wanted to take action herself. She wanted to prove to her father that she was as good as any son he could have. But there was time to think about this later. She must concentrate on what she would say and do with Alex Stainton. One thing at a time.

Just thinking of him got her blood boiling. He made her angry, confused, and jumpy all at once. She could not think straight when she was with him. He was massive in size, making her feel weaker and small. Not a good feeling. This could not be normal. Violet was right. It was an attraction of sorts. She could not sleep...thinking of him. Kissing her, touching her, arguing with her...challenging her. Too much emotion. The butterflies had already taken over her stomach.

Derrick took a sip of strong coffee and stared at the pile of reports on his desk. A little scuffle outside his office and then a ragged urchin burst through his door, hat in hand. His face was dirty, and a red hand print marred his otherwise white skin. He was out of breath standing in front of Derrick's desk.

"Sit down, Mickey. Catch your breath."

The child nodded and sat. "I delivered the note."

"Excellent. Did you let Piedmont know that you did?"

"Yes. Sir."

"Is that mark on your face a gift from Piedmont?"

Mickey nodded. "He thought I returned for more money."

"Bollocks! What a swine…hitting a child."

Mickey knew worse language than this, and Derrick knew it. Mickey had a hard life on the streets, but Derrick gave him work and paid for it. He also offered meals if Mickey were to come by his townhouse. Mickey did not do so often, since he feared that his favor might run out. Derrick reached in his pocket and pulled a coin out, flipping it toward Mickey, who caught it easily. He immediately pocketed it and waited for further instruction.

Derrick had found the urchin two years ago nearly dying in the streets. He was skin and bone, not to mention beaten to a pulp. Derrick had taken him in, nursed him back to health, and paid him to be a junior detective. Derrick often said that Mickey was invaluable for the information he could acquire on the streets. He still dressed the dirty urchin because he was undercover, as Derrick said, but he now owned warm clothing and had enough food to keep his belly full.

"Oh, I almost forgot," Derrick said under his breath reaching for something under his desk. He threw a package wrapped in brown butcher paper over to Mickey. Mickey caught it and stared at it before looking up at Derrick in question.

"Call it a bonus for work well done." After a pause, he said, "Open it."

Mickey ripped the paper and pulled out some shiny new boots a larger size than the worn out, too-small boots he was wearing. He had lived with boots pinching his toes for too long. Mickey gasped in delight as he removed his worn ones.

"My feet like these better, Sir."

"I can only imagine. Put your old ones in the rubbish on your way out. You need only tell me when you require new boots...er...anything." Derrick pulled out a bag containing the lunch his cook made him. "Take this too Mickey." He tossed the bag to Mickey who caught it and stood.

"A pleasure doin' business with yer, Sir." Mickey winked as he opened the door.

"Likewise."

Now, the plan had gone into action and he would get little sleep tonight. Piedmont would make his move, and a trap would be set. He would send a note to Sebastian to inform him all was going as planned. He excelled at strategy, and his eyes sparkled with excitement. Sebastian would be at their mother's townhouse. It was his day to visit her and occupy her time in creative ways.

Sebastian walked up the steps to his mother's townhouse. The door was immediately opened by Jackson, who reached for his coat, gloves, and hat. Sebastian nodded his head to Jackson.

"Jackson. I am early."

"Your Grace. The Dowager Ashford awaits you in her parlor."

"My thanks, Jackson." He climbed the steps two at a time to the second story. The door was open, and a fire blazed in the fireplace. His mother was sitting in one of the matching chairs in front of the fire. She stood to greet him.

"Ashford. You are early, but no matter. I am hungry, so it works out well. Come sit by the fire and warm yourself on this brisk day."

He sat down after she seated herself again and reached over to gently squeeze her hands.

"Lunch is special today. All your favorites. Cook was inspired by your visit, I think. You must compliment her before you go."

The Dowager was thoughtful in that manner, and her boys picked up on that trait. She always said there is not a day that goes by where you cannot find something nice to do for someone…a kind word, a deed…something. If you cannot think of something, then you should reevaluate yourself.

A footman brought in a tray and carried it to the fire. Sebastian adjusted a side table to share between their chairs. The tray sat neatly there. The footman removed the covers, revealing roast chicken, boiled potatoes, glazed carrots, cream spinach and apple tort for dessert. The footman served two plates and then left the room, closing the door behind him.

"Smelling this meal reminds me of how hungry I am. You spoil me, Mother."

"I try."

"You look happy and perky today," Sebastian said smiling at her.

"As well I should. I am quite content with how things turned out with the Dorsey girl."

Sebastian smiled, as he ate a bite of the chicken. "I had no doubt in your abilities, Mother."

She pointed her finger at him. "Do not think for a moment I do not know what you are doing."

Sebastian laughed. "But you are so skilled at handling these issues. I can always use your wisdom."

"Do you know Dexter Manville?"

"I do. Did you know Father sponsored him at Eton because he showed so much promise?"

Ellen gave a tentative smile. "Yes, Dexter told me that. I guess I should not be surprised. Your father did such things frequently. Then he would utilize the talent he nurtured. Brilliant, I would say. Manville married the girl Sunday, and it was a nice affair in the village. By the way, thank you for the dowry. It was a nice touch."

Sebastian helped himself to more chicken. "The Dorsey girl did well. Her life will be much improved from that of a life with a farmer."

"Well, your letter attracted a nice assortment of potential grooms for her to choose from."

"I bet you helped in the selection." Sebastian looked up at her after helping himself to more carrots.

"I did give her somewhat of a lecture on good judgment. Fifteen is too young for all she has been through and even more so for having a child. She is still a child herself."

"Manville will be patient with her. He is a good man."

"That he is."

Jackson tapped on the door and entered carrying a tray with a message. He walked over to Sebastian.

"A message for you, Your Grace."

"Thank you, Jackson." Sebastian lifted the message from the tray and briefly looked at it before sticking it into his pocket. "Ah, a message from Derrick," he said knowing his mother was curious.

"Do not let me stop you. By all means, read your message. Derrick sent it here knowing you would be here. Obviously, it cannot wait," Ellen said as she took another bite of carrots.

Sebastian took the note from his pocket and opened it. He read through the message and silently cursed.

"Bad news. Something you must take action on immediately, I think. I must take issue with Derrick's timing." She smiled. "Truly. Take care of it if you wish. I will survive this interruption to our visit. Perhaps you will owe me an extra visit."

Sebastian got up and kissed his mother on the cheek. "You are always so reasonable."

"You are surprised a woman can be reasonable?" She waved him on. "Oh, bother. Do take care of your business, and perhaps you will share your adventure another time."

Sebastian was seething. With clenched teeth, he read the note again, hoping, just hoping, his brother wrote something different. But no, it still said the same damn thing. Miss Martin was to meet Piedmont, and he needed to stop her. He had no doubt she would do it with no thought to the risk she was taking. Did she even know Piedmont was a trained assassin? No, how could she? She was to be bait, and Derrick said nothing of a plan. What possibly could he be thinking? He was talking to himself now.

Bloody hell.

He seldom lost control of his senses, but this bloody redhead had the ability to make his blood boil. She was reckless, lacking common sense, and she probably thought she was doing this all on her own. Did she not think that his brother was capable? Obviously not. Of all the stupid, idiotic stunts...oh, and she had a gun. Let us not forget that. Perfect. Let us not forget the blasted gun. He was angry enough that he needed to resolve this issue and now.

Hallie got out of the carriage and made her way to the dressing rooms at Drury Lane. She had to make her way through people carrying props, racks with costumes hanging on them, and actors practicing their lines with no care who was listening or watching. They were all in a world of their own. There was energy, color, and excitement. She found the dressing room. She knocked on the door. No answer. A passing actor stopped and addressed her.

"Just go on in. He isn't answering today because he is trying to avoid an abusive patron."

Hallie turned the knob and peeked inside cautiously. Alex was standing with his back to her looking through a script. She came in and cleared her throat. When Alex turned to face her, she looked at him with confusion, and then she was stunned. Her mouth hung open in surprise. Her mouth tried a few times with no success of speaking. A trait she had experienced once or twice before. Finally, she gathered her wits.

"Who are you," she asked.

Alex looked at Hallie with amusement. "I might ask you the same question. You are in my dressing room, after all."

"What do you mean...your dressing room? I happen to know this is Alex Stainton's dressing room," she added with some confidence recognizing the props and costumes.

Alex laughed. "You are correct. It is my dressing room."

"You are an imposter!"

"Not last time I checked." He indicated a chair for her to take a seat. "Why don't you take a seat and tell me what is going on," he said with amusement.

Hallie sat down. He sat in the chair before the mirror and turned to face her. "I do not know what is going on. If you are Alex Stainton, then who is it I know as Alex Stainton?"

Alex was silent a moment. Then he smiled a warm sincere smile and displayed his irresistible dimples. "So someone is impersonating me?" His grin grew and his eyes sparkled with amusement. A slow gentle laugh grew into a riot of thunderous laughter.

Hallie slowly nodded, a slight frown marring her stunned face.

"I see. And how do you know this person, may I ask?"

"Well, I hired him. He does look a great deal like you. You could be brothers. I met him in this very dressing room."

A bark of laughter burst from Alex's mouth and he laughed until he cried. Hallie watched the display and thought he very well had lost his mind. But she patiently waited for him to get control of himself. She was irritated with the wait for his sanity to return. He obviously thought something about this predicament was hilarious. He wiped the tears from his eyes.

"I am sorry. It is an inside joke in my family. You see, I am an identical twin. Very few can tell us apart. In fact, I am amazed that you see a difference…other than how we are dressed, that is. You are special, believe me."

"You have an identical twin?" Hallie asked in surprise.

Alex nodded watching her amazement. Then he watched that amazement turn to rage. Her green eyes were sending sparks out, and her face was a mottled red. She looked like she was about to burst. Her red hair was not just for show, he thought. She has a real temper.

"Why would he impersonate you?"

"I haven't the faintest idea. Why would you hire him?"

She was gritting her teeth. "I hired him…as an actor to play the part of a Duke," she nearly shouted in anger.

Alex let out another bark of laughter that again took some time to manage.

"I do not see what is so bloody funny!" she exclaimed. Alex stopped laughing at her slip of profanity. She was indeed outraged. More like unhinged.

"What I find so funny is that he **is** a Duke."

"What?"

"I said, he is a Duke. He need not impersonate one. Need I tell you that it is a serious offense to impersonate a Duke?"

"Bugger, blast, damn, bloody hell…"

"That is quite a repertoire of curse words. I think you missed a few, though." He filled a glass with a splash of brandy and handed it to her.

She looked at the glass, dumb founded. "I do not drink alcohol." Her hands were shaking, and she looked at them in dismay. What was happening to her?

Hallie looked at him with confusion, but took a sip and felt the fiery liquid burn down her throat to her stomach. She sputtered and coughed handing him back the glass.

Alex smiled at her with genuine warmth. "First come the curse words, then the alcohol. Next you will be picking up men on the street."

"I am teasing you, Miss. Miss…"

"Miss Martin."

"Miss Martin?" He thought for a moment. Does this woman have anything to do with the Martin from America his brother spoke of? So, this was not so random, possibly planned by his brother. This was obviously complicated. It seems his brother had done a switch and not informed him of the ruse. The damage was done, however. He had already let the cat out of the bag.

"My brother is honorable. You must give him an opportunity to explain."

"Who is your brother...the one who impersonates a Duke, but really is a Duke?"

"Sebastian James Stainton, eighth Duke of Ashford."

"I am too angry to decide if I want to give him an opportunity to explain. I feel like a fool. An idiot as a matter of fact." Her chin came up a notch, and she stomped her foot. It barely made a noise since her feet were small and her shoes cushioned.

Alex quirked a smile. "Did you just stomp your foot?"

"I did. I would like to smash a vase or stomp on the foot of a Duke," she huffed.

She stared a moment into space...woolgathering. Her mind was working on all the things said and done with the Duke to capture the full picture of her stupidity. Reliving every embarrassing nuance. Did she not give him advice on acting the Duke? Did she not offer to actually pay a Duke to be a Duke? And did he not say that impersonating a Duke was a serious offense? Then she looked at Alex squinting her eyes.

"When a woman looks like that, it is not good. I am glad I am not my brother."

"He said the same thing you did. That impersonating a Duke is a serious offense...."

Alex shrugged, offering a wry smile. "What can I say? We are identical in many ways. We think alike...sometimes say the same thing at the same time. And, in point of fact, impersonating a Duke *is* a serious offense. Sebastian is a good man, Miss Martin. I can assure you, he must have had reason for his impersonation."

Alex watched her weigh all the information. Her facial features were continuously changing as her thoughts been processed. This was a woman who had caught his brother's attention. She was the kind of woman who swept into a room and captured all the attention for herself. Energy and vitality emanated from her. Everything was alive, even her hands were expressive in their attempt to communicate what was coming out of her mouth.

He could not help but smile. She was a performance of the best kind, and he could observe her for hours. His next thought was she would make a great character for the stage. She was bigger than life. Of course, she was all American."By chance, Miss Martin, do you sing?"

"What? Sing? Are you crazy?" She stared at Alex in near horror.

"Forgive me. I see a rising star in my presence."

She stomped her foot again. Dratted man.

"I think my brother is a lucky man to have such a woman in his life."

"Really? I would like to punch him in the nose."

Alex had not laughed so much in his entire life. He must thank his brother for the amusement.

Chapter 11

London, March, 1870

Sebastian sat in his carriage trying to decide where to go next and what to do. This was an unusual predicament for him, and he did not like the feeling. He had knocked on the door of Harriet and Joseph Pritchard to find that Hallie Martin was not there. He did have a date with her to go to the British Museum, but that was long forgotten and of little interest to him now. He had to talk to her about that blasted note that requested she meet with a "friend." It was a trap, and he had to stop her from putting herself in danger. Of course, Piedmont meant to use her as a hostage. No doubt. He silently cursed again, not that it did any good.

When Martin refused to sell his refinery, Piedmont did not return to the same ineffective tactics. Taking a loved one for ransom was the next logical step. Where could she be? He looked out the window of the carriage and stared at the townhouse, as if the answers lay in the brick and mortar.

How terrible it was to feel helpless. Dukes were just below royalty. And yet, he felt powerless. All the training, all the posturing, the generations of blood titles, the wealth, the power of parliament, and where did that get him in his hour of need?

Bloody damn.

Where was the woman, and what was she doing for God's sake? She stood him up on his date too, not that that was an issue at the moment. Although that did nag him just a little. Who does that to a Duke? He scowled and let out a frustrated sigh of failure. He was not one to give up.

Alex walked up the steps to his mother's townhouse. He wore tan breeches with a gray waist coat and a black wool great coat. His cravat was starched white, tied in a simple knot one that he could manage, since he had no valet nor did he want one. Jackson admitted him. Dressed like this, he could be his brother, but his sassy grin and dimples gave him away. He was too boyish and jolly to be Sebastian.

"Jackson. How is she today?"

"Her Grace is in fine spirits, indeed, Master Stainton. She eagerly awaits you in her parlor. Lunch will be served shortly."

Alex gingerly walked up the steps to the second floor and entered the parlor with a flourish. Ellen awaited him by the fire in her favorite chair. Her face lit up with delight. She looked years younger with such joy in her continence. She started to stand to greet her son.

"Do not get up, Mother," he said, as he bent over and kissed her cheek.

He sat in the chair across from her and smiled in a dashing manner that made women sigh. His hair was windblown, and he raked a hand through the thick locks, trying to straighten the mess. "

"You look quite smug about something, Mother. You must share the story. I always appreciate a good story," he said, adjusting himself in the chair.

"I do hope that you are hungry, dear boy. I had cook make your favorite. Florentine sole. Of course, there are the stewed tomatoes that you dearly love and orange cake to bribe stories and gossip from your lips. I do love a good new piece of gossip."

"You know the way to a man's heart, Mother. I have saved my appetite for this very occasion," he said, winking at her.

A footman brought in a tray with their lunch and placed it on the table between their chairs. He lifted the lid and served them before leaving and closing the door behind him. The room filled with enticing aromas. Alex leaned over the tray and inhaled dramatically.

"Mother. I live for this. The food I have been eating....well, it reminds me how fortunate I am to experience another one of Cook's meals."

The fragrance nearly overwhelmed him with happiness. His mother so dearly loved to please her sons. She was an unusual aristocratic mother, that was for certain.

She breast-fed all her sons instead of the common practice of using a wet nurse and actually spent time playing with them as well as reading to them or telling them stories. She was animated in her story telling and always said that he gained his acting talent from her. He never doubted that. He could not look at her and not be grateful she was his parent. She had actually enjoyed her children. She was a caring mother and sensitive to the needs of her sons. He could not ever remember having a disagreement with her. Not one that truly mattered, that is.

"I met an interesting woman."

Ellen stopped before putting a fork full of stewed tomatoes in her mouth. For an instant, she seemed paralyzed, staring at him in surprise.

"I...did not know you were seeing anyone special..." she said, tilting her head in question.

Alex laughed. "No Mother. She is not a potential wife. Perhaps for Sebastian, but a little too dramatic for me. Funny, is it not? I am not as attracted to a woman who shows her independence and freedom of thought. I like a woman who wants my help, needs me to work out things for her...but I am straying from my point." He gave her a smug smile. "She can tell us apart."

Knowing this would shock his mother, and being dramatic himself, he waited for the shock to wear off his mother's face. And he enjoyed her reaction as he took another bite, watching her over his fork as he landed another taste of fish. He was giving it dramatic timing.

Ellen again showed her surprise. Her dark brows nearly reached her hairline in question. She now looked confused. No one but she herself and perhaps Garret, their childhood friend, could manage that feat.

Of course, it was easy enough when Alex was in costume and Sebastian wore his formal gentleman attire, but when they dressed out of character or alike, it was nearly impossible.

When her sons were young, she was stumped many times and deliberately dressed them differently so she could manage to sort the two out. Later, their personalities helped distinguish the difference, but a woman could do it now? Who was she? She wanted to know everything and as fast as he could tell the story would be best. This would be a unique woman indeed to have such ability.

"You must tell me this story. I will not be able to sleep tonight without knowing this incredible tale. In fact, I will not be able to take another bite." She leaned forward as if to draw the story out sooner from her dramatic son.

Alex laughed his boyish, deep-from-the gut laugh. That, too, was a difference between the two lads. Sebastian was cautious with his emotions, including his laugh, which was stingy and guarded at best.

"I knew this tale would interest you. Frankly, I was amazed myself. It was beyond odd. She was quite the woman wronged...you know, all fire, fury, and spunk. I think my dear brother has done the switch on her. One look at me and she accused me of *not* being Alex Stainton."

He laughed at that as he relived that moment so rare in his experience. He waited another dramatic moment for his mother to catch up. Indeed, she was processing the information as fast as she could, her eyes sparkling with anxious joy.

A slow smile finally spread onto Ellen's face. Her eyes twinkled in merriment. "Now tell me the rest. I hate how you men leave out the detail we women thrive on. I do not care if it takes all night…do tell. I shall starve in the meantime."

Alex adjusted himself more comfortably in the chair preparing himself for the dramatic tale.

Hallie stormed into her bedroom, her skirts swishing about her legs in a rapid wave of stormy seas. She shut the door none to softly and looked about the room to see if Violet was there. She spotted her in the window seat reading a book, but the drama had interrupted her reading, and she was watching Hallie with widened eyes and an open mouth.

"Oh, my, Hallie. What now?" Violet shut her book and moved her legs to the floor to better face her sister. She was attentive now, ready for the drama. Only Hallie could play such a damsel in distress.

Hallie screeched her frustration in an unlady-like, ear-piercing cry of anger. Her face was contorted with rage, reddened and mottled, tears of frustration wetting her cheeks. Her red hair blended with her skin color, giving her devilish appearance.

"He is a villain! A blasted unprincipled cur. He ought to be put away…I will kill him with my bare hands! He is a lying, deceitful scoundrel. He ought to be strung up by his thumbs and eaten by ants."

"Are you speaking of Mr. Stainton, pray tell?" Violet asked as she watched the drama unfold. Hallie had been angry before, but this was near to a tantrum.

Hallie looked at her and screeched again. "Not *Mr.* Stainton. No. No. Not *Mr.* Stainton. He is Sebastian James Stainton, the eighth Duke of Ashford, the bloody swine."

Violet just starred at her. "He did say he was, iIf I remember correctly."

"But he was *acting*! I hired him to *act* the part. Not *be* the part."

"It seems you need not pay him, since he is an imposter. What about Alex Stainton? How did this happen? I thought you met him in his dressing room."

"I am such a fool. An idiot. They are identical twins." Hallie flopped down on a chair before the fire and glanced at Violet for her reaction. "What am I to do?"

"Well, first of all, you planned to fire him. It seems redundant now. You certainly saved your pin money, did you not?"

"How can you joke about this? Or take it so lightly. I have been wronged. Lied to…taken advantage of…I am a blasted victim."

"The fact that he *is* a Duke and not an acting Duke…" Violet started to say, before being interrupted by her snarling sister.

"He is a rogue, a scoundrel, a devil, a…," she jumped up to pace again, her arms waving in frustration.

"He most certainly is taxing your villain vocabulary." She paused. "He was here looking for you. He mentioned you had agreed to go to the British Museum and seemed quite beside himself that you were not here," Violet said, watching her sister for her reaction. "Mother was quite upset that you kept a Duke waiting...er, actually stood him up."

Hallie stopped her rampage and stared at Violet. "British Museum? Ahh. Well, a good thing I was not here. I would not have known of his deception. Yes. Yes...I need time to think."

"Well, it is a deception by way of an omission. Some say that is not as bad as a blatant lie," Violet offered.

"That is bloody ridiculous. Now I will have Mother and probably Father looking to see what I am doing and judging. Have no doubt. Exactly what I wanted to avoid."

Hallie was pacing the floor like a caged tiger. Things were complicated, and she knew her anger was getting in the way of reasonable thoughts.

"He has caused me all sorts of trouble. Another one of my hair-brained schemes gone awry. I can only blame myself. No. That is not right. I blame this idiot of a man who impersonated himself to me."

"Are you listening to yourself, Hallie? You sound crazy. You need to come to terms with this new development and act accordingly."

Violet was always the voice of reason.

Hallie stopped pacing and dragged in a desperately needed breath. Tears threatened to flow. Her frustration was taking on a life of its own. Her throat was raw and ached with the need to cry out her misery. Violet pulled Hallie into a tight embrace, her arms circling around Hallie and patting her back in a soothing gesture. Violet had done this before. Hallie was all fire and spit, and when she lost herself, as she did now, she would crumble into a soppy mess and a much needed cry until the tears ran dry. Although, Violet thought this particular rage incident was the worst Hallie had ever exhibited.

"The trouble is…I was beginning to like him…miss him, and now he has robbed me of that," Hallie sobbed. The tears flowed unchecked.

Violet understood this all too well.

It was not a mystery what was happening between these two people. Hallie refused to listen to Violet, however. Violet was patient. It would take more than this incident to bring Hallie to her stubborn senses. Besides reading, Hallie was her favorite project. She often thought she might write a series about Hallie's adventures.

"I do not know what to do…," whimpered Hallie.

"But you will, Hallie. You always do. You will come up with the answer or another hair-brained scheme at the very least. I just know it." The sisters hugged, the silence that followed not unnatural to them.

"I would ask a favor of you Violet," Hallie whispered under her breath.

"Of course. You know I would do nearly anything…except murder the Duke for you."

Hallie pulled away from the embrace and glanced at Violet through her tears.

"Please tell Mother and Aunt that I am not hungry and that I have a headache. I think I shall go to bed early. You know I am out of sorts and need time to myself to think this through."

"Of course." Violet kissed her sister on the cheek.

"Will you undo the back of my gown?" Hallie asked.

Violet began the tedious job of unbuttoning the gown as Hallie took the pins out of her hair. Her red, riotous hair sprung loose of its confines and flowed down to the middle of her back, causing Violet a grunt of displeasure as she finished with the last of the buttons, shoving the thick hair out of the way as she worked.

After Violet left for dinner, Hallie searched her wardrobe for a worn day dress made of gray muslin. This gown Hallie used to do dirty work such as gardening. She never liked to ruin a fashionable gown and had commissioned their modiste in Ohio with the task of making a serviceable gown.

Her mother had been quite shocked, but finally accepted the need for the gown. The fastenings were in the front. She put on her serviceable half boots and pinned her hair in a tight knot in the back of her head. Hallie wanted to dress so as not to draw any attention. Well-dressed ladies would be conspicuous in the neighborhood where she was going. She dawned a black coat with a hood that was simple and serviceable. She quickly jotted a note to her sister using the small writing desk in their room. She blew the ink dry.

> *My dear Violet,*
>
> *I wanted someone to know my destination in the event I do not return. I am going to The Red Ox to confront the villain I believe is pursuing Father. Please see the note he delivered to me. His intention, I believe, is to take me hostage, but I will outsmart him. I will be armed and prepared.*
> *With Love,*
> *Hallie*

Hallie tucked the note delivered to her from the villain beneath her note to Violet and left it on their bed. She opened a drawer and snatched the loaded gun. She placed it in a large pocket in her gown, one of her reasons for wearing it. She added some coins, and then a knife that lay in their drawer caught her attention. Another weapon she had been trained to use, and she was quite good if she did say so herself. She put that into her boot and smiled in satisfaction.

She took a deep breath. Courage. She could do this. She glanced at the wall mirror and studied herself. Yes, she could pass for a commoner. She could feel the weight of her weapons and knew she could protect herself.

She opened her door and looked both ways to make certain it was clear. Then she worked her way to the servant stairs that would lead eventually to a door at the back of the townhouse.

She would not take the family carriage, but rather a public carriage, to the outskirts of town where she would find The Red Ox. It was a tavern, she heard from one of the servants, that primarily served laborers and seamen. It sounded rough, and although she had been nervous to do this task by herself, something had changed. Anger fueled her energy and determination to follow through with this task, thanks to the "acting" Duke. The cad.

Chapter 12

The Red Ox, London, March, 1870

*H*allie paid the driver and stood at the mouth of a narrow alley, facing The Red Ox, which sat on the street that crossed the end of the alley. It was an old, poorly-kept brick building with a faded sign made of wood that was barely visible. The paint on the sign had once been elaborate, but now was chipped and weather-worn. A street lamp close to the tavern created shadows and strange shapes. Hallie was early intentionally. She watched drunken men stagger out and jovial men enter eager to drink and share their stories.

She wondered who this "friend" was and how she would corner him to get the upper hand. She rested her hand on the gun in her pocket, fueling her confidence. The night was cold and damp, with a marine layer nearly making it dark before night fell.

She was cold in this damp climate, and her thread bare wool gown did little to help. Hallie called it her adventure gown, besides gardening gown, and it came in handy for many a cause and need. It was perfect for her disguise.

A man who could barely stand was trying to get his bearing before going on his way. He looked to his right and then to his left before taking a step forward. Hallie drew in a breath, realizing that one option he considered for his path home was the alley.

If he came her way...she leaned against the cold stone wall and held her breath, praying he would not come her way. Soon, he slowly made his way down the street to his right, and she felt a moment of gratitude.

A heavily painted woman who had seen better days came by and stood a moment in front of the tavern. She ran her hands over her low-cut gown, making an effort to draw the neck line lower to reveal more of her ample bosom. She straightened her hair, which was a messy effort at best.

She finally strolled into the tavern with a confident swagger. Hallie found herself fascinated with the drama unfolding in front of the establishment. A wife dragged her husband from the tavern by the ear, giving him a piece of her mind, which Hallie could hear from blocks away as they disappeared from view. She marveled at the colorful and expressive language from the patrons that came and went.

The Red Ox was a busy business. Suddenly, a noisy, hostile patron was shoved out the door by a large, burly man, who gave the offender a swift kick before closing the door on him. Soon after that, three sailors came down the street, singing a colorful song with many versions of lyrics they could not agree on. There was a lot of laughing and back slapping as they tried to blend their disharmonious voices as one. Hallie watched them, finding it difficult not to smile at their efforts. They managed to open the tavern door and get through the entrance, still singing their hearts out.

A cold gust of wind whipped around the corner, swept under her thin skirts, and caught Hallie unaware. She pulled her wool coat tighter around her frame and bent down to avoid the bulk of the cold.

She leaned against the wall, where there was more protection. Her nose was probably red. Her hands, bare of gloves, were freezing. Her decision to leave her gloves behind was a practical one. She wanted better control of her weapons, but had not thought about the chill that would create an unsteady hand. The time was passing slowly, but the villain would be due soon. She peered around the corner for a better glimpse of the street and its pedestrian traffic.

Suddenly, a leather glove clamped over her mouth and another drew her body against what felt like a brick wall. That second arm was stretched around her middle and solidly restrained her arms against a rock-hard body that could only belong to a man. She tried to elbow him but had no leverage. Her legs, too, were too tightly held against his body to kick.

She silently cursed at being caught unaware.

She could not scream or defend herself. She was caught like a rat in a trap, and it was her own fault for not knowing someone was in the alley behind her. But she had heard nothing. He had been silent, which was curious for such a large man.

She tried to struggle, but she felt her efforts were only going to tire her, so she stopped and waited for what he would do next.

It occurred to her that she might die. He held her in a vise grip. A strategy? What choices did she have? He had the upper hand and there was no getting away...she could not scream since he still had his large hand covering all her lower face. She would like to bite him, but his gloves protected his hands nicely, she thought with frustration. Her hood had fallen away from her head and she felt the cold chill of the air hit her naked ears. Blast it. Now what?

Then his head bent down close to hers, and his lips nearly touched her ears. She could feel his hot breath, which felt surprisingly good and warm. He whispered into her ear so softly she held still to make certain she heard him.

"Relax. Do not move. Promise you will not scream and I will remove my hand."

She did not move for a moment, but then nodded her head in a positive answer. He slowly removed his hand and turned her body to face him. And then she looked up into the familiar face of...Sebastian James Stainton, eighth Duke of Ashford.

Her mouth hung open as she gaped at the last person she expected to see just now.

"Now, close your mouth you little fool. Do you realize what a dangerous position you are in at this moment?"

His voice was soft, but deep, serious and strong. The timbre of his voice sent vibrations through her body. His hands were on her shoulders holding her so tight that she knew bruises were forming along with his verbal reprimand.

"You lying cur...," she nearly shouted.

He placed his gloved hand back over her mouth to silence her, looking toward the street left and right to see if anyone had heard her.

"Control yourself my love, or you will alert every demon in the vicinity," he whispered in a voice not to cross. There was authority in his demeanor, and he was not used to being disobeyed. "Behave or I will have to muzzle you."

"How dare you!" Hallie whispered back. "I did not ask for your help, Sebastian James Stainton, eighth Duke of Ashford."

A sly grin lit his face. "Ah. So, you discovered that I am indeed a Duke."

"You are an imposter, Your Grace!"

He looked at her in confusion. "How so?"

"You were impersonating your brother Alex to me."

He laughed a soft deep rumble. "You mistook me for my brother and I failed to correct you. You wanted a Duke, and you got a Duke. You should be pleased."

Her eyes caught fire, and the green blazed sparks at him. He could see her anger gain force when her entire body seemed to stiffen and her fists were posed to pound his chest. As she laid her fists on his broad chest with all the force she could muster, his hands wrapped around them and flattened her hands above her head against the stone wall. He stood so close that his breath fanned the wisps of hair that had escaped her tight knot.

She was indignant and huffed her displeasure. His rich brown eyes were hooded as he scanned every element of her face, taking note of her reddened cheeks, her lips that had parted to draw in the oxygen that would fuel her fire. There was raw magnetism so intense that she nearly swooned with the power of his presence. His lips came in just a breath from her trembling mouth. His eyes watched her and when his eyes closed, she did the same.

Then she felt the pressure of his lips as they dragged gently across her mouth. His eyes opened briefly and narrowed his gaze to her mouth. Then his lips devoured hers softly at first, touching the corners of her lips, his tongue licking the seam of her mouth, begging entry. Then the kiss grew ravenous, and she lost control of the will to object. Her mouth opened and accepted the first thrust of his tongue. Lava ran through her veins like a fever. She sucked on his tongue and then tentatively tasted the inside of his mouth. He groaned and let loose of her pinned hands. She wrapped her arms around his neck and brought her body against his chest. They fit perfectly.

Hallie smelled him- spices, citrus, and sandalwood. His lips left hers and touched her cool cheek, pressing a gentle kiss there and then down her throat, touching the pulse in her neck. He sucked it a moment and then gently bit her soft, velvet skin, startling a groan from her. She felt warm and protected, safe and comfortable in his arms. She experienced a moment of surprise at that thought. Her mind was obviously fogged and confused.

She was angry, was she not? He had lied and...she must stop this so she could vent her anger. One thing at a time, please. After all, he deserved a piece of her mind. Did he not?

But she could not focus on any train of thought, so muddled was her mind. She could not even think about where she was or how she had gotten here.

She was on a mission.

That much was in the back of her mind trying to find its way front and center…and miserably failing. What was he doing to her?

Sebastian's hand cupped her breast which heaved behind the rough and coarse fabric of her dress. He massaged her engorged breast and felt for the nipple, teasing it through the muslin gown until it peaked into a hard, aching nub. He pinched his treasure, a gasp escaped from Hallie's mouth. Suddenly, she was growing wet between her legs. The shadow of a beard had scratched her cheek raw, and yet she did not mind. She could hear his heavy breathing matching hers.

Hallie whispered in his ear, "You rogue…you lied to me. So angry I could spit."

He chuckled as he covered her lips once again with his, leaving no more opportunity for words. His lips traveled to her ear lobe, where he licked and then nibbled, leaving her more frantic for something she could not identify.

"I am a scoundrel, I do not deny that," he muttered between breaths.

Gathering some of her senses, she shoved him back and asked, "Why are you here? Did you follow me?"

"You must think my brother incompetent to disregard his service. Your father has the best of the body guards, and my brother has a small army on this case. And yet, you foolishly take things into your own hands."

She could tell he was angry, and she also recognized some truth in his words, which put her in a mood. He had a way about him, that was certain. He could make her feel foolish without much effort. Drat the man. She did have doubts about her actions. She knew she was impulsive and allowed her mouth to open and spew words before she thought. She was forever guilty of that. She was flawed, and she knew that. Who was perfect, after all?

"We can catch the man."

"*We* are not going to catch the man. You are going home where you belong. To stay safe and sound. You are a distraction."

Hallie reached into her pocket and produced the gun. "I have a gun, and I will proceed as planned," she stated lifting her chin stubbornly. Knowing she was flawed was one thing. Her pride and ego was another.

"Ahh. The infamous gun. Put that away before you shoot something accidently."

"I am a good shot."

"Maybe in target practice, but this is against a trained assassin. You are in over your head, Red. It is time to cease being a distraction. I will put you in a carriage I have waiting to take you home and keep you safe."

"No. He wants a meeting with me, and we need *me* to flush him out."

She put her hand up as if to stop his objection before he pronounced it.

"He needs me as a hostage and will not kill me." Her chin came up a notch to lay claim to her stubborn streak.

Sebastian was somewhat at a loss. He was not accustomed to being denied his will, and this woman's effort to stand her ground had him at odds. He had been taught since birth that women were to be protected at all costs. Their safety and well-being were paramount at all times. Having this petite woman stand unbending before him caused him anxiety. His jaw clenched in frustration. Another thing new to him. He was flummoxed. Well, there was one thing she could not control, as he had just learned.

Sebastian backed her against the wall and put one arm on either side of her face against the brick wall and trapped her. He leaned his head down to her face, his lips inches from her quivering mouth. Yes, she was affected by him, very much so. Her eyes were blazing and her lips trembling. Her heart was beating at an alarming rate, but so was his. She could be his undoing. The lust he felt was nearly over-powering and he wondered if she felt the proof of his urges pressing against her body. Perhaps she was innocent enough that she did not know about a man's needs.

Between kisses, he whispered, "You. Have. A. Fire. In your belly, and it is all for me."

Between kisses, she muttered, "You. Arrogant. Fool."

Soon the kiss grew to a smoldering fire. Her blood surged through her veins, giving her no relief and little chance to breathe. If his strong arms had not been holding her again the wall, her knees would have failed her and dropped her to the ground. How could he have such control over her body? She must remember that she had a gun, and a gun means she can and will control her fate.

When he pulled away, he studied her a moment and then said in a soft voice, "Do you have a plan, Red?"

She looked into his deep chocolate brown eyes, seeking answers. "Plan?"

"Yes, plan. Surely you were not going to swagger into the tavern without a thought in your brain. He will hardly recognize you in your pleasant girl disguise. He will expect a lady, one dressed as such. And what will you do to catch his attention? In other words, have you thought this out?"

Hallie glared at Sebastian. "My plan is simple, Your Grace. I will identify him and then stick a gun between his ears. At that point, I will have control of the situation." She raised her chin a notch. So there.

A bark of laughter escaped Sebastian's lips before he could stop himself. As the laugh died down, he could see the outrage building in Hallie's demeanor. He realized too late his blunder. Her pride was damaged, thanks to him. Now, how to fix it. She did not trust him, and he had a knack for raising her temper to boiling. In which case, her thinking was impaired.

"I suppose you have a better plan," she spat in return.

Sebastian gave a wry smile. "Detective Stainton, my *competent* brother, has planned a very well thought out maneuver. There are some of his best men inside The Red Ox and have been there since early afternoon. They are disguised as laborers and sailors. The outside is surrounded by men too, including me. His plan did not include you. In fact, you could completely risk this operation, and these men have families that care about them. You could jeopardize everything. One of these men could be killed if things were to go awry. My carriage is around the corner with my driver, who will take you home. It is an unmarked carriage. Do you understand how dangerous this is...for everyone? Not just you."

"Fear of death keeps us alive, Sebastian...." There was a moment of silence as they both took stock of each other.

Hallie locked eyes with him and realized the truth of the situation. The plan was to get the villain was it not? She did not want to risk a well thought out plan. Drat the man. Why was she always looking so foolish? Hallie understood sacrifice well. After all, she had four sisters, and there was a lot of compromise going on if they were to survive to live a tranquil life. She had done her part often enough and swallowed her pride when need be. She was stubborn by nature, and so many times it had been a painful exercise in stamina.

This man would probably drive her to Bedlam. He was so cocksure of himself, and yet she decided that she might actually like him. Even with the deception issue not yet resolved in her mind. She actually enjoyed the sparring. He was interesting and challenging. And he was no fool.

Hallie sighed ruefully. She shrugged her shoulders in defeat and watched a slow seductive smile nearly undo her focus. Sebastian was a seducing scoundrel. Was there nothing else on his mind? His kisses drove her nearly mad. He was quite good at that. She had been kissed a time or two, but nothing prepared her for the depth and passion she felt with his kisses. He was experienced, that was obvious. How many women had he kissed like this, she wondered, not liking the idea.

"I like your kisses," she admitted, her lips twitching in amusement. Her mouth had a mind of its own, and her comment was not planned, as usual. She flushed at her confession. Her mother always said to think before she spoke, and well, it was too late now. It seems the "thought" part always came last, much to her chagrin.

A wicked smile was his response. Sebastian leaned in and touched her lips gently with his and then drew back, as of to seal their bargain.

"We must pursue this when we have more time, Red."

He pulled her away from the wall and directed her toward his unmarked carriage. The carriage was in a secluded corner, hidden by boxes of garbage and stacks of used lumber. The driver hopped down to assist her with the carriage steps. Sebastian shut the door and motioned to the driver that it was time to leave. He turned back to the ally where he was needed to watch the comings and goings at The Red Ox.

Although he was not surprised to find Miss Martin here, none of the others standing watch expected this woman to show up. His woman. He silently cursed his inability to keep her away prior to arriving himself. He shook his head at the thought of her taste of adventure. He was in for a more complicated life, that was for certain.

Hallie sat down on the brown leather, tufted seat and put her hand in her pocket to touch the gun that lay nestled within. She sighed her frustration at again being foiled by the lying rogue. But the outcome was the important issue now, and she understood why she had to stay out of the way. She had to admit she was wrong, although only to herself. It was danger-ous, after all, and there were professionals here who would be successful. Her plans were not well formed and seemed stupid even to her own ears now. Her emotions had carried her away.

Chapter 13

London, The Red Ox, March, 1870

*H*allie wrapped her wool coat tighter around her body to ward off the damp cold. She heard the driver talking to someone, but she did not pay attention. Suddenly, she felt danger…a premonition perhaps of something terrible to come. At first, she thought it silly. She thought of Poppy and her history of illusions and smiled. But it wasn't silly, she realized, as a moment of terror flashed before her. Her hand felt the handle of her gun in her pocket, and she cocked it ready to fire. She took a breath and tried to create calm before the storm. This feeling was real, and she respected her intuition.

Someone touched the handle to the door, and it opened with a creak as a man dressed all in black stepped inside. He wore a greatcoat, hat low on his face, and black leather gloves. She could not see his face, but she knew he was not one of Detective Stainton's men. Again, her intuition. She gathered her coat tight around her body showing her left hand on the outside of the garment grasping the folds of the coarse cloth. Her hope was that if he saw her hand trembling with a grip of the black wool of her coat, he would not wonder where her right hand was or what it was doing.

He was of average height and weight, nothing significant to set him apart. He was not handsome, but he was not unattractive either. No prominent features to set him apart from someone else. His face held no warmth and his eyes were silver gray or perhaps blue…devoid of feeling. They were focused on her. Cold and calculating. He stared, it seemed, for several minutes, studying her features as if to evaluate her character and his strategy.

"Miss Martin." His voice was soft spoken and hoarse. He adjusted his hat again to make certain he wore it low to hide everything down to his eyebrows. He seemed to expel evil. She gave a shiver at the thought.

"You have an advantage, sir. I do not know you, and yet you have entered my carriage. What do you want?"

She was surprised that she had such control of her voice. It was stronger and more forceful that she had anticipated. She felt a moment of pride. She was nervous, but knew she had to be focused and strong. Her life may depend on it.

He sneered a smile. In that moment she felt evil at its strongest. He was dark where she experienced mostly light. He leaned back and made himself comfortable as if he were a guest just invited to supper. The nasty smile did not leave his face, as if he contained a joke meant only for him. She watched him and kept her attention on his body movements as she had been taught in self-defense. She knew some basic facts. He did not want to kill her, for he needed her as a hostage. He was dangerous…an assassin, which meant he was experienced with weapons and killing. He had killed, which meant he may not have a conscience. Never mind ethics or morals. He probably would not blink twice at killing someone. He was not like most people. Of course, in her defense classes, she had been taught how invaluable and essential sizing up ones opponent was. In fact, it was a matter of life and death. This was the test of all she had learned. Would she pass?

"You are an intelligent woman, Miss Martin. You received my note and have come to see what I can do for you regarding your father."

He spoke slowly and distinctly. His eyes were still watching her like a cat watches a mouse. He seemed to be toying with her. He was relaxed and comfortable. In his element.

"I do not think you believe I am a friend, do you?"

There was the twitching of his lips as if he found what he said amusing. But the humor did not reach is cold, stark eyes. She hated him in this moment. She hated how he toyed with her. She was certain this was entertainment to him. He liked to play with his prey. Dangerous. Then suddenly, without warning, his left eye twitched…several times. A sign of stress… nerves perhaps. A weakness, certainly.

Her chin came up a notch as she met his gaze head on. "You most certainly are not a friend. I would never be fool enough to believe your note in its entirety. You want me as your hostage to control my father and get what you want from him. Am I not correct, sir?"

He laughed a cold harsh laugh that was lacking humor. The humor did not reach his eyes. "I must give you credit Miss Martin. You are intelligent and courageous. I must take caution with you I see. If you have me all figured out, why did you come?"

It was then that Hallie realized she may have played her cards wrong. Playing the part of a stupid woman had its advantages. It would have kept him guessing and unaware. Given her the advantage. Now he would know she was smart…bollocks. She had done it again. Her mouth had driven the strategy instead of her brain. It was too late to swoon or play the weak damsel in distress. Drat her mouth. She was thinking fast, trying to cover her blunder. What to do now?

"I thought perhaps I could offer you some money to step off this track and go back where you came from. Everyone has a price."

He laughed again-that humorless deep guttural laugh that turned her stomach. She hated this man.

"Is that so? You do not have that kind of money Miss Martin, I assure you. But I find you interesting. You are not a common woman. Beautiful, intelligent, and courageous. I am quite impressed. You have a plan, do you not? But you shall not succeed."

Hallie tightened her grip on the wool coat, her slim long fingers grasping the fabric in a nervous gesture. The man's eyes lowered to her hand and watched her fingers grip her coat with interest. He had to know she was nervous. Who would not be? He smiled a wicked sneer.

"It is time we go…"

He tapped the roof of the coach to signal the driver. What Neil Piedmont did not know was the vehicle, horses and driver belonged to the Duke of Ashford. It was not a public coach, as he had thought it to be. The driver had left immediately upon the man entering the carriage in search of his employer. There was no one to answer the tap.

Neil waited patiently for a moment and then his eyes darted nervously around. His right hand disappeared to produce a gun directed at her. Her eyes widened at seeing the gun, although she should not have been surprised. It was, after all, expected. Her fingers tightened on her own gun, still hidden in her pocket.

Hallie thought carefully about her predicament. If she allowed him to take her with him in the carriage, all was lost. There was no advantage in going with him anywhere.

If she fired her gun at him, catching him unawares, he was likely to either drop his gun or shoot her, or both. Right now, he was aiming at her middle, and if she shot him, he was likely to lose the aim he presently had. She could dive to the side of the coach after firing in hopes he would miss his shot.

She took a moment to appear desperate and look out the window, as if searching for help. She meant to distract him for only a few seconds. Then, she noticed he too was looking around to assess any risks outside the carriage. She pointed her gun at her target and shot. The blast startled him, and there was a look of shock on his face, the most expression she had seen thus far on his controlled features.

He yelped in pain. Then he grabbed his knee and screamed louder as his gun went off. When Hallie shot her gun, she dove off to one side hoping to avoid getting shot, but she felt a piercing pain and knew she had been hit. It did not seem serious but hurt just the same. Blood was everywhere, and she heard men running in their direction.

Voices shouted outside, but she did not focus on that. Piedmont had dropped his gun and was still barking in pain when she retrieved his gun and leveled the sight on him. He did not seem to notice, as he was busy gasping for air and yelling every obscenity that could be imagined.

Blood was everywhere.

Some was hers, and most was his. The odor was enough to turn her stomach. She gasped for a clean breath. One that might restore her composure. The door of the carriage was yanked open by the Duke of Ashford and he was surrounded by more than eight men, all eager to see into the carriage. His face was a study in rage, hard and unrelenting. She hardly recognized him like this, but she was glad to see him.

By this time, Hallie was holding her side with blood squeezing through her fingers. She had a gun trained on Neil Piedmont and looked at Sebastian with obvious relief. She waved the smoking gun around as she spoke.

"You will need to take over, Your Grace. I feel a little light headed."

With that last comment she fainted, not something she was famous for doing. Before the gun slipped from her hold, a strong leather gloved hand took it from her limp hand.

Sebastian slipped in beside Hallie on the seat and scooped her into his lap, adjusting her onto her side so he could inspect the bloody wound.

At the same time, Derrick slipped into the carriage and grabbed Piedmont by the shoulders and shoved him out of the carriage. An entire slew of curse words followed while Piedmont howled his displeasure of his rough treatment. Derrick's men took hold of Piedmont while Derrick turned to his brother.

"Are you taking her back to your townhouse, brother?" Derrick asked, as he watched his brother fuss over the woman with concern. Ordinarily, he would never assume such a scandalous thing…however his usually very sane brother was acting suspiciously like…well, like he was being reckless over this woman. Something else was at work here.

Sebastian glared at Derrick as if he were an idiot. No answer followed.

"Well, then…you had better send for Mother if you do not want to ruin the woman." The glare Derrick received did not falter as Sebastian tapped the ceiling to give the word to the driver to leave.

Derrick shook his head as he watched the carriage leave on its route to the townhouse owned by the Duke of Ashford.

"I do believe you have found your match, dear brother."

Derrick turned when he heard a scream of pain. His assassin was squirming on the ground in aggravated pain. He turned and glared at the man. Blood was soaking his legs as he held his knee in clear agony.

"I need a surgeon! Bitch shot me in the knee…," he groaned.

Derrick chucked. "Get a stretcher and take him away. I will question him later."

"Question all you want," he moaned. "I will not talk."

One eyebrow rose as Derrick studied the man. "You will if you want a surgeon or something for pain," Derrick said with a wry smile.

As his men dropped Piedmont in the center of a stretcher, Derrick smiled watching the man scream in pain. He could not help himself. The American woman took care of this dangerous assassin. Derrick shook his head. It was ridiculous really… but he could not stop smiling at the absurdity of it all. And the American woman…she was in a carriage traveling to his brother's townhouse. He laughed out loud.

As the carriage seemed to hit every pot hole on the road, Sebastian tried his best to cushion the ride by holding Hallie against his chest, cursing silently. The wound did not seem serious, but he was angry just the same.

Bloody damn.

He was taking her to his townhouse, which would ensure him she received the care he demanded, and he could see her anytime he wanted. She would not be able to deny him. It still rattled him that she had not been waiting for their date to the British Museum, but his deception was one that few women would excuse.

He studied her face. So peaceful. Her long lashes fanning her cheeks made him want to see her brilliant green eyes. He wanted to assure himself that she was all right. Those eyes would be setting fires when they gazed on him. She still had not come to terms with what he had done. He pulled off his leather gloves and stuffed them in his greatcoat pocket. With his fingers bare, he stroked her temples and followed the line of her cheek to her neck. He traced her arched brows with long fingers, marveling at how soft and silky her skin was. Her hair had come loose from the tight coil on her neck, and his fingers stroked the silky fibers.

He knew his driver understood the urgency, which was why the ride was so rough, but it seemed to be taking longer than expected. He must send for the surgeon and his mother. Derrick was right. He could not intentionally ruin her...although that was one way to marry her. He sighed at that thought, because he knew she would not be coerced into doing anything she did not want. Americans. No, she could not be forced to marry him. What an absurd thought. A proper English woman could be coerced into marriage to avoid a scandal, but not his independent courageous American. Not even to avoid a scandal.

He looked at her face again and smiled. "You can open your eyes now, Miss Martin."

Hallie opened her eyes and stared at him in awe. "How did you know?"

He shrugged his shoulders and gave her a wicked grin. She went to pull herself out of his lap and experienced a sharp pain in her side. With a groan, she settled back down where she was and drew in a breath.

"Hurt?"

"Of course it hurts, you idiot. I have been shot...er, Your Grace."

There was genuine amusement on his face. "Ah. Your spirit and sense of humor has returned. I am truly grateful."

She frowned at him. "Are you mad? I could have been killed, you ninny!"

His amusement left so quickly that she actually doubted it had been there in the first place.

"Bloody hell. You damn well could have been killed, and I am angry that you pursued this alone and risked your life so casually...as if it did not matter! You are a little hoyden out of control with not a thought for your own safety."

She could not blame him for calling her a hoyden. She seemed to remember her father using the term once or twice with her in mind. Again, her mouth was a problem. She opened a can of worms with her thoughtless comment.

"I was armed and prepared."

"I see. The infamous gun. Well, you did shoot him in the knee. He will be permanently crippled, which is something. And you did apprehend the villain...but you worried me, and I was not in a position to aid you. I nearly went crazy with frustration."

Her eyes widened and her mouth came open in wonderment of his words. "You worried about me?"

He nodded his head. "You must realize by now that I do care about you."

"I didn't know or think about that." She looked out the window in puzzlement. "Where are you taking me? This is not the way to the Pritchard townhouse…"

"It is not. I am taking you to my townhouse. I want to make certain you are well cared for by the best physician…I want to protect you from harm. I am certain your family means well, but you escaped their oversight, and look what happened. I want to see to your safety."

"But I can't stay with you in the same residence…I would be ruined! What are you thinking? You must take me home. Turn this carriage around."

"I will send for my mother who will chaperone. You will like her." As his last words resonated, she realized he was determined. She drew in a deep breath of frustration. There wills were at odds.

They finally arrived at his townhouse. The footman aided Sebastian in taking his bloody bundle out of the carriage. Sebastian carried Hallie to a guest room and gave orders to send for the physician and his mother. Maids entered the room to aid in turning down the bed and removing her coat and boots, and as they began to remove her gown under the direction of the housekeeper, Sebastian removed himself to write a note to her family. He passed maids carrying hot water and clean linens.

He retired to his library to write his communications and catch his breath. How would he explain himself to his mother? He sighed his frustrations as he sat at his massive desk. He had been impulsive. Hallie came with adventure and challenges, and his life would be forever changed. She did not take direction well, and he was in for some turmoil. But he wanted oversight on her care, and now he had that. He also wanted to have the freedom to see her any time he pleased, and now he fixed things so that he could do that…so why was he so defensive? He had done exactly what he wanted to do. He was a Duke, after all, and in charge of whatever he pleased.

His communication to Hallie's family would be delayed a few hours to make certain his mother would be present as a chaperone and so he could capture some control of the situation. That decision did not feel quite honorable, but risking an invasion of her family too soon was not acceptable to him either.

Chapter 14

Dowager Townhouse, London, March, 1870

*A*lex was enjoying his lunch by the fire, watching his mother eat the cream of onion soup with relish. That was her favorite. She smiled between a spoonful of the rich soup and waited for him to finish his colorful story.

"So, I agreed to do Gilbert and Sullivan. Our actors do sing and dance...so it is not a stretch. It is quite the 'thing' in America and well attended. I look forward to the challenge. Something different, to be sure."

"Anything you set your mind to will be successful, Alexander. You are gifted and I am certain to again be a proud mama." She used her linen napkin to touch her mouth. "What about Maria? Will she be agreeable to the genre change?"

Alex nodded and chuckled. "Maria is quite the prima donna. It will take great strategy and finesse to handle her tantrums. She is worth the trouble since she has quite the talent. And I do enjoy the drama and challenge she creates."

"I know you can handle her. What about her drinking problem?"

"Ah. That is controllable if I keep an eye on her. She turns to the wine and whisky when she is frustrated. I need to help manage her frustrations. Her problem is basically that she is lonely, I think. She was once in love, and he died of consumption. It broke her heart. But that was a long time ago."

"She needs another man to set her attention on then."

Alex laughed. So simple. But his mother was probably right. The symptoms were not the problem. And the problem was the root of the trouble with Maria. Maybe he would spend some time finding a match for her. He chuckled thinking of himself as a matchmaker.

"You are right mother, as always. I am certain the right man would straighten her out. Finding him will be the problem."

Jackson tapped on the door and entered bearing a silver tray with a correspondence on it. He held it out to the Dowager Ashford.

Ellen took the envelope and recognized the seal. "Ah. It is from your brother," she said looking at it with curiosity.

"You must open it, Mother. Do not mind me," Alex said as he finished his soup.

Ellen ripped open the envelope and pulled out the note. She read it and then read it again and frowned. It was a strange message to be sure. She stared into space…thinking and, yes, confused. She looked questioningly at Alex, as if he could clarify her dilemma.

"What is it?" Alex asked since his mother seemed bewildered. When his mother still had not answered, he asked, "Bad news?"

"I don't know," she finally said. "Sebastian simply asks me to come to his townhouse immediately and to pack a bag for several days...nothing else. What could it be, Alex?"

She put the note down and stared at Alex again in question. He picked up the correspondence and read it for himself. It was indeed strange.

"It is a mystery...but I will escort you there. I am curious myself."

The physician had been upstairs with Hallie for over two hours, and Sebastian was frantic. He had tried to cool his nerves with a brandy, but it had done no good. What had taken so damn much time? Maybe the bullet had been lodged deeper than he thought. A parade of maids carrying bloody linens and pitchers of water had been steadily tromping up and down the stairs.

A memory suddenly pierced his thoughts. His mother was having a baby in this very house. There was the same excitement and parade of maids carrying the linens and water. The voices were quiet...whispers in fact. As if in respect for a serious moment. He had been a young boy and did not understand the commotion and concern that filled the house. He also did not understand the need to whisper.

His father had been drinking brandy and had been pacing this very carpet. Sebastian had been told to go to his room, where his brother Alexander was sleeping. But he would be the future Duke and was determined that this...whatever this was, concerned him directly. So, he watched the parade and wondered what all the water was for. Why were there bloody linens? What could be going on with his mother? He wanted to ask one of the maids, but they were focused on their parade and ignored the frowning child who had no place being there in the first place. He was certain he had heard his mother scream several times. He wanted to go to her…why was his father not in there taking care of things? He should be ordering these people around and solving this issue with his mother.

But he was drinking brandy and pacing. Later he would learn that his mother had given birth to a little girl. She had been dead even before birth, and his mother had cried for days following the incident. No one spoke of it again. Not even his mother. His father had refused to discuss it with him other than to say, "Sometimes babies are not strong enough to survive. They die. Now do not bring this up with your mother." And he never did. But he understood more now. More about that damn parade. More about child birth. But he felt some of the same fear. Something he had no control over was happening.

Sebastian was interrupted from his woolgathering by a soft knock on the door. The physician, James Corban, stuck his head through the opening.

"May I come in, Your Grace?"

Sebastian jumped in nervous surprise. "James. Come in and have a brandy and tell me how she is," Sebastian said pouring the drink and handing the glass to James who sat down near the fire. He took a deep breath and a sip of the brandy before looking up at Sebastian, who stood looking at him with a worried frown on his brow.

"Sit down and drink your brandy. You look tired and worried."

Sebastian sat in the companion chair facing James. "Well?"

"She will be fine, Your Grace."

"Stop 'Your Gracing' me James. We have known each other since we were in short pants. I am in need of you as a friend, too."

James laughed. "All right, my friend. It was a flesh wound. I did take at least twelve stitches, however. She should not move or the stitches may open. She will be sore, of course, and may get bored staying bed-ridden…but she needs to stay put for several days at least. I gave her something for the pain. She needs rest. I will come back to check it, although she should have the bandages changed, and the wound needs to stay clean."

Sebastian sighed his relief. "Thank God. I…was worried. Bloody hell. She could have been killed."

James smiled. "There is a good story here. And she is American. And in a bed in your townhouse." He held up his hand to stop Sebastian. "No need, my friend. You know all is confidential with me. I never discuss my cases. It would not be honorable. But I will lay awake tonight wondering…." and then he laughed and drank down his brandy. "I will go home and find my bed. Get some sleep Sebastian, and get rid of those dark circles under your eyes. You need rest, too."

As James walked out of the room, he nearly collided with Holland, the Dowager Duchess Ashford, and Alex on their way to see Sebastian. Alex was carrying a bag on behalf of his mother and both watched as the physician left, their faces etched with concern. They looked to Sebastian for explanation.

Sebastian motioned for them to come in. Yes, he sent for his mother. But he wanted a moment to catch his breath. He wanted to check on Hallie and assure himself that she was going to be all right. Now, with his mother here, it would be complicated. And what was Alex doing here? Bloody hell. And then he remembered that Alex had lunch with her earlier and would have been there when she received his note.

Sebastian directed them to sit by the fire. "Alex, I did not expect you to come."

Alex smiled. "I escorted Mother and would not dream of missing...whatever it is that is going on."

"I see. Brandy, Alex? Port, Mother?" Sebastian asked, as he picked up glasses, ready to pour and serve his guests. Both nodded their need for a drink. It was quiet while Sebastian poured and served drinks. They all understood him well, and knew not to question him. He would tell them what he wanted them to know in his own time. After passing out the drinks, he studied his mother and Alex before deciding how to proceed.

"Mother I have asked you to come to my townhouse to chaperone a woman staying in one of the guest rooms. I would like you to stay next door for the best perception of appropriateness. Both eyebrows raised at once on Ellen's shocked face. Alex did not seem surprised.

"You have a lady staying here?" Ellen nearly croaked. Her face lost its usual composed mask and gave way to surprise.

Sebastian nodded. "I do."

Ellen was clearly stunned speechless, and Alex had a grin on his face a Cheshire cat would envy. Alex sipped on his brandy covering his inappropriate grin waiting for Sebastian to continue. He was used to his brother's boring life as a Duke,, and was delighted for him to have an exciting adventure.

"She was wounded in a CID strategy to apprehend an assassin, and I brought her here for treatment. Dr. Corban left as you came in."

Sebastian watched for his mother's reaction, but she was still quiet...her mouth started to move several times, and then she thought better of it. Obviously, she was stunned.

"Her name is Hallie Martin, and her father had an assassin on his trail," Sebastian offered as further explanation.

"The American," Alex said with a smile and then looked at his mother as if to say, 'You see.'.

Sebastian glared at Alex. "Don't look so smug, brother."

Finally, Ellen found her senses. "But why would you bring her here of all places, Sebastian? You should have taken her to her family. This is highly irregular." Her brow creased slowly, "This woman is important to you?"

Sebastian was silent a moment as he thought how to answer his mother. He never lied to her, and he did not want to start now...and yet how to answer her. She was a patient woman and waited for his answer.

"She is of interest. Yes. I want to make certain she gets the best of care." He said no more and waited to see if that was enough for his mother to accept.

She nodded her head in acceptance. "I will accept that for now, Sebastian. How badly is she wounded? A gun shot?"

"It was a gun shot, but just a flesh wound. She had stitches and is resting. She is not to be moved for several days so she can heal."

"Did you notify her family?" Ellen had found her wits, and now her common sense was kicking in.

Sebastian nodded his head. "I did. I expect they will soon descend on us, and that was why I wanted you here, for propriety sake."

"I see. Well, I think I shall move into the room next door and check in on this American who has captured your interest, Sebastian."

She gave one last glance at Sebastian. A mother's last word.

Both brothers stood as their mother left with Holland following her with her bags.

Sebastian looked at Alex for his reaction and glared at him when he caught Alex smirking.

"This is the spirited American woman you tricked, is she not?" Alex asked settling into a chair.

"She is the daughter of the man I was investigating."

"I gathered that much. She came to my dressing room you know…accused me of being an imposter."

Sebastian looked up at Alex in surprise.

"Yes, she can tell us apart...only she thought you were Alex. I don't know who she thought I was..." He chuckled before holding his glass out for another brandy.

Sebastian took the glass and poured his best brandy into the glass.

"Yes, she never ceases to surprise me," Sebastian muttered.

"You are going to marry her."

It was a statement, not a question. Alex peeked up over his glass to gage his brother's expression, though he understood his brother better than anyone else. He was an extension of himself, after all.

"Yes." Sebastian held his brother's gaze and then a slow smile over took his face. There was no use in fooling himself or his brother. It would be like lying to himself twice over.

"Does she know?"

Sebastian chuckled, and it sounded just like his brother. "No. Not yet."

Alex watched his brother with amusement in his eyes.

"Want me to tell her, on your behalf? I'd be more than happy to do so. Cut right to the chase and save you some time. I could be Sir Lancelot and recite poetry to her...on your behalf."

"I will string you by the thumbs if you do. She is an independent woman and not too keen on marriage at the moment. But with her stay here...I plan to change all that."

"I believe you have met your match."

"You approve?" Sebastian asked.

"I approve." Alex smiled and took another sip of brandy.

"Don't you have to be on stage...?"

Alex smiled and shook his head. "I allowed my understudy to have a night in front of an audience. I did not want to miss... whatever this is, dear brother."

Ellen walked up the stairs with Holland on her heels. She would occupy the room next door to Hallie Martin. These rooms were two of the best for their ample space and decoration, as well as their proximity of the ducal rooms. Ellen noted Sebastian's choice of rooms and how near they were to his own.

Very interesting, to say the least.

"So what are your thoughts on her, Holland?"

Holland was silent for a moment. "Not for me to say, Your Grace."

"Oh, Hogwash!"

Another silence. "I have not seen her since she was carried up to bed. She is quite a beauty, if I do say so, Your Grace."

"Is she?"

Then Ellen smiled a warm cozy smile that lit her face. Oh, this was going to be quite the project. Her son favored this woman, and she was in the opportune position to witness it all unfolding before her very eyes. She was in a front row seat to watch this relationship blossom, and it would blossom, she was certain.

Brilliant.

It seemed to be hours before Sebastian could get rid of his brother. Finally, Alex went to his room, the same one he grew up in, and retired for the night. Sebastian took the stairs two at a time until he found himself in front of Hallie's guest room. He was going to knock but thought better of it with his mother next door. She most certainly would hear the knock. He opened the door quietly and peeked inside. Hallie was snugly in bed, but he could not see her face.

He walked quietly into the room. The thick carpet kept his steps soundless. Her head was propped up with two pillows, her eyes closed, her mouth slightly open in sleep. He stood over her, watching for something. He wanted to be convinced she was all right, but he noticed no frown marred her face to indicate pain or discomfort.

He should leave.

Then he found his hand reaching for the stray hair that covered one eye and pulled it to the side. Someone had released that tight bun she had been wearing. Her hair was like silk, and he squeezed the strand between his fingers before releasing it to the pillow. Her red mane was spread on the white pillow case around her head like a wild flame in the fireplace.

The covers were neatly tucked in, holding her in place on her back with her hands neatly folded on her chest. The sleeves of the night gown were white linen, and flowered embroidery ran around the cuffs covering her wrists. It was the work of his mother, he was certain. So, the maids had produced one of his mother's night gowns for Hallie's use. His mother was taller than Hallie so it would be long...if she were to stand up. Her nails were short and neatly kept. Small delicate hands with long fingers. They were soft hands…hands he imagined stroking his back, wrapping around his neck, threading through his hair…

It was foolish of him to stand here and imagine her doing erotic things to him. He felt himself grow hard, his cock straining his trousers. He sighed his frustration. He should not have drunk two glasses of brandy.

His imagination was running amok.

He came into the room to satisfy his need to know that Hallie was well, and he still did not feel convinced. Her eyes were still closed, and he could not see within the deep green depths to know she was recovering. She was too quiet. Peaceful…and he had never seen her like this. He was unnerved. Rooted to the spot and unable to move. He touched her cheek, so velvet soft. His eyes had softened as he gazed at her in such a vulnerable state. He wanted to protect her. Keep her from harm. He felt so helpless and useless. He wanted to spar with her, hear her arguments, see the fire ignite in her eyes. He could smell the scent of her-roses. He wanted to wrap his arms around her, feel her body against his chest, run his hands down her back and trap her within his embrace.

Just then, the door opened. He impulsively stepped away from the bed and tried for a bland face. His mother came through the door, and they stared at each other a moment. She did not seem surprised to find him by Hallie's bed.

"Sebastian. I see you are worried. How is she?" Ellen asked, as she too approached the bed. Ellen looked Hallie over from head to foot in a casual manner. "Ah. She is a beauty. Her hair is glorious, I would say."

Ellen was not fooled by her son's detached expression. She had been just in time to catch the softening of his features, the open sincerity he displayed watching the woman sleep, and it stirred her heart like nothing had recently. She should be reprimanding him for being in the woman's bedroom, especially unchaperoned.

But she knew and understood her eldest son. He knew what he was doing, and she knew what he was doing. He also knew she would not reprimand him. Yes, he was caught in this woman's web. Ellen knew he would marry her. All she could do was control things long enough so there would be no scandal and he could then marry when he was satisfied he was ready for the event. Otherwise, it would be out of his control, and that would be disastrous, because he always wanted to be in control.

"I know how you feel, Sebastian. Your father was in a state for two days before he died, and I could barely tolerate watching him unresponsive. I wanted to see him awake one more time. It is a terrible feeling being so helpless. I will sit with her and read my book. You must go to bed so that you will be well rested when she wakes. Do not worry. I have a feeling she will be fine, and I will watch over her."

Sebastian dragged his eyes from Hallie's face and looked at his mother with appreciation. She was always there for him. He was tired and saw no reason to argue. He kissed his mother's cheek.

He nodded his head, knowing Hallie was now in the best of care. His mother would wake him if there was a change or a problem.

As he approached the door to leave, he turned and looked at his mother.

"You know, she could have been killed...died. I should have been able to stop her," he said softly, so softly that his mother strained to hear him.

She stared at him, struck to see his raw pain and vulnerability. He left the room, closing the door softly behind him.

Ellen stared at the beautiful woman a moment and sighed.

Then, she opened a book and started to read. It was a book of poems by Elizabeth Barrett Browning she admired and always carried with her.

> *"How do I love thee?*
> *Let me count the ways.*
> *I love thee to the depth and breadth and height*
> *My soul can reach when feeling out of sight*
> *For the ends of Being and ideal Grace..."*

She would read a few lines, lines she already knew well, and then look up to see if there were any changes with Hallie. Hours passed and her eyes grew tired, but the chair was comfortable, and she did not mind. Her eyes opened and fastened on Hallie when she heard the rustle of bedding. Hallie's eyes were open and staring at Ellen.

"Ah. You have finally awakened."

She laid her book of poetry on the table next to the bed.

"I am Sebastian's mother, the Dowager Ashford, Miss Martin. How do you feel?" Perhaps you require water before you speak."

She proceeded to pour a glass of water from a pitcher on the small table beside the bed. She stood up and stuffed another pillow under Hallie's head, allowing her to sit up. Then she handed the water over to Hallie, who drank it down.

"Thank you, Your Grace. Where am I?"

"You are at the Ashford townhouse under the protection and care of the Duke of Ashford."

Ellen took the empty glass and returned it to the side table.

"You are a heroine it seems. Shot the bad guy in the knee and managed to get yourself shot in the side. You are fortunate to be alive, I think. I must ask, however, why did you risk your life with such a dangerous task?"

"I thought I was in the best position to apprehend the assassin. The note came to me, after all. My father was under quite a bit of stress, and I wanted to assist in…"

"My son was quite beside himself with worry for your safety, Miss Martin. You know my younger son, Derrick, is quite competent." Ellen offered as she measured Hallie's character.

Ellen watched the changing expressions on Hallie's face. She was not an English lady that was certain. She was one of these new independent women America was known for creating, and her son was interested…more than interested, she corrected herself.

"What do you think of my son, Miss Martin?" Ellen asked deciding to change the subject.

"Which one?" Hallie retorted without a blink.

"Why, His Grace, Sebastian James Stainton eighth Duke of Ashford, of course." This young woman would most certainly try her patience in no time whatsoever.

"He is an arrogant horse's ass, Your Grace." Hallie had raised her chin just a notch to deliver her this answer and then, realizing her rash comment, actually reddened in embarrassment. Again, she spoke before she thought.

Ellen sucked in air at that very bold statement and was silent for a moment while she digested the comment. Then she roared with laughter. Tears came down her cheeks unchecked as she threw her head back in an uncharacteristic manner. Hallie watched at first in horror and then she sighed her relief.

"Well, that certainly sums him up nicely, does it not?" Ellen responded after catching her breath and getting some control back in order. "I do not think I have laughed so hard in years. I think you are delightful, Hallie. Does my son know how you feel about him…the Duke son that is?"

"I think so. I have told him once or twice. He seems unimpressed with my thoughts on the matter," Hallie responded, watching the Dowager Ashford with interest.

Ellen did not seem stuffy at all. She expected an uptight, very proper lady who was unyielding and formal. The Dowager was smiling now, obviously enjoying herself.

"You are not at all what I expected," Hallie admitted.

"Oh, what did you expect, pray tell?" Ellen responded with curiosity.

"Well,…"

"Do go on, my dear…I am waiting to hear this one. I expect honesty, as you are obviously used to supplying."

"I did not expect to like you, Your Grace. But I do. Very much. He looks so like you that it is difficult not to think of him when I look at you. Your eyes…hair and…"

"But that is not bad, is it?" Ellen said, watching Hallie's face for her expression. She was very expressive, but then she was American. Americans seemed to be bold. Hallie had no fear. She said what she thought. Interesting.

"I admit he is quite handsome."

"But you can tell him apart from Alexander?" Ellen found this ability very interesting and unusual. Not many people could tell them apart, except when Alexander was on the stage or Sebastian was behind his desk at the Ashford townhouse barking orders. She did it on pure sight alone and after being deceived into thinking Sebastian was Alexander.

"Apparently so. They are very different…" Hallie said.

"Not many people think so. Of course, one is an actor and one a title, but looking at them…few can tell the difference.

"The trick, Your Grace, is knowing the correct name for the correct brother."

Ellen laughed. "You are truly a delight, my dear. You have been asleep for several hours. Perhaps you would like a tray of food sent up?" Ellen asked.

"Thank you, Your Grace. I am starved. I could eat a feast for ten!"

Again, Ellen laughed. A woman with an appetite. How refreshing. She shook her head in disbelief. What a rare find this woman was. Certainly not boring. She speaks her mind. No wonder Sebastian found her appealing.

Ellen pulled the rope to signal a maid. She had not been so amused in ages. This "favor" Sebastian demanded of her was nothing short of pure enjoyment. She felt a surge of happiness that had been remiss before.

Chapter 15

Ashford townhouse, London, March, 1870

*S*ebastian had not been asleep very long when Holland touched his shoulder. Holland shook him twice before Sebastian realized he was not dreaming. It was such a deep, comfortable sleep. Bloody damn. Sebastian growled his displeasure.

"Your Grace, sorry to interrupt your sleep…but you have a house full of visitors downstairs, and they are quite vocal and demanding."

Holland stood back a step and waited for Sebastian to acknowledge him. Sebastian opened his eyes just enough. Ah, a mint green cravat to greet him.

"Bloody hell. What time is it?" Sebastian asked, rubbing sleep from his eyes and sitting up. "Who the hell has come at this hour? Are they mad?" He snapped, as he stood up and grabbed his robe. His hair was mussed, and he ran his hand through it in an effort to neaten it. He tied the robe hastily while stuffing his feet into his slippers. He mumbled under his breath.

"I believe your guests are Miss Martin's family, and they are quite distraught, if I do say so myself. I could barely keep them contained in the parlor. They would not accept anything save your presence, Your Grace. They are Americans I believe, which would explain a lot, I dare say."

Sebastian made his way to the door. "I will take care of this Holland...but you had better come along. I have a feeling they will not leave any time soon. I will need you there as...well, I will need you there."

As Sebastian descended the staircase, he heard a commotion coming from the parlor. It sounded as if a crowd of people were all speaking at once. Women's voices and men's voices alike were all collectively creating a racket of biblical proportions. They needed a ringmaster, because it was most certainly a circus with no leadership or direction. Holland was a few paces behind him as he entered the parlor to find the source of this riot.

Everyone was standing and speaking at once talking over each other like an uncivilized bunch of baboons. The women were colorful, all dressed as if out for afternoon tea. And it was the middle of the God damned night. Who does this? He stood in the threshold and watched in awe. Alex would be amused at this drama. When they noticed Sebastian standing there, the crowd grew quiet. It was truly amazing. It was utterly silent for several seconds. Even Sebastian was spell-bound. Ah, he had power it seems. Good. Let them be speechless.

Benjamin Martin stepped forward and stood at attention. He seemed to be their leader, Sebastian realized. He was dressed up like he was ready to go to the opera. All black and carefully groomed. Everyone looked to him in eager anticipation. One could hear a pin drop it was so silent.

"Your Grace. I believe you might remember me from the Bickford ball. I am Benjamin Martin. He bowed. And this is my wife, Alice Martin."

Alice stepped forward curtsied and joined Joseph standing beside him. Sebastian noticed she took his hand and held it in an affectionate gesture foreign to Sebastian. When Alice noticed Sebastian looking at their held hands with curiosity, she delicately dropped his hand and smiled nervously her face reddening. She smiled and encouraged her husband to continue.

Benjamin continued his introductions.

"This is my wife's cousins and mine by marriage, Harriet and Joseph Pritchard. You met Joe at the Bickford ball...in the card room."

The Pritchards stepped forward together and bowed and curtsied.

"These are my daughters Violet, Poppy and Iris."

The girls all came forward and curtsied together. Sebastian stared at each one as they were introduced, spell-bound. Good God. This was the bouquet. What the dickens? What were all these people doing standing in his parlor in the middle of the night, for God's sake? It was a comedy. Have they no sense? Why were they not in their beds? Do they not know this is not an appropriate hour to come for tea? But then, he had to admit, they were concerned family members. He just didn't want a house full of people, if truth be told

Benjamin resumed his role as the leader.

"I heard from you that my daughter is here, Your Grace," Benjamin continued.

Alice Martin began to sob. This drew Sebastian's attention to her as she sniffed and dabbed her nose with a lace handkerchief. It was no act. Tears ran down her cheeks, and Harriet Pritchard patted her shoulder for comfort. Alice covered her hand with an affectionate gesture. These people were acting like they cared for each other...a support system at work. Interesting. Powerful. Alex ought to put them on the stage, for surely this was entertainment at its best.

Benjamin again took charge.

"Now, now Alice. Calm yourself. We shall get to the bottom of this."

Then he turned again to Sebastian.

"We received your note. We had been out for the night and did not get your note when it arrived. We had been missing Hallie and wondering where she was, and then she is wounded...with a gun! Our Hallie has been hurt, and we are all..."

Sebastian held up his hand to interrupt. "Yes, your daughter is here. She is well. One of London's best physicians has already attended her, and it is a flesh wound with a few stitches."

"Stitches?" Alice croaked. And her eyes rolled back. Oh, no. She would not faint, would she? She took a shaky breath and sighed.

Everyone gasped in unison at the word stitches, so it was not only Alice Martin who found the idea horrifying.

Sebastian continued. "She needs rest and she is in one of my finest guest rooms with my mother, the Dowager Duchess Ashford, personally seeing to her needs. The doctor has recommended rest. Her stitches must heal. You may all see her in the morning after she has rested the night without interruption."

Sebastian knew he was probably over doing it, but this blasted circus had been more than he could tolerate. There were things even he could not control, and that irked him.

The room was quiet.

Not a sound permeated the air. Sebastian looked from face to face and each of them stared at him, waiting for him to satisfy their concerns. Obviously, they were not satisfied with his perfectly articulated speech.

Alice opened her mouth as if to speak but thought better of it. Then, everyone in unison started talking at once. It was chaotic panic. Sebastian clenched his jaw. Bollocks! How was he to handle this mess? His entire purpose was to have Hallie to himself for a spell, and now this. Hell and damnation. Things had gotten out of hand. Thank goodness his mother was here to chaperone. What a scandal this could have been. Sebastian could feel Holland's tension too. All these people were expecting him to do something...something that would be of comfort to them. It was obvious that they had no intention of waiting until tomorrow. All stood paralyzed in their spots, waiting for him to solve everything. Sebastian dragged in a much-needed breath.

"I do not think it is wise to interrupt Miss Martin's sleep. She has experienced some pain...and trauma." On that word, there was a unified voice of groaning. Sebastian turned to Holland and sighed. He was defeated.

"Holland, see them to some guest rooms. It seems we have guests for the night," he muttered under his breath, and only Holland heard his groan.

Holland stepped forward and announced; "Follow me. I will show you to your rooms."

The talking started up again but in a more joyous manner as they paraded out of the parlor, bowing and curtsying as they went. Hallie was located in the family wing next to his mother, not far from the suites he occupied. The third floor housed all the guest rooms where Holland was taking this mass of noise and upset. Far away from his living quarters where he would shortly find peace and quiet.

Sebastian needed a brandy.

By the time he crawled into his cold bed, he was worn to a frazzle. His patience was gone, and the brandy he had gulped down did nothing to settle his nerves. He tossed and turned trying to find a comfortable position when he realized it was his thoughts keeping him from sleep. Could he not shut down his bloody brain?

All his work to bring Hallie to his home and now his house was full of her deranged relatives, leaving him little privacy. They had descended on him like a swarm of locusts, and somehow it would be a long time, if ever, that things returned to normal. He had the respect of parliament, the regency, his peers...but this swarm of Americans did not seem to take him seriously. They questioned his judgement. Or so he thought.

He was laying on his bed tracing the pattern of his quilt with his fingers for God's sake.

His eyes were wide open. Common sense told him if he shut them, he might find sleep. Eventually. But it did no good to shut his eyes. He could still see a riot of flaming red hair and flashing vivid green eyes mocking his fatigue. He wanted to caress her smooth skin, run his hands through her silky hair and hear her moan for his touch. He was reacting like an untried school boy. He was hard and aching for need of her and had never experienced such an unrelenting drive for one woman. He had not felt this for Marlene or any other woman in his past and no other woman would do. He was out of his depth and uncertain of how to handle himself.

She was an innocent, not some doxy waiting for his attentions. He had never been attracted to an innocent, and, of course, they represented trouble. Designed for marriage, one wrong move and a man found himself shackled for life. Although he did not mind the idea of being shackled for life with this hoyden. He was already thinking of her as his permanently. Curious. He might want to examine this thought more closely. She would certainly make his life interesting. Being his wife floated in and out of his consciousness constantly demanding attention. And blast it, it was not an unpleasant thought. It actually brought him a certain level of peace.

Sebastian realized after laying in his bed an hour or more that he would not be able to get the minx out of his mind, so he got up and put on his robe, tied it and put on his slippers. He combed his hair with his fingers and then marched down the hall toward the guest room, which was drawing him like a serpent and leaving him weak with the need to see her again. Once her family had her again, he would be left with no time of his own with her. Well, that was not exactly true. He would have to court her, of course, and that was new to him. But courting entailed carefully chaperoned excursions…and he wanted to kiss her, touch her. Yes, more than kiss her. How was that going to work?

He carefully turned the knob to her door and entered the room. There was a candle lit on the table next to her bed. Hallie was sitting up reading a book, much to his surprise. She instantly saw him standing in the doorway and put her book down in her lap.

"Well, come in or go out…before you ruin me, Your Grace," she said in a husky voice that nearly undid his courage.

She was a saucy wench. He stepped into her room and closed the door quietly. He turned the key in the lock and pocketed it and then stared at the vision before him. Her red hair was wavy and thick tumbling down her shoulders in wild abandonment. Her skin was pale, and yet pink cheeks and lips brightened an otherwise colorless face. Her lips were full and kissable he thought, intently watching her form her words. He wanted to kiss her senseless. She was wearing a plain white linen nightgown from his mother's collection, he realized. Tiny purple flowers were embroidered around the high neck. The nightgown was modest, and yet he found her very alluring. The folds of the cloth were graceful and hinted at her full breasts which he would give his best horse to touch. None of these thoughts were helpful. He was hard just gazing at her. She had a sleepy, sultry expression that made him want to tumble her in her comfortable bed.

"I see you are feeling better. Good book?" he said nodding toward the book in her lap. She looked down at the small, black, leather-bound book and smiled seductively.

"It is your mother's book. Poetry by Elizabeth Barrett Browning. Not exactly something to keep me awake. But I was bored, and it filled the time. I have had enough sleep. I could use some distraction."

Sebastian could not help but laugh. He walked closer to her bed and sat in the chair his mother had occupied. He could smell roses. His mother wore a similar scent, but it was distinctly Hallie's too. He inhaled and sighed. Her hair was the most beautiful he had ever seen. It was a cloud of sunset. Shades of red, orange, and yellow. She shined and glowed with energy and happiness.

Like sunshine. Happiness. He could not help but smile.

"How is your wound? Should you be sitting up?" Sebastian asked with concern. Those stitches had to be stretched tight with her sitting up like this.

"It feels tight, but I need to sit up for my sanity. I have never felt so cooped up before. I am used to being active...busy. I feel like a butterfly pinned to a..."

Sebastian cleared his throat. "I cannot express how much you have ravaged my thoughts." Hallie frowned at that comment, not certain where he was going. "You risked your life. And now your family has descended on me. I am a bit rattled."

"My family?" She asked with curiosity.

"Yes. They are all here in this house, hopefully sleeping on the third floor. Your sisters, parents and even your aunt and uncle are all here. They are all concerned for you. I would not allow them to see you before the morning. I thought you would be resting."

One eyebrow came up. She was questioning his judgment.

"I wanted to see you myself before I turned your family on you," he admitted. Honesty. He thought it prudent to tell her the truth, although now he felt vulnerable. Her eyes suddenly changed, and she was obviously sympathetic. She relaxed and a soft smile lit her face. Like she might say, "Aww."

"You care," she uttered in a gentle voice.

"Of course I care. What the blazes have you done to me? You must be a witch. I am a wretched mess."

A soft musical laugh brought him out of his morose thoughts. Her face was lit with amusement and even her eyes danced with laughter and sparkled in the dim light. "You are so dear...at times."

"Really? Is that all that comes to mind?"

"Well, on the other hand...you upset my stomach and make me hot and sweaty. I do not like that part."

Sebastian roared with laughter. "I see. Perhaps you feel some lust for me after all."

"Lust? Are you addled? Lust is when one wants to kiss someone, is it not?" She was serious now, and the innocent question gave him a moment of tenderness that was a rare feeling for him. A new feeling, in fact.

"Desire, my love. Lust is a desire to possess another sexually. A kiss would hardly suffice."

His eyes were hooded and his gaze intense. His brown eyes were smoldering fire and Hallie felt a raw magnetism draw her bodily toward him. She leaned toward him as if he were a lifeline drawing her into his space. She reached out with her finger tips and caressed his unshaven beard. It was course and prickly, but not unpleasant.

"Do you need to shave every day?" she asked without thinking, but now that she asked, she really did want to know. Her eyes were large and luminous waiting for his response.

He gave her a wicked smile. "I do. Quite a nuisance, I might say. By the end of the day...I have a beard again, giving me a shadow and rough whiskers for you to touch."

She drew her fingers away and still held his gaze.

"I like your touch. It is like butterfly wings tempting me to touch you in turn," he admitted.

The comment startled her at first. She withdrew her fingers, and they stood in mid-air for a moment as if confused. Then she rested her hand over the other one in her lap, covering the book. She smiled at his words.

"Hmmm. I have frightened you. I regret that." He slowly extended one hand toward hers, lifting her right hand and bring it carefully to his lips. He kissed each finger while she watched with interest. Then he let her hand lose, and she held it still close to his lips as if she were unable to take ownership of her hand again. She looked at her fingers as if they had changed somehow. His touch had warmed every body part she had.

He flashed her another wicked smile. "I would like to kiss every inch of your beautiful body slowly."

"*Every* inch? Because of lust?" She whispered in a hoarse voice, making him hard all over again.

"No. More than lust. I do not have a name for it as yet. I am uncertain exactly what I feel for you, Hallie, to be honest. I admire your courage. You are intelligent and witty. I like how you speak your mind and then wonder why you did so. I like how your green eyes sparkle when you are passionate about something, and I like the colors of your hair. Vivid. I like how your lips move, but no words come out because you are spell bound. You make me happy to be in your vivacious presence. You have a temper that does justice to your red hair, and you are too stubborn for your own good, but it is all what makes you who you are and who I admire. You are truly a treasure, and I value my treasures."

"You. Admire me?" Hallie frowned in her confusion.

No one had ever admired her. Or treasured her, for that matter. Well, maybe her parents. In fact, she spent most of her time trying to stay out of her father's line of fire. Trouble was her middle name, her father often said. But this…felt good. Someone…admired her and not just someone, but Sebastian James Stainton eighth Duke of Ashford. Someone important found her a treasure and something to value. That changed things somehow.

"Excuse me, for I have trouble staying focused, but why did you pretend to be Alex? Once you knew why I was there at the theatre, why did you not correct my mistake? I need to put my anger to bed, and I would like to understand your motives. It was an act of dishonesty, and yet you strike me as honorable and honest in nature. I am still puzzled by that."

Sebastian studied her a moment before answering. He took a deep breath.

"That's a fair question. I have pondered this myself wondering what my motives truly were. I take pride in the fact that I am an honorable man...and honest. I think that I was so enamored with you, I could not let you go. And then when I discovered that you wanted my brother...quite frankly I did not want to consider not seeing you again. I wanted to proceed with your plan to spend time with you, to get to know you. Of course, I was asked to assist your father by the Home Office, and it seemed plausible to carry on with the ruse. Probably a bad idea. I will give no apology, because I am glad to have spent time with you. I have grown quite fond of you."

He seemed frustrated and he struggled with some emotion.

"I find it difficult to express exactly what I feel with you. It never seems to come out right. You rattle me." His eyes seemed to be pleading with her to understand.

Hallie liked watching him express himself. His lips were generous. Sensual. When he talked, she saw a hint of dimples-a promise of some humor she wanted from him. His voice was rich and smooth, the rumble so masculine. She could hardly concentrate on what he was saying so swayed was she by his delivery. She thought he must be quite effective speaking before the Parliament. Who would not be riveted by his voice and cadence?

He was intelligent and well read. He had a powerful, rich voice that was soothing and peaceful to her. Why was she dwelling on his voice?

She had grown to trust him, which was odd considering his deception. His eyes were warm and reminded her of smooth rich chocolate…comforting and calm. Seeing him rattled over her was interesting and exciting.

He wore a silver and black satin robe tied at the waist. Inappropriate and sexy. She stared at the V neckline where black chest hair curled from his neck down disappearing beneath the V neckline. He caught her eyes and where they focused, and his lips turned a slow seductive smile that sent chills throughout her body. She blushed crimson. What must he think of her? Was she wanton? He seemed to be undressing her with his eyes. His gaze was so intense that she wondered if her nightgown was transparent. She wanted to look down and see, just to make certain, but he would definitely know what she was doing and thinking. Although, he seemed to already know her thoughts. He was raw and sensual, and heat spread to her thighs. A wetness settled into her private parts that seemed unnatural to her. What was happening to her? Lust?

Sebastian stood slowly and leaned over her, placing his lips on hers ever so gently. She gasped her surprise and that is all it took for his tongue to find its way into her mouth. His tongue dueled with her tongue gently but thoroughly, teaching her what he wanted, what he needed. His right hand held her face in position for his thumb to caress her cheek. Her eyes closed, and she breathed in his essence.

Sandalwood, brandy, leather...and something else she could not identify. Oh, she was smitten, no doubt about it. His hand was large but gentle on her face, and she felt cherished and valued...even needed. A treasure. He did treat her like he treasured and cherished her. Broad shoulders, muscled body, tall and strong and yet more gentle than she could imagine. She hoped this moment would never end. She breathed in a sigh of contentment.

Something was going on with her body...her stomach had butterflies, and there was an ache between her thighs that craved his touch.

She groaned.

There was a smoldering fire building between them that promised pleasure like she had never experienced before. It was a demanding fire that seemed to build with intensity. He pulled away only slightly and gave her a measuring glance. They were breathing heavily, both trying for an element of control.

"You feel it too. We have something special between us," he whispered in a hoarse voice she did not recognize. "We are well suited, are we not?" His voice sounded raspy and sexy.

Her eyes filled with tears. She had no idea why. Please, she prayed, don't spill onto my cheeks and give me away. Her feelings were intense and barely controllable. She was out of her element.

"There are several more hours before dawn. I must leave you to rest. Your family will descend upon you soon enough. I am guilty of keeping you from rest, but I was selfish for your company."

He smiled at her as he stood. He gently pulled the book from her fingers and set it on the table beside the bed. He pulled a pillow out from behind her back and helped lower her body flat in the bed, tucking the covers firmly around her. A kiss on the forehead, and then he blew out the candle.

She looked at him in wonder. Before she could gather her thoughts, he was unlocking the door and gone.

She was tired, exhausted if truth be known, but she could not sleep…not yet. She needed to process what had just happened. Sebastian. There was no doubt they were attracted to each other, but what did it all mean? She definitely liked him… well more than liked if she was honest with herself. She often had these discussions with herself to keep her head on straight, but this…whatever it was had her baffled. Lust. It must be lust she felt.

She had wanted to put off marriage indefinitely. Frankly, it scared her. A man having total power over a woman. The 'woman' had no rights. Since she had a large dowry, she had hoped to talk her father into allowing her to have possession of it and enjoy freedom. But the plan was ludicrous and her father would never buy into it. But she still dreamt of such a life, and now Sebastian had her at odds with herself. What to do? Nothing would be solved tonight, so sleep finally over took her.

Sebastian heard the commotion in the breakfast room as he descended the stairs. Who was up at this hour? He was an early riser and enjoyed an early morning ride on his favorite horse. His black Hessian boots were contrasted by his tan form fitting trousers that showed off thick, muscled calves. He usually had morning coffee and scones…but his usually good mood took a dive. Bloody hell. The circus was here. He had nearly forgotten. He paused while he got a grip on himself. He had had sweet dreams of Hallie and finally slept well. Her kisses, although innocent, were like magic. He craved more. He would never have enough of her, he thought.

They were all talking at once. Is this what American families were like? Chaos. Utter chaos. How did they get anything solved or carry on a simple conversation? He sighed his frustration as he walked through the door to find all of them seated at the table eating and waving their forks and hands like lunatics. He had never witnessed such drama and racket. It wasn't until he was nearly upon them that everyone stopped the chatter and looked up at him. As the men started to rise off their chairs, he held up a hand to stay them. No need for formalities.

"Please continue. I trust you all slept well." There was nodding among the circus. He followed each with a glance to acknowledge them. "As soon as you are finished, I will escort you to Miss Martin's room. I know she will be pleased to see you all." He wondered if that was true.

With that, he went to the buffet set up and helped himself to sausages, buttered toast, and eggs. Eating a major breakfast was unusual for him, but today was unusual. His back was to them so he was surprised it was still quiet. No one spoke a word. It made him nervous, for God's sake. Why were they quiet? What the dickens were they all doing so quietly? Not a fork or spoon clanked on a plate. He did not trust the silence.

Sebastian turned and walked to the head of the table, his usual place. A footman poured his strong, black coffee and placed it before him. He put his linen napkin in his lap before the footman could do so and began to wonder why he was nervous at his own table. He looked around to see why it was still quiet and he realized they were all watching him. Why was that, he wondered? He proceeded to dig into his meal.

Alice Martin spoke up. "Your Grace, I wish to thank you for your hospitality. Is our daughter doing well?"

She was staring at him with his fork suspended in the air, a nice bite of scrambled eggs waiting for his mouth. He put the fork down and addressed Alice. He could see Hallie in her face and hair. There definitely was a resemblance. She was still politely awaiting his answer.

"Your daughter is well, Mrs. Martin. She has the best of care, I assure you." He picked his fork up again, his mouth open to receive the eggs when Harriet Pritchard spoke.

"Will she be able to come home today, Your Grace? We would not want to impose on your household any longer than necessary."

Again, Sebastian put the fork down and addressed Harriet this time. He smiled at Harriet Pritchard, who looked at him expectantly. She reminded him of a bird, her nose looking like a beak ready to peck. She seemed a harmless woman leaning in for his answer. These people were not like the ton, who were ruthless at times and carried all sorts of ulterior motives. He was accustomed to vindictive people who searched negative bits of knowledge to keep the gossipmongers happy and thriving. These people seemed supportive of each other.

"I hope you understand that one more day, if not more, would be best for your daughter. The physician will be checking her later to see when the stitches are ready to come out. We should wait and see what his recommendations are," he offered. Good. He handled that well.

There was some nodding and whispering, as they all pondered the news. Sebastian waited for the next interruption before resuming his breakfast, and when there was none, he ate with gusto.

Some spirited conversations began awkwardly at first, and then they were back at it. All talking at once like a pack of magpies. He blocked it all out and concentrated on his meal, which began to taste better with each bite. He mastered the circus and felt a moment of success. Just tune them out. That was the secret, it seemed. Concentrate on something else to block out the nonsense. He sighed as he took his last bite of food, never enjoying his breakfast so much as he did right now.

Alex walked into the room and looked around in amazement. He looked to Sebastian for an explanation, but was ignored. The circus grew quiet again when they saw Alex. He was not dressed as an actor, but as a gentleman. Sebastian smiled at the obvious confusion. He never saw so many faces turn to him to explain. Of course, the twins looked very much alike dressed as they were. Most were wide-eyed and some held their mouths open in surprise and confusion, looking at one twin and then the other.

Sebastian stood and looked at Alex. "May I present my twin, Alexander Nathan Stainton, who would like to be referred to as simply, 'Alex.' Alex, may I present my house guests, Alice Martin, Benjamin Martin, Harriet Pritchard, Joseph Pritchard, Poppy Martin, Violet Martin and Iris Martin."

He looked at each person as he stated their name ignoring the dumb-founded expression on Alex's face. Each person nodded as they were introduced. But the shock of seeing the identical twins together had not worn off. There was some whispering between the guests trying to make sense of what they had witnessed.

Alex bowed to the group, and the men had stood and bowed to him. The women nodded and smiled. Alex was obviously stunned and walked slowly to the buffet to help himself to breakfast. His hands moved with uncertainty as his mind was processing all the people talking at once. Americans. He kept sneaking a peek over his shoulder to see that the circus was still there. They were. And they were all chattering again, which made Sebastian smile ear to ear. Alex filled his plate with eggs, kippers, and sausages and looked for a place to sit. He sat in an empty seat between Iris and Violet. He nodded to each in turn and began to eat his meal. A footman brought him coffee.

As the circus continued to talk over one another, he looked around at the chaos and confusion. How can a man think with this racket? He glanced over at Sebastian, who smirked at him.

Alex scooped a bite of kippers and started to put them in his mouth when Iris turned to him with a little frown on her face.

"You look exactly like the Duke. That must present some problems for you. I would love to have an identical twin who could take the blame for my indiscretions. That would be capital."

Alex nearly choked on his bite. What was she…all of eleven or twelve? She was waiting for some response, although there were no questions asked of him. He smiled at the precocious child and realized she wanted him to respond in some way. He put his fork down and studied her a moment, trying to decide what to say.

"My brother and I used to trade places when we were at University. We fooled a lot of people." He continued to eat, thinking he had satisfied her issues. No such luck.

"I would have a smarter twin and ask them to take my tests…also any punishment that comes my way. That seems a good use of a twin to me."

"My brother did take a few tests for me to ensure I passed and did not create undo stress on my father. Come to think of it, he admitted to some of my folly and took my punishment too," he added as he shoveled another bite of kippers into his mouth.

"He sounds like the perfect brother. And what did you do for him…I mean in return?" she asked innocently.

Iris had stopped eating and gave him all her attention. Freckles dotted her face, but did not detract from her crystal-blue, intelligent eyes. She had strawberry blond hair arranged in braids, tied with colorful ribbons. She knocked the braids behind her, as if they were a nuisance. Her eyes never left Alex and eagerly waited his answer. She was a pretty child likely to be a great beauty someday.

"Well, I will have to think on that one. I honestly don't know." Alex frowned at that and realized she had challenged him in some unknown way.

He was puzzled by the thought that he had no positive contribution for his brother. Damn. What did he offer his brother in return? His brother paved a path for his beloved theatrical career, and yet…how had he thanked him? Besides verbally, that is.

"It does not sound like a very good bargain, if you asked me," she responded. Then her fork started to move around in the air in front of his face. What the hell was going on?

"If you don't want those potatoes, I would like a bite." With that little warning, such as it was, she pierced her fork into his potatoes and removed her bite from his plate with clever expertise. She had done this before, he reasoned. She was too good at it. He was speechless.

He watched her squint her eyes in pleasure as she put her lips together, sucking the morsel off her fork and groaning in pleasure over the potatoes au gratin. He was surprised, and his mouth was probably open in amazement. No one had ever speared anything off his plate. And with such finesse. She was a pro. Clever little chit.

"It is not polite to take food from another plate, Iris," her mother said from across the table. "You know your manners.

I am certain Mr. Stainton wanted those potatoes or he would not have taken them." Alice was gentle with her reprimand.

Iris nodded and looked at Alex. He smiled at her, and she smiled back. A beautiful, flawless smile with perfect white teeth. These Martin women possessed real honest beauty, Alex thought. She looked not a bit remorseful, he noticed. He would have to protect his potatoes.

"How is the heroine Miss Martin today?" Alex asked, and his question stopped all discussion, which meant the chattering crowd was capable of focusing on several conversations at the same time. Amazing. What an interesting talent. Alice became solemn as all faces turned to her. So, they were all tuned into each other after all.

"His Grace reports that she may come home shortly. We plan to see her this morning after this wonderful meal."

She looked at Sebastian as if to get approval. Alex, too, turned to Sebastian for further information. Alex had never felt so much like he was participating in a play. He wondered how it all would turn out.

"Miss Martin had some stitches, and luckily it was just a flesh wound. She has been resting comfortably," Sebastian said.

"I am happy to hear that good news," Alex responded smiling.

But Alex became distracted, reflecting on his conversation with Iris. Quite simply, the child reminded him all that Sebastian had done for him as a child, and yet what had he done for his brother in return? A dark cloud settled over his head. His brother had always taken care of him, protected him, and helped him get established in his beloved career. He acted like a protective big brother…and he was only five minutes older, for God's sake! Oh, he loved his brother…no question there. But what had he done lately for his brother? Hell. Iris, in her innocence, had unplugged a jug of guilt he needed to deal with now.

Holland came in and whispered something in Sebastian's ear. Sebastian nodded and looked at Alex. He motioned for Alex to come to him. Alex stood and walked over leaning in to Sebastian for his direction.

"Alex, Derrick is here to discuss the issue of the assassin. I do not think I will be long, but if I am, will you have mother go to Miss Martin and await this family's arrival to Miss Martin's room? There will be introductions of course, which I know you can manage," Sebastian whispered for Alex's ears only.

"Of course. Never fear. I can handle this small task with the utmost efficiency," Alex responded in a whisper and then returned to his chair and to his conversation with Iris, who was interested in his business. They seemed to be new best friends. And a twelve-year old. What next?

"What secrets do you carry Mr. Stainton? I can keep secrets," she offered in a low whisper.

Alex whispered back to his new friend. "I am to arrange for you to visit your sister after breakfast. But remember you claimed you can keep a secret. And I must say I never met a woman who could keep a secret. It seems to be against their nature."

"I will be the exception to your rule, Mr. Stainton. I would love to give you some references, but then I would be giving away my secrets and failing your test." Alex laughed. She was delightful, he decided.

Chapter 16

Ashford townhouse, London, March, 1870

Sebastian greeted Derrick in his library. His brother was already seated in front of the fire waiting for him. Derrick stood, but Sebastian motioned for him to sit. Sebastian stood at the mantel one arm leaning against the pillar and looked at his brother, who wore a conservative gray wool waist coat and starched white shirt. He looked stylish, although his hair was wind-blown and gave him a boyish appearance much younger than his years. His observant brown eyes were studying Sebastian.

"It seems you have a house full of guests. Noisy guests, I might add," he said smiling.

Sebastian arched one eyebrow at his brother before answering. "I took your advice and sent for Mother to chaperone. Then...they all came...her family, that is."

Derrick let out a roar of laughter.

"Not so surprising actually." Derrick crossed his legs and leaned back in his chair. "How is the infamous Miss Martin?"

"A flesh wound with some stitches...a little rest and she will be good as new."

"Miss Martin is quite the woman. She is creating quite a stir among my peers at the CID. The woman who shot the villain in the knee," he chuckled. "He has a brace on his leg. He is in constant pain, cursing his life away. The Americans want him. It seems he has quite a list of offenses. My superiors have not decided what they want to do with him as yet. There is talk of sending him back to America, throw him behind bars here, send him to Australia...the usual. Meanwhile, he is in constant pain befitting a villain. He is a royal nuisance."

"Did he talk?" Sebastian asked.

"Not at first. But holding out on pain medication and medical care loosened his tongue. Funny how that works."

"He can rot in hell for all I care," Sebastian grumbled.

"His injury creates its own hell. He did work for Rockefeller, but failed to get Martin to sign over the refinery. At least trying to obtain it legally. But then Rockefeller has a partner that is rumored to be...history. That was incentive enough for the partner to hire Piedmont to get Martin to sign under stronger physical pressure, making him a hero of sorts." Derrick gave a wry smile.

"The partner wants to keep his partnership and reasons that if he can produce the much-desired refinery...it may convince Rockefeller to see value in him," Sebastian added.

"Exactly. The partner was in London, but departed for America a short time ago. I believe the Americans will take care of him. We sent word to Rockefeller, which should also cause some issues with the partner, who was acting on his own."

"Have you told Martin yet? I am certain he will be glad to know he can get rid of the two security guards he grouses about."

"Derrick chuckled. "I talked to him personally last night and relieved his security guards of their duty. My visit got him out of bed. I knew he would sleep better knowing. I gave him no details, since he was not happy to leave his bed. The visit was short and to the point."

"Well, now he is sleeping here under my roof," Sebastian returned with a sigh.

"How did you acquire the Martins?" Derrick asked with a smile.

"I had to send them a note about their daughter's part in the drama, did I not? And the result was *all* of them showing up on my doorstep last night. The middle of the night. I could not convince them to go home and come back this morning. And besides mother, Alex is here too, lending his humor."

Derrick laughed. "I think you can handle this, brother. And I might add, you brought this on yourself."

"I am certain this drama is all quite funny to you Derrick. Come have some breakfast and meet these Americans before they excuse themselves to see the patient upstairs."

Hallie stretched beneath the cool linen sheets and felt a stab of pain in her side where the stitches stretched. It was sore, and it itched too. She dragged herself up and stuffed an extra pillow behind her back. Her first thought besides the pain in her side was of Sebastian. She wanted to see him again.

His kisses were exactly what she needed to…what was she thinking? Was she giving up on her goals? Giving her father what he wanted of her? Hells bells. She was in a fix of her own making.

A scheme gone wrong.

She had to admit that thinking of Sebastian made the blood surge through her veins hot and intense. Butterflies made her stomach pitch in a most uncomfortable manner. And yet, she wanted more. He was certainly handsome. No denying that. Warmth centered in her loins and created havoc with her attempts to regain control. She yearned to have his fingers touch her bare skin.

Was she wanton? Was this natural?

She loved how he touched her, his tender kisses, his concern for her welfare. Yes, he was controlling, but it was for the best of reasons. There was no question he cared for her…but was it enough? She loved how he treasured her and appreciated her courage. She was in trouble with him, just as she was with her father, but this was different. A nice different.

Just then, a soft tap on her door interrupted her thoughts. The Dowager Duchess of Ashford, in her elegant black gown, stepped into view. She was a beautiful woman. She stood tall, regal, and carried herself like a duchess, confident and graceful.

"I am happy to see you awake and sitting up. It is time to ring for your breakfast. Your family will soon be descending on you for your assurance that you are well."

She pulled the rope for service and went to the dressing table, and snagging a hair brush and mirror.

"Perhaps you would like to brush your magnificent hair. I have never seen such glory." She handed the brush and mirror to Hallie and sat at her side.

"Thank you, Your Grace. There must be snarls upon snarls in this rats' nest."

She started to gently brush while Ellen watched with amusement. Snarls jerked her head right and left and caused her to squint her eyes in displeasure. She worked the brush underneath and then took small bunches of hair at a time and worked diligently and thoroughly as her mane crackled and glowed with her actions.

"I apologize for not having a maid braid it while you were unconscious. That would have been a fine time to do that chore, but I was not thinking. I was too surprised to find you here and Sebastian at wits end. I have never seen him so rattled regarding a woman. It was a pleasure, to be sure. Never doubt that. It is time he settled down."

"Settled down? We have only known each other a few weeks," Hallie said with concern. "That is hardly time to decide if one wants to spend the rest of their lives together."

"I had an arranged marriage, and I grew to love my husband. In fact, I will never marry again. No man could stand in his shoes."

"But knowing what you know now, would you not want to marry for love? You would not take a risk and marry a tyrant who would control you at every turn, would you?" Hallie asked in a serious tone that stopped Ellen in her tracks.

"I suppose you have a point. You are straight forward and honest. I like that in a woman. No wishy-washy thoughts come out of your mouth, that is for certain. I suppose that is one of the reasons my son is infatuated with you."

"I am certain he will tell you that I drive him mad. We argue and spar, and he gets red in the face and looks as though he will have an apoplexy. He thinks me a hoyden, spoiled, sassy, and insolent. I dare say he does not think to bind himself to a crazy American."

Ellen watched her, wide-eyed and barely able to hold her mouth closed for wanting to drop it in shock. "How are his kisses?" she muttered without thinking.

"Oh, they are divine…" Hallie was now the one wide-eyed and shocked, because once again her mouth spoke before she thought. "You tricked me."

Ellen held a smug expression but fought the urge to expose it. "Just as I thought. He is in love with you, my dear. Plain and simple."

Hallie was shaking her head in denial. "That cannot be true. He barely knows me, and I have been a pain in his arse… excuse me," she stammered, ashamed how her emotions had gotten the better of her.

Ellen smiled and started laughing. Understanding this young woman's need for independence, another strategy crossed her mind.

"Marriage can give a woman a level of independence," Ellen said.

Hallie looked at her with skepticism. "I do not see how that can be true."

"Well, a woman does not need a chaperone once married. She can wear nearly any style and color..."

"I do that now." Ellen widened her eyes in surprise. "That is no reason to marry! I am surprised at you, Your Grace!" Hallie finished with one eyebrow raised.

Ellen laughed again. "I see that I cannot outsmart you, my dear."

Ellen still had a grin ear to ear which was irritating, Hallie thought. The woman had a one-track mind. But she liked the Dowager Duchess. She was kind and good hearted. She also had a tolerance for independent women. One had to excuse anything else at work here.

Ellen watched Hallie eat her breakfast. She seemed to be particularly fond of the hot chocolate. But then she ate the eggs and ham with gusto, as if she were starved. Her appetite was that of two women her size, but then she had been unconscious a long time.

Ellen found her subject fascinating. She was beautiful, courageous, honest, and outspoken. She would make a fine duchess. Her smug smile was hard to hide. She was satisfied that Sebastian had found his match. She truly liked this American. Hallie looked at Ellen with interest.

"Would you like a biscuit or some tea, Your Grace?" Hallie asked, now feeling guilty she had eaten like a pig with no thought to the woman sitting next to her.

Ellen smiled her appreciation. "No, child. I had my tea and toast hours ago. But I will stay and keep you company and ride rough-shod over your family. I understand there are quite a few people ready to see you."

"I do have a very large, noisy, but loving family," Hallie said between bites. "And they are in each other's business, which can be a nuisance at times."

"It sounds very American."

"My sister Violet is my best friend. She is two years younger than I, but so much older in intellect. She reads all the time and is her own best friend, I think. I used to play pranks on her to take her away from her books. I regret that."

"What kind of pranks?" Ellen asked, watching Hallie with an amused smile.

"Once I tore an important page from a book she was reading just to frustrate her. I was not there when she discovered it, and she suspected me of the mischief. Although I thought it funny when I ripped the page out, later I was ashamed and embarrassed. I begged her not to tell our mother."

"And did she?"

"That is when I realized she was my friend. She did not tell, and she was angry that I would think she would."

"I think you share a rare relationship with your sister...and your family for that matter. I envy someone who has a genuine friendship. I have so many people who treat me as a friend just to be associated with the importance of my position. Being a Dowager Duchess has its drawbacks. People admire power and status and attach themselves to me for what I can do for them. I cannot think of a time where I had a true friend," Ellen admitted woefully. "Perhaps my sons are the closest I have to true friendship. At least I can trust their motives, and they are all honorable."

"That is truly unfortunate that there is such deceit and lack of honor within society."

Ellen lifted the breakfast tray from Hallie's lap and placed it on a nearby table. Everything was nearly gone. Amazing Ellen thought. Hallie might be a friend to her, she suddenly thought. Hallie was not afraid of her or intimidated by her status. It was refreshing and comfortable to be in her company.

Yes, she liked Hallie very much.

Her son could do worse. Some money grubbing, spoiled, haughty, insensitive, social climbing, ton approved, woman who treated her beneath her notice would be a nightmare and yet the usual selection within their ranks. That would be the expectation, of course. But none of her sons did the expected, and for that she was grateful and took a bit of credit for herself.

A knock on the door interrupted Ellen's thoughts. Alex peeked inside.

"Ah. Alexander. Come in and see how well our patient is doing," Ellen responded.

The door opened wider, and it was then that Ellen heard the chattering coming from the hallway that rose in volume as Alex grinned and opened the door wider to admit a crowd of people. Ellen turned in her chair to see where the commotion was coming from as Hallie's family flooded into the room and spread themselves around her bed. They all looked upon her from head to foot with rabid concern. Alex took a position behind his mother and watched the drama unfold with a grin on his face. His dimples were displayed, adding to his joyous expression.

Ellen did not know who to look at next.

"First, allow me to present you to my mother, Dowager Duchess Ashford. Mother I will do my best to get everyone present straight." Everyone watched Alex with interest as he attempted to introduce each family member.

"The little poppet on the bed is the youngest Martin daughter, Iris. Poppy is the daughter straightening her hair. Violet is the eager one ready to pounce on Miss Martin. They are tight, I understand from Iris. Mrs. Alice Martin and Mr. Benjamin Martin are at the foot of the bed and Mr. Joseph Pritchard and Mrs. Harriet Pritchard are standing behind. Did I miss anyone?"

"I am pleased to meet you all," Ellen nodded to them as a group.

"We are all so worried and cannot thank you enough for taking care of our dear Hallie," Alice said, gazing at Ellen with warm gratitude. They all performed curtsies and bows.

"Yes, we thank you," Benjamin added.

As this family constantly talked over each other, they began to confuse each other in their effort to be heard. Harriet Pritchard started a conversation with Ellen and soon Joseph joined in, while Iris got off the bed and walked over to Alex to contribute to their budding relationship. One suitable to a twelve-year old and an adult male.

Violet soon took Iris's place on the bed and leaned over to capture Hallie's hands and squeeze them while she searched her sister's face.

"I was so worried about you Hallie. Shot...for goodness sakes. Another adventure to add to your collection. How are you, really? They are saying you are a heroine. Imagine that, Hallie," Violet said with a fierce expression on her face. "I must write a story about you. You are a very interesting person. Mother is out of her mind with worry. You just disappeared. We searched the house many times. If you were not wounded, I think Father would have considered wounding you himself," Violet continued. Hallie had never heard her talk so much all at once.

"I am sorry to have worried everyone. I only wanted to help Father." Hallie sighed in defeat. All this drama over her antics. She did not like being the center of attention. Especially when the attention is for a plan gone badly.

The room was buzzing with separate conversations, and even the Dowager Duchess was engaged in a separate conversation with Aunt Harriet. Alex was leaning over to talk to her sister Iris in an animated fashion. Her head was spinning. Her mother was rubbing her feet with motherly devotion and her father had his arm around her mother, watching her fondly. Poppy was begging their father for ices at Gunter's later, and her father was ignoring the request from Poppy. Poppy was waving her arms in frustration. Violet smiled at Hallie and smoothed her hair away from her face.

"Are you courting yet, sister?" Violet whispered under her breath. Her smile turned coy.

"How can you ask such a thing, Violet? I was busy saving Father. And I might add...I am wounded." She did roll her eyes for effect.

She looked around her and saw her family all here out of concern for her welfare. She was truly blessed and sighed in satisfaction.

"Father has lost his two baboons, I suppose. That ought to be worth something to him," Hallie muttered under her breath.

Violet laughed. "I rather enjoyed that drama. He tried to act normal with a big gorilla, as he called them, following in his wake. It was a sight to see," Violet said smiling. She gazed at her father with appreciation. "I am happy you shot the bad guy. You live such an adventurous life. I envy your courage."

"I did not have courage. I was scared out of my life. I asked myself more than once what the bloody hell I was doing. To quote Father," she added as an afterthought. They both laughed.

Alice stepped closer to Hallie. "I am sorry to interrupt Violet, but I must be assured that my dear Hallie is well." She looked Hallie over as only a mother would and sighed. "You are naughty. You left your room and put your life in danger. We were all so worried. I cannot believe the trouble you find," Alice said with a sigh. "What am I to do with you? I suppose it is a good sign the Duke wanted you here...he has not spoken to your father as yet. But he must be interested," she added nodding her head in agreement with herself.

"Mother. You are getting ahead of yourself. Please. You frighten me with talk like this. The next thing you know Father will be involved in this. You know then he will not be able to leave it alone."

"He already has his hopes up, and why not? The Duke has been very attentive, would you not agree? He is so handsome too. Ah. My daughter to be a duchess."

"Mother." Hallie rolled her eyes. "You must not get overly excited about this...."

"Of course. I must allow you to recover from your stitches." Alice cringed at the thought of stitches in her lovely daughter. "Violet found the two notes you left, and we were all so disturbed that this assassin would contact an innocent woman to get at your father. I cannot believe you thought it a good idea to respond to that note. Detective Stainton was taking care of everything, dear one. You are so precious to me."

Violet was behind their mother making dramatic faces, which Hallie tried to ignore. She wanted to burst out laughing. Violet crossed her eyes once and that nearly did Hallie in.

Alice leaned in and kissed her daughter on her cheek, sighing as she said, "I love you so much Hallie. I wish I could better protect you. Maybe it's time for His Grace to take over. He would be more competent."

Chapter 17

Ashford Townhouse, London, March, 1870

The door opened wide with competent force. Sebastian stood there glancing at the crowd surrounding his future wife. His mother sat regally next to Hallie. Alex stood behind his mother with his hands braced on the back of her chair. Alex was watching the drama before him with amusement. The rest of the circus was standing around her bed, and, as usual, they were all talking at once. He waited patiently for the right moment to interrupt.

But it happened suddenly. When one person noticed him, all the others stopped what they were doing and turned to see him standing at the threshold. There was some curtseying and bowing and then they patiently waited for him to speak. They were respectful, he would give them that. But then his over-six-foot stature demanded attention. With his broad shoulders and muscular build, he took possession of a room simply by being there.

"I trust you all have seen how well our patient is fairing. Detective Derrick Stainton is in my library awaiting Mr.

Martin and Mr. Pritchard. He thought to fill in the blanks for you regarding Piedmont." Both men nodded their interest.

"Ladies, I have tea trays in the downstairs parlor with the best lemon cakes and berry tarts you have ever tasted."

There was a moment of silence and then all the women paraded out, following the men. Except for Alex and his mother. Sebastian stared at Hallie. A moment of tenderness crossed his face at seeing her sitting up in bed looking glorious with her riot of red curls lighting up the white pillow case behind her head like a sunset. He seemed prone to lunacy at the moment, but he did not care.

Ellen watched her son. He was over the moon for this woman. It was clear as the day is long. She looked up at Alex.

"Alexander dear, please have a cup of tea with me in my parlor," she said still staring at Sebastian. Alex took the hint and offered his arm to his mother as they left the room. Ellen was satisfied at this moment that Sebastian would make this women his duchess. Alex turned and looked behind him as he left the room. He saw his brother and the American woman staring at each other as if there were no others in the room but themselves. He smiled as he closed the door behind him and wished that some woman would look at him in the same way Miss Martin looked at Sebastian.

Hallie missed him when he wasn't here. She was attracted to him. She liked having him close, his scent so rich and vital to her comfort, and hearing his strong, rich, baritone voice rumble created a sense of soothing peace that made her feel protected. She liked that about him. She smiled as he watched her adjust herself on the bed.

"I have missed you," he said softly.

"We just saw each other hours ago, but I know what you mean. I missed you too."

She felt embarrassed by her admission and looked down at her hands folded in her lap. As much as she treasured his company, there was also a level of discomfort that she truly did not understand. He would never harm her, she was certain. But the lust... the attraction was new to her, and she had no idea how to behave.

"I will formally ask your father to court you."

"Why? Are you not courting me now? Or is it because I hired you to court me that..."

"Forget the blasted 'hire' and let us start anew. You do understand what is meant when a man asks to 'court' a woman?"

"Are you saying that you wish to marry me?" she asked with astonishment.

Sebastian nodded. "I am."

"But why? We are enjoying each other now. Why ruin it with marriage?"

Now Sebastian looked astonished. "Most women want marriage. A Duke is considered quite a catch."

"I am not *most women*. I want independence. Freedom. I want to explore, experience adventures..."

"And you do not think marriage to me would offer you those things?"

Hallie stared at him a moment, taking his measure. "I honestly don't know what marriage to you would be like. Why don't you tell me?"

Sebastian laughed at her candor. "You are correct. You are not like most women. Most women would marry me for my title and money. They would marry me for the status in society. They would be ordering a new wardrobe, redecorating my estates, and going to all the functions entitled to them as a duchess."

Hallie frowned at that. "But I don't care about those things."

An infectious grin brought out dimples that gave Sebastian a boyish look that Hallie liked. "I know. Perhaps that is one of the many attractions you have for me, Red."

Hallie suppressed a smile although her lips twitched. She liked that he had nick named her "Red." No one else called her that. Ever. It was as if she had a secret name that only Sebastian used and that made it personal and intimate. Special to them.

"But you need a duchess…one that is trained to do all the things necessary of that position."

"You would do just fine, Hallie. You vastly underrate yourself. You would find freedom in our marriage because I would want you happy. Of course, I would not want you to risk your life," he added under his breath.

"What about travel? I have only been in Ohio and London. I have always wanted to see the world."

"Perhaps you might consider a wedding trip to Italy, Paris…" he said, shrugging his shoulders.

Hallie laughed with glee. "Oh, yes. That sounds divine."

"Then we are in agreement."

"Well, I don't know. I want to consider all this…"

"Do you have other questions or concerns that I can help with?"

"Would we visit Ohio? Where would we live? What would life be like married to you?"

"Ah. You are wise to ask these questions. Yes. We can visit Ohio. Our primary home would be here in London. Although this townhouse is my seat, you could select another home here in London if you do not like this townhouse. I do have estates in Kent and Mayfair. I do have responsibilities with tenants, parliament, shipping businesses and such, which might have timing issues. It might affect when we do things, and it may dominate my time on occasion."

Hallie was listening to him intently. Sebastian took a seat in the chair by her bed where his mother had recently sat. He took her hands in his and was studying her a moment.

"I think we would be a good match. We would both have to be willing to work at this. It could be an adventure as you say…"

"You will expect an heir and a spare. What if I do not have sons…what if…"

"It is not important to me. I would like children, of course. But I have brothers…spares as you call them, and if I do not provide an heir, perhaps Alex or Derrick will. It certainly is not a concern to me."

"Really?"

"Really." Sebastian smiled confidently and squeezed her fingers.

What an interesting dilemma this was. She had not thought to marry for several years and maybe never. Suddenly Sebastian presented an appealing offer. Most men she had met had no interest in a woman's freedom or interests. They naturally thought her crazy.

Of course, most were intrigued with her fortune and found her tolerable due to that appealing advantage. Her father was very discriminating, since he did not want to entice a total buffoon. He valued his fortune because he had worked hard for it and would not approve of a fortune hunter. Hallie did think that buying a title was somewhat going against his principals, although he did not seem to mind that exception to his rule. This title, however, did not need her father's money. She would like to be valued for herself and not her father's fortune. There was a great deal to consider. Perhaps he was not being honest about…no; he was an honest and honorable man. His entire family were good human beings, in her estimation.

"It is a serious step, Your Grace."

"Sebastian. And indeed, it is."

Most people considered the advantages of title, social standing, finances, family blood lines and then, if all measured up, the marriage was approved and done. In this case, his intended was considering happiness, independence, daily structure, and likes and dislikes as if they were of upmost importance, and he found himself intrigued and actually in agreement. He did not relish being unhappy. Why not examine some basic reasoning on what their life would be like together. Not an unnatural concept. Divorce was not something easily done without scandal. A happy marriage was naturally appealing. Her priorities were interesting and refreshing, he realized. He liked negotiating, which he was good at in business. It was the name of the game. He knew his mother would be delighted with this conversation. She liked the challenge a woman could bring to a man, and she admired women with a mind of their own. Sebastian found himself comparing women to his mother since he respected her so much, and most women came up short. Somehow, he thought Hallie measured up quite nicely.

"Perhaps you will give me some time to consider this…," Hallie said, watching for his reaction.

She realized most men would be astounded if a woman needed to consider such a good proposal. They would find her request for time insulting and ridiculous. She could hear her father saying, "What is there to consider?" It is a grand proposal, certainly. No question. But she had a tendency to be rash and impulsive at times, and this was important enough to take some time to consider all facets of the marriage proposal. He said he would be talking to her father. Her father would be over the moon with the idea that she had attracted a title.

Sebastian did not seem offended. He was measuring her with his gaze, but he seemed to look at her with respect.

"Of course. Take some time. You will be going home shortly, the stitches taken out, and you will be good as new. I will eagerly await your decision to court you properly."

She had been watching his lips as he spoke and hardly paying attention to the words coming out in a deep, poetic rhythm. He gave a devilish smile when he saw where her attention lay. He leaned over and brushed his lips over hers. She instinctively wrapped her arms around his neck and held him in place, hoping for more. His lips left hers a moment while he looked into her eyes. He lowered himself on the edge of the mattress still watching her and plundered her mouth with his. This was no innocent kiss. This was a ravenous meeting of two souls who could not get close enough, deep enough, or thorough enough to satisfy their urges.

His hand moved the quilt impatiently away. Once the quilt was folded at her waist, his hand rested comfortably over her breast. Her eyes widened in surprise and pleasure as he kneaded her breast gently bringing her nipple to attention. He rubbed the hard nub back and forth until she had to gasp for breath and yet leaked a deep, husky moan from her lips.

She did not recognize the sound coming from her own mouth.

His eyes watched her with interest as he broke the kiss briefly to see her reaction. A tiny frown marred her expression. She was confused. Such a gesture as touching her breast had nearly undone her sanity. How odd. She had never had a man so intimately touch her. It only created an ache, a need or yearning for more. She felt wanton. She now understood the gossip of servants on their escapades with lovers. She had never understood the attraction to have a lover and perform love-making. It had seemed one-sided, favoring the man. She must reexamine this entire idea. Perhaps she was mistaken. She had thought the bed sport was something to do to only create children. Although, all the sneaking around servants did for a private moment seemed to deny the validity of that. Well, perhaps she should explore this more...it certainly was not unpleasant.

"More," she muttered in a throaty voice.

"More?" he repeated with a wicked smile. She nodded her head. He needed no other persuasion. His hand went behind her head and held it in place for his lips to lick and suck hers as if she were a succulent peach. Heat surged through her veins that created hot waves of pleasure. He slid his tongue into her mouth pillaging the recesses in a thrusting motion reminiscent of lovemaking. Her tongue met his and dueled in an effort to participate in the thrusting. He groaned in pleasure. He breathed a soft chuckle and drew away, using the time to study her a moment.

"You catch on quickly. A little more of that and I will not be able to stop myself from ravishing you."

"I do not want you to stop. It felt too good." She ran her fingers through his thick, silky, dark hair. He had recently cut the length, and it now was short, curling at the neck. "Why did you cut your hair?"

He smiled. "You like it long?"

"I like it both ways. I like you."

He laughed. "I cut it in respect for my mother. She did not like it long, so I cut it for her. It seemed a small thing to do to make her happy."

She loved that about him. He respected his mother that much. To cut his hair. She looked at the short strands of hair waving with a mind of their own. It was as if the long hair had dragged the waves from his hair, and with the heavy length gone, the rest was free to dance and curl. Her fingers followed the waves brushing them back from his face. One stray lock danced over his forehead and captured her attention. This stray lock would not behave even after an attempt to brush it back.

"Your hair is wavy. It seemed so straight long. It makes you look younger and more boyish." She smiled at him. "I think I like it this way."

"Then I most certainly will keep it short for you, too."

His fingers slid down her side and touched the bandage there. "Does it hurt?"

Her lids closed over her eyes in rapture feeling his fingers move artfully down her side. She shook her head. His fingers touched her hip caressing the bone gently before dipping lower and cupping her woman's mound. She arched into his hand and moaned.

"Nothing and everything hurts. You drive me mad," she moaned. "I want it all…do not spare anything…please."

"Hallie, you tempt me…but you are here under my protection. I cannot take advantage…"

"You are not taking advantage. I am taking advantage of you. I know you can take this yearning away…"

"Yes. I know a way to please you. It will relieve your anxiety."

His hand pulled her nightgown up and found her smooth bare skin inside her thigh. He gently touched the soft velvet skin that led to her sex. Then his fingers expertly found the soft hair covering her mound and parted her sex ever so gently. Her eyes widened in surprise and embarrassment. But she did not stop him or discourage him.

She arched her back begging him to continue and being impatient for something, she knew not what. He waited a moment watching her reaction, and seeing her eyes close in pleasure; he found her nub and teased the hard bud back and forth slowly and persistently. Hallie bucked her hips in what seemed agony, when his middle finger suddenly dove inside her deep, quickly rubbing her clitoris as he did so. A spasm rocked her so hard that she let out a silent cry. Her eyes opened wide in wonder, her mouth still open in surprise. Her body continued to spasm for several moments in uncontrollable seizures.

Hallie was speechless. How did she lose such control over her body? She looked at Sebastian with a thousand questions marring her face. Was she so innocent that she did not know this would happen?

She looked out of breath and so dazed that he had to suppress a chuckle. She shivered several moments in aftermath, again adding to her wonder. He loved that expression of pure joy and puzzlement on her face. How happy he suddenly felt that he had provided that moment of ecstasy for her. A new experience that gave so much joy. He had not had an experience such as this with his experienced partners of the past. They were long over such innocence.

"Sebastian. I do not know what that was, but it was indescribable. Incredible. No one ever told me that…wait a moment. Am I not still a virgin?"

Sebastian laughed. "You most certainly are still a virgin. But a wiser virgin. There is pleasure to be found in lovemaking. That, my dear, was your first orgasm. Men expect them, but many men do not see to their lover's pleasure. A little more work and patience, but as you can see, well worth it."

"But you did not experience a…orgasm?"

"No. But I found pleasure in your pleasure." He leaned over and kissed her forehead. "The physician is due here this afternoon to check your stitches and see if you are well enough to go home. I will be disappointed to lose you…but I still plan to court you. Be ready, Red."

Hallie laughed at him and then her eyes watered. She had a sentimental moment, and he waited patiently for her explanation. She blinked back the tears that she hoped would not spill.

"I do not know what to say, Sebastian. I think we shared some beautiful moments, and you make marriage to you sound very tempting when I had my mind made up to avoid marriage for a long time…I never imagined that there were such beautiful experiences in lovemaking…." She blushed at the subject she just opened up. Drat her mouth.

"I think I need to thank you for your careful consideration of this serious proposal. I cannot yet name what I feel for you Hallie, and I know that is an important thing to some women. I have never felt this way before…that I know. I am not a man that throws the word 'love' around aimlessly."

"That is good to know."

Hallie was not bothered by his confession. Sebastian was honorable, and he seemed to care for her. That was obvious. He was careful about his emotions, and she was happy he did not throw the word "love" around to get what he wanted. She knew there were men that did so. She was not discouraged. She always thought if she did marry, it would be for love, not a title or any other reason. She was confident that he would love her soon. How difficult could it be to make Sebastian love her? She just had no idea how to do that.

Chapter 18

Pritchard Townhouse, London, April, 1870

Hallie admired her scar. Not much of a scar, but evidence of an adventure she was rather proud of. It was a red line, but it had healed without much pain, and she was happy it was on the mend. The physician had been excellent at stitching her up. Her sisters had all seen the scar and shown their admiration. She took a look at it each time she dressed, and it had become part of her process of dressing. A little war story of her own. Something that gave depth to her character.

Daisy helped her with her gown-layers of sheer, rose-colored silk with tiny roses embroidered in silk thread. The square neckline was cut just low enough to display the swell of her rounded breasts. Tiny embroidered roses danced around the neckline. Seed pearls were sewn around the roses, representing the stems of the flowers. The pale color brought out the vivid, rich shade of her hair. Daisy was dressing it up on the crown of her head with several stray curls escaping the elegant sculpture. Tiny matching roses were set into her hair with hair pins of small pearls.

Tonight was the Harrington ball, and Sebastian was escorting her. The gossipmongers were saying that there would be an announcement of engagement. The eldest Harrington daughter was to marry a Viscount.

But that was not the only excitement expected at the ball.

The ton was anxious to meet the American heroine. She was sought after, and invitations arrived daily. More than she could accept. Her entire family was of interest due to Hallie's adventure. They, too, would be attending the Harrington ball. Violet was none too pleased for the attention, but Poppy was glowing with the extra focus. Poppy answered questions with great enthusiasm, enhancing the story to biblical portions. She seemed to be a natural for poise and refinement with the interrogations. She was obviously shining in the spotlight.

Poppy at ten and seven years was becoming a beauty. She was willowy, and her curves were just starting to develop with promise. Her golden red hair and bright blue eyes were attracting attention, and she was delighted. Her mother, Alice, was none too anxious to allow her daughter out into the courting arena. But then Poppy also had some oddities about her. She had some experiences with deja vu and attributed it to reincarnation. This had Alice very concerned, and she was praying it would all go away. Just like her desire to become a nun. That had only lasted a few months. Otherwise what sort of man would Poppy attract? Some lunatic? Poppy practically demanded she be allowed go to the Harrington ball, and Violet yet again winced at the thought of attending.

Poppy's gown was pale yellow crepe with a cream lace trim. Although Poppy preferred bright colors, it was not acceptable for young, unmarried women to wear such vivid colors. She sighed at the indignity of it all, trying to convince her mother that she lived her life before as an older woman. That only drew more concern from her mother, so she swallowed her need for color. Her hair was dressed in curls tied back from her pale face with a yellow satin bow. Her pink cheeks were brightened by her excitement for her first ball. Energy and vitality flowed from her like rays of sunshine.

Hallie arrived at the ball on Sebastian's arm, just before her family had arrived in another carriage behind them. Sebastian patted his hand over her arm in encouragement as they were greeted by the host and hostess, Viscount Harrington and his wife. The event was well attended, with hundreds of people already swarming the entrance and ballroom eagerly greeting each other.

Hallie drew her own crowd of fans as young ladies wanted to know all about her adventure. Sebastian smiled and stepped back a moment to give her time to share her story with the ladies, who gasped at the right moments and leaned in with eager anticipation for more. Hallie glanced at Sebastian several times as if for aid, but he just smiled and nodded for her to continue.

Poppy nearly skipped by Hallie as Hallie reached out to slow her sister. Poppy immediately realized her blunder and corrected herself in a lady-like walk. Alice was quick to catch up and take her daughter in hand. Soon Poppy was standing with her mother, watching the ballroom fill and the musicians tuning up for the first dance…a waltz. Not a dance for Poppy or anyone of her age. She watched longingly as couples began to pair up for the first dance.

Sebastian took Hallie's hand and drew her onto the dance floor.

"I believe this first waltz is mine, Red," he whispered in her ear.

Hallie took her position as the music began, and they whirled around the dance floor in perfect harmony. Sebastian was an excellent dancer, even if he held Hallie a little closer than was proper form. She did not mind. He looked down onto her smiling face.

"Your sister Poppy is going to break some hearts."

Hallie laughed. "She is quite excited to be here. My mother is not so happy to have her growing up. She has only Iris left to baby."

Poppy stood near her mother, watching the colorful gowns twirl around the dance floor. She took a few steps away from her mother and was satisfied that she had her own space. Alice was busy talking to Harriet Pritchard with great enthusiasm and did not notice Poppy removing herself.

Soon, Poppy was tapping her slipper to the music. Her hands trailed down the skirt of her gown and moved the fabric to the music. Her eyes were aglow with excitement. Then, as if she sensed someone watching her, she turned to look across the room. There standing by himself was a young man, watching her. When she first spotted him, he made her uncomfortable.

He was staring at her, unblinking with a strange, intense, rather intense expression marring his face. After he realized that she had discovered him staring at her, he gave her a lopsided grin. He was not very old…perhaps twenty if that.

Poppy gave an uneasy smile back to the young man. He was not handsome, but he was acceptable looking, Poppy thought. She liked having a man notice her. It made her feel pretty and feminine. She went back to watching the dancers and decided he would lose interest. But several moments later, she peeked in his direction and found him still looking at her with some intensity. She finally gave him an expression that said, "What are you doing?"

He nodded and tipped his head in the direction of the balcony as if inviting her to join him. Her first impression was… bad idea. Then she looked at her mother, so intently talking to her aunt with little interest to her, and it was then that she decided to walk his direction.

She knew she had no introduction to this man, and it was highly improper to walk alone toward him, but she did not care. She was stretching herself, she thought. Adventure, like Hallie. She walked with proper posture and swayed her hips as she had seen other ladies at the ball do.

It seemed a long distance as she took one step at a time. The man had a satisfied grin on his face that suddenly questioned her judgement. The grin was almost sinister. She wanted to look over her shoulder to see if her mother had discovered her absence, but her focus was locked on the man she was approaching with some trepidation.

Sebastian glanced over at Poppy through the crowds of people and then at the man luring her over to the balcony and frowned. He did not have a clear view of what was going on, but as he glanced back to where Poppy should have been, he spotted Alice Martin in conversation with Harriet Pritchard, and she seemed oblivious to the disappearance of one innocent Poppy Martin.

"What is wrong, Sebastian?" Hallie asked, as he watched her sister cross the room toward the balcony.

"Wait here for me, my love. I shall be right back. I must check on a matter," he muttered as he squeezed her gloved hand and disappeared into the throng of people. Hallie watched him artfully weave around the dancers, as people tried to address the Duke. But he was set on a mission, and as he nodded to people, he was not taken from his focus.

A beautiful woman slipped to Hallie's side and watched Sebastian disappear. She turned to face Hallie and smiled. Her gown was a vivid crimson, her lips painted to match her dress. Her breasts were nearly bursting from the daring gown, and jewels decorated her chest and wrists. She was older than Hallie by perhaps a decade, but it did not matter. The woman was confident and beautiful. Hallie had a difficult time not staring. Her beauty took one's breath away. The woman seemed to know that and smiled a knowingly.

"Perhaps I should introduce myself, Miss Martin...er... may I call you Hallie? We ought to become friends, after all."

Hallie was speechless. She was still paralyzed by the woman's beauty and vivid colors that were so brilliant it made Hallie feel drab in her pale rose colored gown.

A soft throaty laugh permeated the air. "I see I have surprised you. Or are you meek...perhaps shy? I cannot see Sebastian interested in such a woman. Not for how I know him."

This brought Hallie out of her woolgathering. She turned her head and looked closely at this bold woman. "Who are you, may I ask? You seem to know of me...and Sebastian..."

The woman nodded. "Indeed, I do, Miss Martin. My name is Marlene St. John. I am a widow and Sebastian's mistress. You do know what a mistress is? I would have married him, but I value my freedom," she boasted. Then she delivered a wicked smile that did not reach her cold eyes.

Hallie closed her mouth with some effort. She hoped it was not open for more than a second or two. She did not want to draw attention. The woman was not only beautiful, but rather brash and confident of herself.

As she finished her comments with a wave of her arm, she saw that Hallie obligingly caught notice of the emerald bracelet on her wrist said, "Ah, I see you have noticed the bracelet that Sebastian gave me. He is generous, so you are smart to attach yourself to him. I am certain he may decide to give you a piece of jewelry, too." She smiled but her eyes remained cold.

"If I decide to marry him, Mrs. St. John, he will give you up," Hallie retorted smugly. Hallie did not know why she said that. She had no idea if that was even feasible. But one thing was certain; she would not marry a man who kept a mistress. How humiliating. This was one subject she had not thought about when she and Sebastian discussed marriage. She heard that some men kept mistresses, but she never thought she would be faced with this herself. In fact, the practice seemed quite common.

Marlene laughed. "How naive you are. But you are but a child. Oh, ladies do not discuss a gentlemen's mistress. Let it just be between us that we know about each other. It will make things more civil, don't you think? Perhaps I can give you a few suggestions of his...well, what he likes in bed sport."

Hallie's eyes widened at Marlene's words, and then her eyes narrowed in anger.

Marlene chuckled her way toward the refreshment table, leaving Hallie to stew. Hallie watched her sway her hips, catching the eyes of men hoping that her breasts might pop out of her gown. She seemed to be admired by nearly every man she passed. Marlene's head turned to the left and right, capturing the gaze of her admirers and nodding her head in greeting. Flirting seemed to be natural tendency for her.

Drat the man. How could she compete with that beautiful woman, she wondered? A streak of jealousy struck her without warning. Good heavens...she could hate that woman. Why did she not say more? She was a speechless blob without an ability to put that woman in her place. It also made her angry at Sebastian. How could he do this to her? He said he had cared for her deeply. Why does a man need two women? What does that say about her? She was obviously lacking in some area. She was also angry at herself. She wished she had discussed this subject with Sebastian about marriage. But to meet this woman at the Harrison ball! She was unprepared. She refused to be a victim. She was a strong woman. She could handle this. Her chin came up a notch in a stubborn gesture. A lady did not discuss this with a gentleman! Bah! Ridiculous!

Sebastian had his eye on Poppy, following her movements toward the balcony. So many people blocking his view. And yet, he did not want to draw unneeded attention to his quest, so he moved with purpose, and yet he had to navigate his way to greet people as he passed them on his journey. Fortunately, a nod here and there did the trick. He did have to tell one titled gentleman that he would address business with him later. Even that went well, he thought. Maybe they all sensed he was preoccupied and determined. He made his way across the crowded ballroom in due haste. He watched the man pull the unsuspecting Poppy onto the balcony with a hard tug. He cursed silently. People watched him. He was a Duke. He had to be very careful. He did not want to be the cause of ruining Hallie's sister. For God's sake…what was she? Ten and six, or ten and seven? Definitely too young. He dreaded being a father of daughters. He might kill a man over something like this…ah but the scandal. There was that to consider, after all. Then he asked himself, what kind of man preferred a child? Bastard. He might be worth killing after all.

Poppy stopped just short of the balcony, perhaps regretting her decision. The man smiled a knowing grin and reached his hand out for hers. She placed her gloved hand in his larger hand and he tentatively pulled her toward the balcony where the doors were open and fresh, brisk night air felt good against the stale perfumed swelter of the ballroom. Bodies crushed together created an intense perfumed heat that begged relief. She resisted the last few steps, but he gave a harder pull to get her through the doors and outside to privacy. Then he laughed, as if getting her outside under his control amused him. Actually, it was a victory for him.

"You are a vision. So sweet and young. Is this your first season?" He asked, leaning closer to her face as if he might steal a kiss. His voice was hoarse and throaty.

Poppy was definitely out of her element. She knew she had made a serious mistake. This man was very aggressive and assertive. She was not experienced with such bold behavior from a man.

Now she understood better her mother's concern for her entering the world of courtship. There was obviously much to know. She regretted her rash behavior and was not certain what she should do. Her face reddened in a deep blush, and her hands were shaking as she considered her options.

"I think, sir, I have made a mistake. I should not have come out here with you. I do not know you." She turned to go, and he grabbed her wrist. She looked at his hand. "Please unhand me, sir," she said with more force than she had expected.

He laughed. His face was not as attractive with the evil sneer. She tried to tug her wrist free, but he dragged her closer to his body, which smelled of tobacco, liquor, and perspiration. His breath was foul, too, she realized. She looked up at his face and wondered how she had come to be here with such a dreadful man. His hair was oily and slicked back in a severe style. He was older than she had originally thought. His skin was a sallow color, his eyes intense with purpose, and it was then she saw he had no alluring qualities what-so-ever.

Poppy had never been so sorry for her judgement than at this very moment. She gasped for a breath, thinking she might scream. Probably not a good idea when she thought more about it. Scandal. She did not relish the trouble she faced from her mother...and her father if he were to find out. But there seemed few options that made sense. Was she to grin and bear this behavior and then get herself out? What could possibly happen?

Then suddenly, without warning, she was thrown aside by a strong arm. The Duke of Ashford threw his other arm against the villain's neck and crushed him with tremendous force against the wall. After releasing Poppy, he used both arms to grab the man by the shoulders and shook him, banging his head against the hard surface, nearly knocking him unconscious. The man's face was red, and his body was trembling. Perspiration gathered on his forehead and dripped down his face. His hands were shaking if not from fear, then from too much drink. He winced in pain.

"What is this about, Your Grace," he muttered in fear.

"You over step yourself, Boswell." Sebastian grumbled. "Are you not the groom-to-be announced tonight by the Harringtons?"

Sebastian nearly choked the man out. Boswell was nearly unconscious, but nodded his head. His eyes rolled back in his head several times, warning of his weak state.

"I pity the bride-to-be." Sebastian let the man loose to slump down the wall to the ground in a crumbled heap.

Sebastian turned to Poppy. He offered his arm. "Come Poppy. I will escort you back to your mother. Are you all right?" He asked as a second thought.

Poppy nodded her head. "Will you tell my mother what has happened?" Poppy asked with concern as they strolled back into the ballroom.

"No. You must promise not to do that again. Stay with your mother, and it will be our secret."

Poppy smiled at Sebastian. "Thank you. You saved my life."

"Well, I don't know about that…"

"Oh, yes. My father would have killed me for certain."

Sebastian laughed. She was a bit dramatic, but she was also right. Someone might have been killed. If he were her father, he might have killed Boswell. The coxcomb.

"You had better be more careful. You would not want to find yourself married too young and to a scoundrel like Boswell, now would you?" He offered as a moral to the story.

Poppy shook her head. "That was a near disaster, and I thank you for assisting me. If you had not come, well…"

"It was my pleasure."

Sebastian delivered Poppy to her mother and looked for Hallie. She was still standing where he left her, talking to her sister, Violet. She was lovely. He admired her from her dainty slippers to her beautiful hair.

Gerald Boswell sat on the ground a moment gathering his thoughts. He wished he could punch out the Duke of Ashford for not minding his own business, but then one did not punch a Duke. He got a handkerchief out of his pocket and ran it across his face. It would not do to have someone come out on the balcony and find him in a heap on the ground to answer unwanted questions.

With some effort, he dragged himself up and leaned against the wall for some support. He took a deep breath. He needed a drink. He must not risk his commitment to marry the Harrington girl. She was nothing to look at, but her dowry would get him out of debt and set him up in style. He was the second son of an Earl without much promise. The creditors were after him, and his father had refused to support him.

He took a deep breath and straightened his clothes. They were wrinkled, and there was a tear in his sleeve. Luckily, the Harrington girl had been easy to court and wanted him, so her parents reluctantly agreed to this marriage. He did not want to change his standing with them, so he must find help to straighten his appearance. His slick hair was a mess. He snuck out of the balcony area and sought aid. He did not have much time before the announcement was made.

Viscount Garrett Montjoy came into the ballroom late. He scanned the crowd and spotted his friend Sebastian talking to the Martins, but he was not looking for Sebastian. He was searching for a beauty he met at the last ball he attended and then at Gunter's. He was not certain he wanted to court, or marry for that matter. But he could not get the unusual beauty out of his mind. He liked that she did not know she was a beautiful. She had interests other than gossip and the weather. She was educated in a way he was not accustomed to for a woman. He liked her. He finally got a glimpse of her talking to her sister.

She was wearing a pale blue voile gown that looked nearly silver in the light. Delicate lace trimmed the bodice and accentuated her small waist. Her neckline was rounded, hinting of full breasts. Her golden red hair was shiny and piled on her crown in artful curls.

Violet was focused on a conversation with her sister. It was not gossip, fashion, or the weather. Her face was too serious and intent to be talking of a frivolous subject. He smiled at the notion. She seemed to be considering something her sister said and nodded her approval. Her curls bounced when she nodded. He could watch her all evening. She was interesting and well read. He enjoyed conversations with her and had thought quite a bit about seeing her again.

Garrett was a catch. He had a title, was attractive in a boyish sort of way, and every mother with a marriageable daughter wanted him to court their little darling. He had to be careful or a trap might be set. Every available title had that concern. Sneaking off to a dark corner for a kiss could lead to the parson's mousetrap. Staying away from innocent girls barely out of the school room was the smart way to live one's life. That was why he was confused by Violet. He knew better than to show an interest that might lead to more than he was ready for. But he still found himself staring at her and thinking about talking to her again. All innocent, or was it? No matter how much he thought about the issue, he could not solve it. She would still occupy his thoughts.

Perhaps he should get himself a drink and have a conversation with Sebastian to see how his love life was going. Besides, he wanted a first-hand account on how Miss Martin ended up shooting the assassin in the knee. Everyone was talking about it. Talk about gossip. He smiled at the thought.

Sebastian brought two cups of punch to Violet and Hallie. He smiled at them both and handed them the small cups.

"I thought you ladies must be parched from all the conversation. And it is warm in here, is it not?"

They took the punch with smiles. Hallie gulped it down in nearly one swallow. Violet sipped hers and glanced over at her mother and sister.

"I think I will see what mother is talking about with Aunt Harriet. I will leave you two to another conversation." With that, she made her way across the dance floor.

Hallie placed her cup on a passing tray a servant offered and stared at Sebastian with some displeasure. He frowned a moment in confusion.

"Shall we take a stroll in the rose gardens, Hallie?" He asked with a tentative smile. "I think you have something on your mind that needs attention."

"How intuitive you are. Yes, I would like that," she responded.

She put her hand on his arm, and they made their way out the French doors toward the rose gardens, which were lit for just such an occasion. There were other couples spaced adequately apart as to allow for private conversations. Couples spoke in low, hushed voices lending to the ambiance of the natural environment.

"You are quiet Hallie. I am intrigued as to what has been gnawing on that intelligent brain of yours."

"I met a very beautiful woman tonight."

"Not as beautiful as you are, I am certain," he smoothly replied.

Hallie stopped a moment and studied him. He smiled and leaned in to brush his lips across hers, but she did not respond and held her continence.

"Ah. I see this is about me. What have I done Hallie? Better tell me now so I can fix it." He held a wry smile, and they started walking again.

"You seem to read me well, Sebastian. I am impressed. A husband that can sense trouble with his wife is invaluable, I would think," she said, stopping to smell a soft pink rose. She looked up to see his puzzled expression.

"Her name was Marlene. Do you know her?" She asked coyly glancing up from the rose.

"You know damn well I know her. Let us not play games Hallie. You are an honest and forth right woman. Get to the point."

Hallie stood taller with those words from Sebastian and took a breath. He sounded gruff and impatient.

"I will not marry a man who has another woman on the side. I would be the only woman in his life."

Sebastian laughed. "I don't know what Marlene told you, but she **was** my mistress. I gave her up some time ago. You certainly would be woman enough for me, Red. I plan to honor my wedding vows."

Hallie frowned. "She said...she showed me..."

"Listen Hallie, Marlene is rather bitter about our split. She can be vindictive. She had hope for a marriage proposal, and I made myself clear about our relationship from the beginning."

"I see."

"There should be trust between us. A marriage without trust could be disastrous, do you not agree?"

Hallie looked at him a moment and found him sincere. He was so handsome tonight in his black formal attire. He was sensual, and yes, she lusted for him. She nodded her head in agreement, admiring his appearance. There was something about being around Sebastian that took all thoughts but his charismatic attraction from her mind. He occupied her dreams at night, and a yearning to be with him even to touch him, played havoc with her sanity during the day.

"It is just that we did not discuss this subject before and…"

"Usually proper young ladies do not know about mistresses…but I admit you are not ordinary by any means." His wicked smile caught her unaware.

"You are right. I am an American. Outspoken and opinionated. Not your usual English proper lady."

Sebastian laughed. "Yes. I must agree. But that is what I find most appealing about you. I think we make a perfect match."

He turned her by her shoulders to face him. He measured her expression and touched her face with his fingers, following the curve of her temple to her cheek and then cupped her chin.

"I want to marry you Hallie. I would make it my goal in life to create happiness for you. I cannot sleep without thinking of you. You have become my world. I want you to stay in it. I love you, Hallie. I know that now. I can get a special license, and we can be married as soon as you are willing."

He wondered if he had over-stated his position. Maybe it was too much all at once. She was surprised, that was clear. It was the longest few moments of his life. What was she thinking? Why didn't she say something? He sighed. This made him vulnerable.

"Yes." Hallie said it so very quietly that he could barely hear her.

"Did you just say, 'Yes?'" He asked, not certain he had heard her correctly.

She nodded her head smiling.

"I must formally ask your father, so do not share this with anyone as yet."

Chapter 19

The door to the study stood open. Alice flew through it like her gown was on fire and landed in the arms of her husband, Benjamin. He wrapped his arms around her waist and held her. He was enjoying this moment. He liked having his wife in his arms and all by her own actions. He smiled down into her radiant face.

"Oh, Benny. Is it true? Is our Hallie to be a duchess? Tell me everything." She looked up into his face to see if she could read any of it in his expression.

He took his arms from around her waist. "Do sit Alice. I know you want all the details, and I am afraid you would not be able to stand still one moment."

He directed her to the fireplace, where two comfortable chairs faced each other. They sat after he poured them two glasses of port. Alice was anxious but knew better than rush her husband. He could not be rushed from his purpose. She dragged in a sigh, barely able to contain her excitement and joy. He looked into the fire as if the flames held answers to how he would proceed. Again, she understood this of her beloved husband. Most of the time she could read his thoughts and say things just a moment before he was about to say the same thing. It seemed at times they thought from the same brain, but then he was very smart about business, and she was not.

"Little did I know that when we came to London this time, Alice, my dreams for my daughter would come true. All that work I put into snagging a Duke for..."

"Now, Benny. You snagged no Duke. Your daughter captured a Duke fair and square, and you had little to do with it...I do admit you wished and prayed for it a great deal."

"Does it matter? The Duke of Ashford has asked our beloved daughter Hallie for her hand in marriage. She will be a duchess. Is that not grand?"

"Benny, why did it take over an hour? I know you men like your brandy, but surely...." Alice watched her husband sip his port and swallow before answering.

"You know the Duke of Ashford is very wealthy? One of the wealthiest in England, in fact? He had a great deal of property beyond just what is entailed with the title. I had no idea...he even has stock in business here in England as well as America, Paris and Italy. I was willing to buy a title, but I never dreamed...." Benjamin was staring into to the flames of the fire with wonder and amazement.

"You told him about the dowry?"

Benjamin nodded. "I did."

"Did he want it, or was it insulting to him, Benny?" Alice sipped more Port and held her empty glass out for more. Benjamin stood and took her glass from her and poured more Port.

"He wanted it. But strangely not for himself. He asked me to write it up as a gift to Hallie to do with as she pleases." He smiled at his wife. "He really wants to take care of her...protect her."

Tears flooded Alice's pale blue eyes. "Oh, Benny. How wonderful. He is a dream come true, is he not?"

Benjamin nodded. "That is not all, Alice. He has given Hallie property and funds, also to be strictly hers. She can someday give them to her children or whatever she wants."

"I am happy. So very happy," Alice said as she dabbed tears from her eyes. "What of Hallie?"

"Sebastian, as he asked me to call him, says she will marry him. Evidently, our daughter is ready to marry him. A miracle, really. She is so stubborn that I thought she would never marry, let alone a Duke. Just to show her independence if nothing else. I have created independent monsters..."

Alice laughed. There was silence for a moment. It was not uncomfortable, because they used the silence to gather their thoughts and enjoy their happiness. Not a moment wasted.

"Benny, does he love her?" She finally thought to ask her husband.

Benjamin looked at his wife with surprise. "Why Alice, I am surprised you asked that question. A man who gives back a woman's dowry for her and takes care of her future with generous funds and property loves his bride, does he not? But do not worry my darling Alice. He told me he loves our daughter."

Soon, the entire house would be celebrating, but for now, there was time to enjoy the moment, and they knew how to do that. Benjamin leaned over and kissed his wife. First Rose and now Hyacinth. Good marriages for them both.

Poppy was on a quest. She could not sleep the night through. Her mind was cluttered with guilt. She spent the night stating and restating her issues, rehearsing as if for a play. Once in the night, she even got up and paced the floor, but nothing helped her sleep or resolve her problems. She was going to fix things, and she would do it first thing in the morning and that was the cure for her sleepless night. She slept for two hours before dawn.

Daisy helped her dress and tried to talk her out of her excursion. She was wearing her walking gown that showed off her developing figure. It was her favorite. It made her feel grownup and powerful. Her mother had had it made for her, along with several similar gowns, but this one was special. There was something about the cut of the gown that just seemed perfect. The skirt was full and floated around her ankles like a cloud and made her feel graceful.

"If you do not chaperone me, Mother will be angry," Poppy said with authority in her voice. "And please put my hair up so that I look more sophisticated."

Daisy worked for all the sisters, but Poppy was a challenge. She was on the peak of growing up, and she was a handful, to be certain. Daisy always got an earful of interesting thoughts from Poppy. Reincarnation was an interesting subject that

Daisy decided just to listen to and not argue. She was able to become more of a friend doing so and could influence her charge into being more reasonable, at times.

Daisy sighed in defeat. "You still look your age, Miss Poppy, if you don't mind my saying...and I may lose my position if I go with you...and I may lose my position if I do not accompany you. Where is your Mother?"

"She has gone out shopping with Aunt Harriet and won't be back for hours. We will not be missed. I have to do this Daisy...so I can sleep tonight."

"Drinking warm milk would do the same thing, and we will not face trouble!"

Poppy gazed at herself in the mirror. Daisy had talent, that was certain. Her strawberry gold hair was a mass of perfectly-formed curls that hung down from her crown to her neck. She was happy with her appearance and turned a grateful smile on Daisy.

"Would you like ribbons that match your gown, Miss Poppy?"

Poppy tilted her head back and forth considering. "Would we match the gown or the trim, do you think?"

"I think we should match the trim," Daisy said, reaching for the blue ribbon that matched the trim to her pale pink gown. She began to thread the ribbon through the curls with expertise. Soon they were speeding down the steps out the servant entrance to the carriage house behind the townhouse.

The footman helped them into one of the Pritchard carriages after Poppy gave the driver directions. The two women settled onto the forward-facing bench. Both women were quiet on the short trip. Daisy was not approving and was brewing like she sometimes did. Poppy was rehearsing in her mind what she would say. She did not have calling cards printed as yet, so she had taken a blank card and carefully written her name in her best penmanship. It was a short ride, not much time to prepare her speech.

The driver stopped in front of the townhouse, and Poppy peeked out the window to assure herself that they were in the right place. It was a beautiful townhouse built of brick. Colorful flowers decorated window boxes, which gave the residence a friendly, welcoming feel.

"It is not too late to change your mind, Miss Poppy," Daisy whispered in her ear.

Poppy shook her head in denial and waited for the footman to put the step down and assist them to the front door. Poppy told the footman they would not be long, as they knocked on the door. A butler opened the door and looked at Poppy and Daisy with a raised eyebrow.

"Miss Poppy Martin to see Viscountess Harrington," Poppy said, in a strong, rehearsed voice.

The butler nodded and waved his hand to direct them past the door. He held out a silver tray for her card. Poppy dropped her card on the tray and looked up at the intimidating butler for direction. He was tall and regal with graying hair and spotless livery.

"I shall see if my Lady is receiving."

Then he indicated a marble bench where they could sit while they waited. Both women sat and looked at each other.

As determined as Poppy was, her hands still trembled. She had never done something like this before and without her mother's blessing, to boot. But she could not imagine her mother agreeing to this meeting, and she knew she had to do this. She was certain it was the right thing to do. Do the deed first and ask for forgiveness later. That had paid off more than once for Hallie anyway....

"It is probably too early to come calling, Miss Poppy," Daisy whispered. "Perhaps we should have come later at a more fashionable hour."

"I know. But I had to get this over with. You understand, do you not? Besides, if we had come later, the more fashionable hour, there would have been more visitors. I need to see her alone."

Daisy nodded. She understood the impulsive Poppy Martin very well. They waited nearly half an hour before the butler showed them into a small parlor decorated in pale yellows with pale blue accents. In one corner of the room, a piano with well-worn ivory keys. Fresh flowers permeated the air. Pale yellow velvet drapes hung on either side of one large window overlooking the street. Blue tiebacks held them in place. Poppy could see their carriage sitting on the street in front of the townhouse.

"Tea is coming ladies. My Lady will join you shortly." The butler bowed and left the room. A maid brought a tea tray and put it on a table in front of a vacant sofa. There were tiny cakes and sandwiches on a bone china, flowered plate. Daisy and Poppy faced the sofa, waiting for their hostess.

Daisy sighed. "I hope this is not a disaster, Miss Poppy."

"I know. But I have to do it anyway."

Viscountess Harrington gracefully entered the room in a beautiful flowered gown that nearly matched the wallpaper in the room. It had pale yellow roses with blue Forget-me-nots trimmed with lace and satin ribbons. Viscountess Harrington was a handsome woman with bearing and strength. Her broad face was kind, her blue eyes set wide, her nose larger than acceptable, but her mouth was smiling in greeting.

Daisy and Poppy stood and curtsied before being motioned to take their seats.

"Miss Martin, what do I owe the pleasure?" Upon seeing the young Poppy and taking her measure, she frowned a little in confusion. "May I call you Poppy? You were in attendance of our celebration, were you not…with your family?" Waiting for answers to her questions, she began to pour tea. "Is this your maid?"

Poppy almost laughed at all the questions that had been asked. "Yes, my Lady, do call me Poppy. I was here with my family for your special occasion. And, may I present my maid and chaperone, Daisy."

The Viscountess nodded. "Do you take anything in your tea?"

Daisy declined.

"Lemon please," Poppy responded.

After everyone had their tea and a small cake, the Viscountess waited for the purpose of the unexpected visit.

Viscountess Harrington was amused. First, the handwritten calling card and then this young woman, barely out of the schoolroom, sitting in her parlor, just as grown up as can be.

Most unusual. Highly irregular.

Her life for the most part she thought boring, but it was instances like this that brightened her day. At first, she thought there must be some mistake and that this young woman was here for her daughter. Now, she was curious. She waited patiently for her guest to sip her tea and eat her cake before she spoke.

"I must say I am curious about the purpose for your visit. It is not social, is it? " the Viscountess asked between sips of tea, looking over the rim of her cup.

Poppy shook her head and took a much-needed breath. "I came to ask you to reconsider the engagement of your daughter."

The Viscountess' eyes widened in shock, and she nearly choked on her tea. Daisy wanted to crawl into a corner. Now came the drama. The Viscountess put her tea cup down and looked at Poppy for an explanation.

"I know you must love your daughter…it is just that Mr. Boswell is not a good man."

The Viscountess smirked a little if one was fast enough to catch it. "Why would you say such a thing, Poppy?" she asked, as Poppy too put her cup down.

"Mr. Boswell behaved badly at the ball, and I just think…"

"Badly how, Poppy? You came all this way to say this. Let us be honest. Tell me exactly what you know."

Poppy nodded and told the Viscountess about her experience with Mr. Boswell, leaving nothing out. The room became quiet. There was silence for what seemed hours, however, Poppy waited.

"Does your mother know what happened to you Poppy?"

"No."

"How old are you Poppy?"

"I am ten and seven."

The Vicountess nodded her head. She picked her cup again and took a sip. "It was very brave of you to come and tell me this. Why?"

"It seemed the right thing for me to do."

"I see."

Poppy stood. "I think I should be going."

"Sit a moment more, please."

Poppy and Daisy sat back down.

"I want to say, your trip here is appreciated. I do love my daughter. She has not had offers of marriage except this one… her father and I do not like Boswell, but my daughter wants to marry him. I will talk to her father, and I think you are right, Poppy. I do not think she should marry him. I would like to compliment your mother on your upbringing. You are a delight, I must say. I wish my daughter had friends like you, Poppy."

As Daisy and Poppy rode home, they both gave a sigh of relief.

"You are very fortunate she took that well, Miss Poppy."

"I realize that. I still had to do it even if she was not happy with my message."

The next morning, one Miss Poppy Martin received an eloquent thank you message written on fine linen paper from one Viscountess Harrington. Furthermore, there was an invitation for tea from the Viscountess that would include her daughter, one Margaret Harrington.

It was late. Too late to be running figures and making important decisions. Sebastian stretched his legs under the massive desk where he worked. His business manager had taken a holiday with his family. Who does that in April? Normal people. He sighed. There was so much business to catch up on, and he was not focused as he should be.

The Kent estate needed a manager. He was daft to think he could do it all. He pondered the idea of hiring a young man named Dexter Manville. His mother had just selected Manville to be the groom of the Dorsey girl. He was a smart young man, good with figures, and had attended university, thanks to Sebastian's father. Manville would grow into the job, he was certain.

Yes, that was decided. And on doing so, it would relieve him of a huge burden. It would also delight his mother, who loved fairytale stories. He chuckled to himself. Perhaps now he could take himself off to bed and actually sleep. It had been difficult to keep his mind on business after meeting with Martin. There would be an engagement announcement and then a wedding. He would have been satisfied with a special license and a quick wedding. All the faster to get that redhead in his bed. That, too, would be a relief from all his day dreams of the little minx.

Sebastian thought about how Martin was over-joyed his daughter was to marry a Duke. He was surprised by Sebastian's generosity with the dowry and offer of more funds and properties. Sebastian was amused at the shocked expression on Martin's face. After he got over that initial surprise, he had wanted to crow about it with a big wedding. And, of course, every girl wanted her wedding celebration. So, there would be much ado about this. His mother would be happy and delighted, too, with a big wedding.

He had sent Holland to bed. Now he would straighten his desk and get a good night's sleep. He stood and stretched. All his paper weights held down important stacks of paper. He gazed at them with satisfaction. How he loved organization.

Then, he heard a knock on the massive front door. Who could that be at this hour? He moved toward the door and thought perhaps one of his brothers had a problem. He ran his hand through his messy hair. He had worked it over with his hands many times while working out business strategies. He wore no cravat, his shirt was open at the neck, displaying dark curling hair, his sleeves rolled up as he often did when he worked, and he sighed, as he was not fit for guests. But what kind of guests came calling at this ridiculous hour? The knocking persisted. Finally, he swung the heavy door open and gapped with surprise at the woman standing on his threshold.

Hallie Martin stood wrapped in a hooded wool gray coat her gloved fist posed to knock again. She wrapped the coat tighter around her body to ward off the cold. She had never done such a bold thing before, and although she had no regrets, her courage was being challenged once again.

"What the blazes are you doing here, Red?" he asked, dragging her inside, looking both ways to see if she had been seen. But who was out at this hour anyway? He saw a public carriage leave from in front of his townhouse. A public carriage? What the deuce was she doing?

Hallie took down her hood and exposed her mane of red hair. He was paralyzed, still waiting for an explanation. But he could not help but admire her beauty as she removed her coat and handed it to him. He tossed it on a bench near the door. He was spellbound. Flummoxed. No lady came by herself to a single man's home. And no lady was out at this ungodly hour. It was difficult to surprise him, and yet she had.

"What has happened? Are you all right?" he inquired with concern. What the devil had gotten into her?

Hallie Martin stood proudly in front of him. She was magnificent.

He gasped in awe at how beautifully dressed she was. She wore a silver-threaded, rose pink damask gown cut low in the bodice, exposing the tops of her rounded breasts. It was trimmed in a darker rose lace around the low neckline and waist. The gown had cap sleeves covered in delicate lace.

"Nothing is wrong. Are you going to offer me a drink, Sebastian?" she nearly purred in a raspy voice.

She was rather proud at the control in her voice and body language, since her nerves were out-the-window frazzled.

Was she out of her mind? What the dickens was this? Did she not understand what a scandal this could cause? But then, she was to be his wife. What did it matter....?

He waved his arm to indicate the study where he had just been working. "By all means, come in and join me for a drink. What is your pleasure, Red? Port, brandy?" His voice sounded husky even to his own ears. Was she aware that she was driving him mad?

She moved with her usual grace into his study and settled down gracefully into a chair in front of the fire. She adjusted her skirts around her legs and then looked up into his face. She was so dazzling, he blinked his eyes to give them a rest. He watched her a moment and then went to prepare the drinks. She slowly removed one glove and then the other. He could hear the movement as he arranged the glasses.

"I think I would like a brandy," she said with conviction. Her voice was husky.

One dark brow raised in question. "Certainly. Whatever the lady desires."

He watched her adjust herself in the chair, folding her skirt neatly around her legs again in a nervous gesture. She was not as calm as she seemed, he assessed. He handed her a glass of brandy and sat in the chair opposite hers with his own glass. He took a sip and watched her over the rim of his glass. He was curious. What was she up to? She never ceased to surprise him.

Hallie took a cautious sip of the fiery, deep amber liquid and seemed to have difficulty swallowing. When she finally swallowed, she took a deep breath to cover her discomfort.

Her eyes widened in surprise. He suppressed a laugh. He dragged his eyes slowly over her body from her delicate feet to her red flaming hair.

She was luscious.

Provocative.

His. He definitely was aroused.

Hallie turned and stared at him, centering her attention on his lips, as if she was asking for a kiss. It was nearly his undoing. He could not imagine himself squirming, but he was squirming in his chair. His pants were suddenly too tight, and he was definitely too warm. Good God. She was a sight. No paid courtesan could do this better.

"Are you trying to seduce me, Hallie?" he asked softly.

Her long lashes fluttered in a nervous gesture. To a woman practiced in flirtation, it might have been intentional, but not Hallie. His Hallie. She was too innocent. Her eyes searched his for a signal perhaps, and then her lips parted. He wanted to kiss her then and there, but he wanted her answer. So, he patiently waited, and it was not an easy task.

"Yes, Sebastian. Am I succeeding?"

"Oh, yes, my love, you are definitely succeeding."

Chapter 20

Sebastian had a difficult time stopping himself from grabbing the glass from her hand, throwing it into the fireplace, scooping her up, and carrying her to his bed. What the blazes was she expecting from him? Certainly not patience. She crossed the line in that category.

"This is a dangerous conversation, Hallie. Do you not know that?"

She nodded her head. "I do hope so, Sebastian."

He was staring intently at her.

Predator. She nearly wavered. His scent was strong.

"I may not be able to stop myself…"

"I am counting on that…husband to be." Did that really come out of her mouth?

Hallie was not as brave as she was pretending. She was out of her comfort zone. But she had been ravaged by lustful thoughts, and enough was enough.

There was to be a ball for an engagement announcement, then a wedding, and all the planning that took. She could wait months, and it would be months of suffering this lustful thinking that made her unfocused and sleepless. She was burning up like she had a fever. Being this close to him was nearly her undoing. She wanted to touch him. Run her hands over his chest and through his hair.

Experience wicked behavior. Naked. Body to body.

She was nervous and afraid he would not accept her offer of seduction. What then? Humiliation. But it would be worth the risk.

Sebastian stood up in front of her and took her hands in his. He pulled her up to a standing position and reached around her waist to pull her closer to him. His hand found her chin and tipped her face up to his. His rich brown eyes were intent and focused on hers, seeking her motives. His eyes were warm and intense.

"How should we proceed, Hallie?" he whispered in a deep husky voice that felt like music to her ears.

"I think you should kiss me, Sebastian."

With that, he bent down and brushed his lips on hers tentatively. Her eyes closed, and she sighed her satisfaction. A smoldering fire started to build momentum with little hope of dying. Hallie wrapped her arms around his neck, feeling the soft strands of his hair with her fingers. His tongue sought the recesses of her mouth, tasting her, demanding her surrender. Her blood surged in hot molten paths through her body, making it nearly impossible to breath. She felt like she could swoon in his arms as he held her tightly against his hard, sinewy chest. She inhaled his fragrance. Sandalwood, spices, leather…rich aroma that was him. At this moment, she knew she had made the right decision. This would sate her need.

His tongue was thrusting in her mouth, and soon she was matching his rhythm discovering that she could breathe through his mouth. He groaned and pulled away to look at her. She was a fast learner. There was more, she was certain. All she had to do was keep the fire blazing.

"What now, Hallie? Much more and I will not be able to stop. Do you want me to stop?"

Hallie took his hand and placed it over her breast. His eyes widened and one eye brow shot up.

"You like this?" He asked, gently caressing her breast. She nodded and moaned her delight at his experienced touch. He reached behind her and released the pearl buttons from their loops with practiced ease. He dragged his parted lips down her neck as her gown loosened. He reached inside her gown and realized the minx had no corset on. He felt himself get harder, if that were indeed possible. His hand traced her skin beneath her shear chemise. Her skin was soft like satin. His fingers pinched her nipple pulling a gasp from her lips. She leaned into his hand, wanting his touch, needing and craving it.

"Sebastian, what are you doing to me?" she asked in awe.

"Seducing you, what else?"

"Ah. Perfect."

His head bowed to her breast and he took her nipple into his mouth and suckled it, finishing with a lick around her are-ola. Her wet skin shivered in the cool air, drying as he looked up with a hooded gaze. A tension coiled deep within her was yearning for more.

Sebastian gave her a wicked smile. "I think we need to take this to my bedroom now, while I still have an ounce of control."

He scooped her up easily in his strong arms and marched toward the door. Hallie leaned her head against his chest and listened to his heart beat. The heart she knew belonged to her now. She was certain.

He took the steps to his suite with a strong stride, holding her as if she were the most valuable treasure. Her arm wrapped around his neck and her fingers found his dark chestnut curls, twirling them within her fingers. She inhaled his addicting aroma again, as if she could never get enough.

She was dizzy watching the ceiling pass by knowing she had passed the point of no return. Not that she wanted to undo what she had started. She wanted to curl up against his naked body and touch every inch of him. Was that not wanton of her? But she did not care.

He opened a door and slipped through with her still in his capable arms. He closed it and locked it with a key that remained in the keyhole. He then let her slip down his body, every hard inch of him, and watched her scan his bedroom as her feet touched the floor.

It was a male room. No question. Large, dark, massive, carved walnut furniture with tall ceilings to accommodate the proportion of the furniture. The room smelled of lemon oil and beeswax. It was clean and organized like Sebastian. She smiled as she took in every detail that was him. Large windows with heavy, dark crimson velvet drapes gave the room warmth. The carpet was dark floral in burgundy, green, rose, and gold.

His dresser held personal items like his hair brush, a comb and ornate jars with perhaps his scents. She walked the parameter of the room inspecting each item. Then she spotted a small desk with a neat stack of papers on top held by a glass paper weight.

So Sabastian.

Her fingers trailed along a stuffed chair near the lit fireplace. The fabric was pale rose and green floral, the only feminine thing in the room. There was a duplicate chair opposite it, both facing soft burning wood with flames that gave off just enough heat to make the room comfortable. She smiled, knowing that this room held no surprises. It was him. It was comfortable and felt like home. Each item had a purpose and was placed with care and thought. She noticed a small framed portrait of his mother. She was younger, but it was clearly her and valued in a gold, ornate frame.

Direct, simple, straight forward...like him.

Sebastian watched her peruse his private quarters. No other woman, other than servants and his mother, had graced these four walls. He wondered what she thought, what she was thinking...she was taking in every inch, considering every item, touching his things. He was transfixed. She was a wonder, a miracle really. Her fingers sought out her hair and casually removed hair pins as she looked over his room from top to bottom. She set a stack of hair pins on his dresser, as if they belonged there, and maybe they did. She shook out her hair and ran her fingers through it casually...slowly. Seductive. It was sexual although she probably did not know it. Her mane cascaded down to her waist in gorgeous shiny, red-flamed ripples. He nearly said, "Ahh." The breath he let out of his lungs escaped without notice. Control.

Her hair was thick and glossy and bounced with her movements. He wanted to touch it, feel the strands with his fingers. It seemed alive, wild, untamed, like her.

And then she stood before the massive canopy bed. He liked this bed. It was big-big enough for his height and weight. The headboard was carved walnut; the posts were large columns sporting light fabric tied neatly back to expose the bed. Satin quilts of burgundy and rose were turned down, inviting occupants. There were pale rose satin pillows stacked at the headboard. Hallie stared at the sexual invitation. She put her arm around one of the thick posts and leaned over to caress the shiny quilt. She turned her head to see his reaction. Her eyes lowered and then widened in realization.

"Was this your parents' room?" Of course it was. She was being an idiot.

He nodded once and smiled a slow lazy grin.

This was no time for a case of nerves. She wanted this, planned for this, needed this. She would not question her gut feeling on this subject. She looked to him for guidance. She had no idea what to do now. She let go of the post and swung around to stare at him. He was beautiful. All strength, yet he watched her with what? Tenderness, warmth...confusion, perhaps amusement?

"Why don't you take off your clothes, Sebastian?" She found herself asking. Her eyes scanned his body casually. Oh, how she wanted to see him naked. Could he tell what she was thinking? Sometimes she thought he could actually read her thoughts…see deep into her mind.

Sebastian quirked a smile that turned into a full, deep, resonate laugh. "Ah, a woman after my own heart." He pulled off his shirt over his head. His broad, muscular chest was sprinkled with dark, curly hair. His arms were muscled and thick, tanned from the sun in a rich golden brown that looked healthy and virile. He was perfection. Not the usual form one saw in Greek Gods, but more, so much more. There was strength, muscle, tone, and yes, beauty. She could look at every inch of him for hours….

She walked up to him and put her small hand on his chest feeling the muscles, the coarse hair, and the warmth of his skin. She liked the feel of his skin, and the coarse hair felt prickly to her fingers. So different than her own body. Where hers was curvy, soft, and slick, his was coarse, angular, and textured. She wanted to feel him body to body…hold him against her and feel his heart beating in rhythm with hers.

"It is time for you to take a piece of clothing off," he said, watching for her reaction. His eyes were warm, the deep chocolate brown color capturing her soul, his eye lids drowsy and sensual. He watched her…now he was the predator, watching his prey. A thrill went down her spine and settled in her stomach, causing a moment of dizziness. Swoon? Not her.

Her gown was already unbuttoned from the back, so she let it fall to her waist and worked it down slowly over her hips onto the floor. She picked it up with a sweep of her arm and tossed it on a nearby chair. She looked at him with her chin tilted up in a stubborn gesture he recognized. She stood in her chemise and petticoats. The chemise was shear silk with tiny roses embroidered around the neck. Her breasts could be seen through the fabric, the dark shadows of her nipples poking hard against the fabric. The scent of roses filled the air. Her nipples were pressed hard against the soft fabric, aching to be set free.

"You are so beautiful. Perfect in fact," he said in a husky voice.

"I was thinking the same of you," she responded in a whisper, which he barely heard. She smiled. Her lips quirked with promise of another scandalous request.

"Take off your pants, Sebastian. It is your turn."

He gave her a wicked smile and reached down to unbutton his dark, wool, pin-striped trousers. She watched his long fingers work the button.

"You are wearing something under those, are you not?" she asked with honest curiosity.

A slow, seductive smile followed by an expressive eye-brow lift. "It would be more convenient if I did not wear smalls, is that not true? Besides, you did not wear a corset. That was scandalous, don't you think?"

"No. I think going without smalls is worse by far."

"I did not say I was without smalls," his lips curving in a sinful smile.

He lowered his pants and stepped out of them. He also picked up his trousers and tossed them over her gown. He stood in his smalls, and she gapped in astonishment at the sight before her. She had never seen a man without clothes. He was magnificent. His thighs were muscled and thick and sporting dark hair. His smalls were budging with...what? She stared at the budge and cocked her head to the side in question.

"I do think you are making my...er...man parts grow. Please look at something else so I can gain control."

"What are you talking about?"

"Just look elsewhere," he said sternly.

She looked up into his face, hoping for an explanation. None came. It seems he wanted to change the subject too.

"Take off your petticoats. It is your turn."

She looked down at her petticoats and nodded. Her fingers worked at the ties and lowered her petticoats to the floor. Again, she scooped them up and tossed them on top of his trousers. Now she stood in her chemise and stockings held up with lace garters.

He stared at her a moment in perplexity. His desire of her was raging. With other women...he, well, he was attracted to a woman and then he took her to his bed and all was under control. Hallie was a different matter. She was a virgin, for one. And usually virgins did not interest him. He enjoyed experienced women. He did like to pleasure a woman, but virgins were a lot of work. There was drama, pain, and sensitivity involved. But this desire he felt was raging to a point of being unbearable. It took all he had in what little control was left just to play this silly game of hers. Bloody hell. He wanted to get on with it, and they were playing a stripping game that might cause him to organism in his smalls like an inexperienced school boy.

"Well, if I take off my smalls next, the show is over. I think you should take something else off. Allow me to take your stockings off, hum?"

He waved her over to the bed, where she could sit on the edge. He deftly removed her slippers and caressed her feet each in turn, watching her reaction. Hallie gave a start at the tender touch of his hands on her feet. She lifted one shapely leg offering him the task of rolling her stocking down her leg. He untied her garter and reached up her thigh. His fingers were calm and gentle as he carefully rolled her stocking down her leg, watching her face to gauge her reaction. His touch was extraordinary. Provocative. It sent tingles and goose bumps up her legs. His long fingers traced the skin on the inside of her thighs.

Slowly. With agonizing purpose.

She knew he was experienced, but could not get beyond the anticipation of what was to come. He drew out every second. His fingers softly, tenderly moving toward her apex. He watched for her reaction as if she were in control. What rubbish.

She was trembling. He was very, very good at this. What did she have to offer? She had no idea how this worked or what she should do. She laid one hand over his as if to stop him. Slow him down. He looked at her in question. Poppycock. She removed her hand so he could continue. So much for slowing down...she did not want it to stop. Could she have a heart seizure? Her heart was pounding so fast and hard she felt it would pop out of her chest.

He carefully laid her stockings aside and looked up at her. "Lights on or off?" he asked. But then he voiced his desire. "Let us leave one on. I want to see you. All of you."

Hallie nodded. He pulled back the quilts and adjusted her to the center of the bed admiring her beauty and every inch of her curvaceous body. Then he put out all but one lamp, leaving shadows. He slipped under the quilts, removed his smalls in one fluid motion and settled next to her. He turned to his side and held up his head on one arm gazing down at her. Her hair spilled over the pillow like a breathtaking sunset, her green eyes wide and questioning. Her vivid red hair against the white pillow was startling.

"You truly take my breath away. You are so beautiful."

She smiled and brushed her legs over his in a tender caress.

His hand touched her cheek, and his thumb was moving over her lips in a tender gesture. Then he kissed her mouth, first on one side and then the other, his tongue licking along the seam of her mouth begging for entry. It was sensuous and luscious. Her mouth opened slightly to create a deep moan allowing him his much-desired entry. He tasted of brandy.

The kiss grew more ravenous in their mutual need. The slide of his tongue combined with his whiskered, roughened cheeks caused heat to surge through her veins. His mouth dragged down her neck, licking and kissing, his rough whiskers causing a friction that built an inferno, starting in the pit of her stomach. But just as she thought she could take no more of his succulent kisses, his lips jumped to her nipple where his tongue licked and nipped in wild abandonment. First one breast, then the other. He teased and pulled on her nipples with his lips. Her fingers found his back and stroked him with her nails.

She arched into his embrace trying to get closer, begging for more. Relief. She needed relief. There was a raw magnetism that created a desperate need, causing their bodies to grind together with recklessness. The straps to her chemise were down to her waist, exposing her breasts and stomach. It was not enough. He dragged the chemise off her body and threw it aside. His mouth followed the trail down her satin smooth stomach licking her navel on the way. Shivers ran down her body.

Sebastian made his way down to her woman's mound, parting the folds tenderly. He licked and plunged his tongue into her depths, tasting her. She tasted sweet, salty, and musky all at the same time. The thrusting of his tongue made her buck and moan at the unexpected pleasure. Her hands stroked his hair. With his persistence, a flame much like a volcano ready to erupt began to create a desperate need she hadn't known before. A silent scream threatened as tension built within her.

"Almost, Hallie. Hold on," he hoarsely whispered.

Then, without warning, his fingers pinched her nub, and series of spasms jolted her entire body. She would have screamed, but Sebastian covered her mouth with his for a scorching kiss. She gasped for a breath and wilted in his arms from exhaustion. She was winded gasping for a breath.

Her head rolled onto his shoulder, and his arms wrapped around her in a protective gesture. She felt safe and cherished. And exhausted.

"There is more?" Hallie asked as she took a long, deep breath.

He turned his face to her and flashed a smile. "Ah, yes there is much more. We could spend days, weeks, months, years and not experience it all."

"But, I am still a virgin."

He nodded his head. "Indeed."

"What about you?"

What about me?"

"What do I do to make you happy? Feel pleasure like you showed me?"

"I am happy making you experience pleasure. I do not want to rush you into…"

"But I did not take this risk coming here to go home a virgin. I want it all now."

He gave a bark of laughter. "I see," he said between chuckles. "So, you want to be totally ruined. Compromised beyond doubt?"

"Sebastian. I am already ruined and compromised. I am lying in the middle of your bed naked, for pity's sake."

He rolled over on top of her and began kissing her again. It was not long before their ardor was heated again. Hallie caressed his back with her fingers scaling his bronzed skin. Between kisses, he muttered in her ear, "It may hurt at first, and once I start…I do not know if I can stop."

"Do not ever stop," was her answer.

His fingers traced her curves, marveled at her silky, soft skin. She worked her hands over his hips and felt his bun which got an instant reaction from her touch. She felt empowered as she discovered his coarse hair on his body, so unlike hers. His back was muscled and broad. His leg insinuated between her legs separated them. His breeding organ was hard as it dragged down her stomach and found its way to her center. She felt him nudge her there between her folds. Then he was inside her just a little, as he kissed, her taking his time so that she could become accustomed to his size.

She was tight and small, he realized. He worked his way in slowly, worried that he might hurt her. She bucked trying to force him in further. He felt the barrier and took a breath before thrusting all the way.

Hallie jerked at the intrusion, which was foreign and uncomfortable. She was far too small for this, and there had been a stab of pain. She took a much-needed breath of air.

"Is that it? It hurt, and I did not like it. You are too big for me, I think." There was a moment of frozen silence.

"It will feel better, Hallie. It will never hurt like that again. I promise you."

He started to move slowly at first drawing nearly all the way out of her body and then thrusting in again gently. He was stretching her, and the discomfort went away. She began to feel pleasure. Astonishment spread over her face. Then she matched his thrusts with her own and found his rhythm. Soon he began slamming into her and she matched his thrusts. Their skin was moist from perspiration, and the sound of smacking bodies created a rhythm. There was a shocking bolt of heat that took them both higher and higher. The pounding became faster and more intense, and she cried out as he plundered her mouth with a demanding kiss.

She rocked first, her body jerking with an intense spasm. He followed after her, coming just in time to spend his seed on her belly.

She looked down at her belly in wonder. "What is that?"

"That is my seed or sperm. By pulling out when I did, we will not worry about a child before we are married." He was out of breath. It was as if he had been boxing for several hours at his club.

Hallie was gasping for breath, panting with wonder and surprise too. "That was good."

"Just good?"

"It was really wonderful." She stared at the ceiling of the canopy for a moment and then said, "So this is bed sport. I have been wasting my time waiting."

Sebastian laughed. "I am happy you waited for me. I will enjoy teaching you."

He pulled her into his arms and after turning out the lamp, drew her back against his chest. They fit perfectly, and she was content. She thought about why she waited so long to experience such joy and pleasure. Soon, she was fast asleep, and her soft breathing lulled him to sleep. He spooned against her back and tucked her against his body. They fit perfectly. He could smell the scent of roses in her hair. This felt right.

Chapter 21

Pritchard townhouse, London, April, 1870

Hallie opened the door to her bedroom to find Violet sitting on their bed, dressed and staring at her with concern. A pile of paper and pencil sat in her lap.

"Where have you been? You were gone all night, and you worried me sick. I did not know if I should sound the alarm or cover for you. I did not want to spoil one of your adventures, and on the other hand, I wondered if you might have found trouble."

Violet was in a stew. She never reprimanded her sister, but this was beyond the limit. She did not consider that she would be in a stew, too, for not reporting Hallie missing.

"I have blundered."

"Oh, is that all? That is not surprising at all. That has happened before, and you always pull through famously." Violet waited for the seemingly distraught Hallie to explain.

"No. This is worse. I had it all planned. I slipped out undetected. Accomplished my goal, but did not consider getting myself back home without detection." Hallie wandered into the room in a daze. She sat down on the bed near Violet.

"Here I am in my evening gown, trying to slip into the house in the morning like a lady of the night. I never thought about that. Of course, showing up at the Duke of Ashford's townhouse with an overnight bag with a change of morning clothes may have caused gossip too." She seemed to be almost talking to herself.

"You were at the Duke of Ashford's townhouse all night? Doing what?"

Hallie looked at her sister as if she were an idiot. "What do you think I was doing?"

Violet slapped her hand over her mouth at the same time as she shrieked. "Are you ruined?"

"Of course I am ruined. To the first degree. And Father is talking to Sebastian in the study at this very moment. He saw Sebastian escort me into the house."

Sebastian accepted the glass of lemonade from Benjamin. They sat in front of the fire in the Pritchard study.

"I must say, Your Grace, I am curious. My daughter just slipped upstairs in her evening gown of last night." Benjamin muttered between sips of his lemonade. He studied Sebastian with amusement.

A muscle twitched in Sebastian's temple. "Please call me Sebastian. We are practically family."

"Sebastian it is."

"I have compromised your daughter," Sebastian boldly said.

He did not believe in small talk under the circumstances. It seemed in bad taste. Ridiculous in point of fact. He was one to be honest, and getting straight to the point seemed the best course of action.

"Is that all?"

"Is that all? What the dickens? We will at the very least need to set a date with no haste, is that not so?" Sebastian said with some impatience.

If he were a father of a daughter, he would be outraged. Of course, they were to marry. He dreaded this meeting, however. It did not feel right to sneak Hallie to the back of the house up the servants' stairs. He boldly took her to the front door and escorted her in like it was a normal courting engagement. She had gone upstairs, and he had been captured by Benjamin standing just outside the door of the study in the hallway. He looked straight at Sebastian and waited for an explanation. Benjamin had seen the carriage pull up with the Duke of Ashford crest on the front. He watched his daughter step down in her evening gown and decided to meet them outside the study. He could not wait for the explanation.

Sebastian felt like a school boy caught stealing candy. He was certain his face had reddened in embarrassment. It had been ages since that had happened. He had dragged in a deep sigh and followed Benjamin into the study and closed the door.

"Is there need to be alarmed? Could we not plan a ball to make an announcement?" Benjamin asked.

Sebastian could read people well. And this man wanted much attention for the fact his daughter snagged a Duke, a title.

He did not want to be disappointed. He was like a little boy who was begging for a treat. He was asking Sebastian for a ball…attention, the opportunity to flaunt it like a peacock. For an American, this was something to crow about.

"Let us compromise on a family event with close personal friends and an announcement in the papers. Could you put that together in less than two weeks?" Sebastian knew it could be done. He wanted to allow Benjamin some room to play a part in this discussion. But one thing was for certain, time was of the essence. Hallie and Sebastian had a taste of their passion, and neither one wanted to wait. They were asking for trouble.

"I know my wife was counting on a ball, but I am certain I can encourage her to down size her thinking. But you also need a wedding, and I take it, that too is time sensitive."

Sebastian nodded his head. "The sooner the better."

A small gathering of one hundred people. Absurd. But then Alice Martin was compromising. If there was to be no ball for the engagement announcement, then a small gathering of one hundred family and close friends was the result of her compromise. Her task to have planned and executed in less than two weeks was barely possible. Invitations went out immediately before any plans were made for the actual event.

This would cost her husband a pretty penny. But even Benjamin was not immune to the importance of the event. Their daughter was to be a duchess. Even as a small intimate family event, it had to be done with careful thought and precision. She would need a small army of assistants to accomplish this in two weeks…and the trousseau. Hallie would need the finest dressmaker. She must find Harriet and start on this massive event.

Violet stacked her papers and gazed at her sister with interest. Finally, she gathered the nerve to ask her question of Hallie.

"Hallie, it seems you are to marry the Duke of Ashford. I have a favor to ask…it is a huge favor, but important to me."

Hallie turned to look at her sister. Violet never asked anything of her, and she was curious as to what had made Violet so serious.

"What is it Violet? I am sure I can do whatever you need… always, you can count on me."

"Well, you will be living here in England, and the rest of the Martin family will return to Ohio. I want to stay here. Maybe you could convince Mother to allow me to stay with you. She might listen, since you will be a duchess."

Hallie was surprised. She had not thought of separating from Violet until this moment. "Of course, you can stay with me. I am certain since I will be a duchess; there is much we can do that we want. Why…is there someone…"

"Oh, no. Not that, Hallie. I have been writing stories, and I want a chance to see if I can publish…but Mother would not understand. If I could stay here and have some freedom…"

"What kind of stories, Violet? I did not know you were writing."

"I do not know if I am any good…so I kept it a secret." Violet looked down at the stack of papers and gathered her thoughts. "The stories are about a courageous young woman who creates adventures." Violet looked up at her sister, who was stunned.

"Are these stories similar to my adventures, Violet?"

Violet nodded her head and shrugged her shoulders.

"I could not help myself. You present an opportunity that cannot be ignored."

"Are you changing my name, for goodness sakes?"

"Of course. I am not a total idiot. Besides, you inspire me to create more adventures using the character of my heroine, which is you. I do enhance the stories…for interest sake."

Hallie smiled. Her sister was her champion. "I would love to read your stories, Violet."

"Not yet. There is too much work before it is ready for someone to read. I am forever checking the dictionary. So far, it is just rough ideas and needs polishing."

"I think that is so exciting. I am certain you are very good, Violet. I will help you in anyway I can."

"Just staying here would help me. Under Mother's doting eye, I will never get a chance to publish. And with you almost wed, I will be the next project. I want to avoid that prospect as long as I can."

"I had not thought of that. You are correct. You will be the next project for marriage. What's her name?"

In typical Hallie manner, the subject changed, and Violet looked at her sister in confusion.

"What? Who?" Violet asked, frowning.

"The adventuress. Your heroine in your story." Hallie asked, nearly giggling in her amusement.

"Ah. Charlotte."

Hallie thought for a moment her finger tapping her chin. "I like it. It is a strong woman's name. You need that for a heroine. Certainly not a flower...."

Both girls laughed and then hugged.

"Actually, her family calls her 'Char,' but her character that finds mischief and adventure is 'Charlie."

"Oh, Violet. I do like that. A tom boy name, to be certain."

Alice swept into Harriet's parlor with paper in hand. She sat in her favorite chair next to Harriet's writing desk.

"I do not know how to keep this list under control. Benjamin said more than once that it is to be family and close friends, and only they would understand the short notice to this event. How do I distinguish close family friends? If I invite the Bickfords...how can I not include the Harrisons?"

"You do have a challenge keeping this a small gathering," Harriet said, blotting a letter she had just written. "What is your count now?"

"With the Harrisons it will be 203. I do not think Benjamin will think that I kept the gathering intimate. He did want a big event at first, of course. He is quite proud our Hallie is marrying a Duke. Of course, he is taking full credit."

"Perhaps he will be agreeable to the number."

"It is just that in such a short time frame, the small event makes more sense."

"It sounds like you have not come to terms with this as yet, my dear. Why not let my Isabella handle this. She is very good at control, which is what you need right now."

"Perhaps you are right. Maybe I am too close to this to do it any good. When could Bella come?"

"I will send word, and I am sure she can be here tomorrow or maybe even tonight since it is urgent."

Alice sighed in relief and laid the crumbled papers on Harriet's desk. Alice had had not slept since worry and stress had taken over her senses. She smiled at Harriet with gratitude.

Isabella was delighted to take on the planning, and Harriet and Alice spent the time fussing about their gowns. Two weeks flew by.

Sebastian climbed the steps to his mother's residence. He was escorting her to his marriage announcement event, hosted at the Pritchard townhouse by Benjamin Martin. He was happy the event was kept under one hundred. He hated large events. They seemed impersonal and lacked the warmth he envisioned for this event. His brothers would be there as well as his friend Garrett. He was dressed formally, as was expected for such an occasion. He wore black, with the exception of his white, starched shirt. His black cravat was tied in an elegant waterfall. His trousers were black pin-striped, which accounted for the only variation of black. As he mounted the steps, he could not ignore the carriage in front of his mother's townhouse.

It was James Corban's carriage, and suddenly all thought but his mother's welfare disappeared. As he approached the door to knock, Jackson opened it.

"Mother? Is she well?" Sebastian asked, hardly waiting for an answer as he mounted the stairs toward her rooms.

"She is in excellent hands, Your Grace," Jackson replied, although Sebastian was nearly all the way to her rooms, not hearing any reply.

Sebastian burst into his mother's bedroom. Ellen looked up from a chair where she was sitting across from James Corban. Her foot rested on a stool, with a bandage around her ankle and a bag of ice resting on top. James looked up with amusement.

"Ah, Sebastian. Look what I have done." She sighed. "I will make you late to your engagement soiree."

"I have told her she needs to keep her foot elevated, but she is stubborn," James said, closing his medical bag. "She should keep the ice on the sprain for 20 minutes. It will take down the swelling and help with the pain."

"How did this happen, Mother?" Sebastian asked with concern.

"Oh, how does anything like this happen? An accident, dear boy. I missed a step on the stairs."

"Thankfully, the last stair or she might have had a more serious tumble," James added with a wink to Sebastian. He stood and took another appraising look at his patient.

"Don't you dare tell me to be more careful, Sebastian. I did not go looking for a sprained ankle, and it is damned inconvenient. I could use a shot of brandy."

Sebastian looked at James for approval, and James nodded his head. "I actually think that is a brilliant idea, under the circumstances.

"I will see you to the door James."

"No need. I know my way out. And I think you had better scrounge up that brandy."

James passed Jackson on the stairs, who was coming to seek direction from Ellen. Sebastian leaned out the door.

"Jackson. You can see the doctor out, and bring up some brandy would you please? Her Grace has a need for it...it seems."

"You don't approve?" Ellen asked.

"I approve. I would want several if that happened to me. I am not a good patient. I must send word to let..."

"Oh, no you don't. After my brandy...you will carry me to the soiree and set me gently on a chair with a stool...and brandy nearby. I would not miss this."

"We can postpone the announcement."

"Over my dead body."

"We will see after you have had that ice on your ankle for 20 minutes."

"Oh, rot and nonsense!"

Sebastian smiled. His mother forever had spirit he admired. Did nothing get her down?

She sat a little straighter in her chair, if that were possible. Never mind the back of the chair. Her back was ram-rod straight, her chin held high and her mouth set. Stubborn.

"Did you not notice I am wearing purple? I have retired my black, and in honor of your special occasion. I now wear color," she added, with a flourish of her arm.

Sebastian laughed. "Your gown is so dark, one has to squint to catch the light just so to see any purple."

He held up his hand to ward off her protest.

"But I appreciate the gesture. You have moved on, and that makes me happy. You are the best of mothers. Father would be proud of you...as I am."

He kissed her forehead, and she covered her hand over his which he had rested on her shoulder.

"Now, let me take a look at that ankle, and we shall go from there."

Chapter 22

*T*he small quartet was tuning their instruments. People had already collected in groups to admire the flowers, the buffet, the decorations, and congratulate the lucky couple, although no announcement had been given as yet. The anticipation was flickering in the air like the candles that permeated air with the aroma of flowers. Voices rose and fell with anticipation.

Hallie made her grand appearance down the decorated stairs in a silver threaded, rose- pink damask, which glimmered in the romantic lighting. The gown swayed in rhythm with her graceful walk, shimmering. Her red hair was coiled on top of her head, giving her a regal appearance. Several curls were artistically left to drag down her long neck. Her eyes were shining with excitement. She scanned the ballroom, looking for Sebastian. There, by the punchbowl, she spotted his broad back.

He was talking to her father and Uncle Joseph. He was dressed in black, his hair slicked back formally. She liked his posture, his wide shoulders that made her feel safe, his aroma that was always true to him. Just smelling him gave her peace and comfort and yet challenged her wits. Yes, she had made a wise decision. They were well suited, and she looked forward to their life together. He respected her wishes to be independent, and for that alone, he had won her heart. She could not imagine life without him. He was now essential...needed.

She greeted some family members and sauntered up behind him ever so quietly. She boldly placed her hand on his back to capture his attention, knowing he would turn to see who it was. She readied her smile for him.

He turned, and she fought the gasp that threatened to escape her open mouth. Her eyes widened. Before she could utter a word, he put his arm around her waist and pulled her close to his body, bringing her full into the circle facing her father and uncle. She struggled to gather her wits.

"Ah, Hallie, my love. You look beautiful," he stated with confidence.

What was at work here, she wondered? She knew better than blow the cover. She took a breath of air and looked straight into his eyes.

"You're quite handsome yourself,... ah, Sebastian," she returned with more confidence than she felt. Something was afoot, and she had not been informed. This did not mean she could not play the game. Adventure was her middle name, after all. She could be patient...or maybe that part was a stretch.

"I think, gentlemen, I will ask my finance for a dance." He turned and took Hallie's hand and led her to the dance floor.

The musicians got their cue and played a waltz. Once in the center of the ballroom, away from the guests, Hallie waited a moment for others to dance and create some cover noise.

"So why the switch, Alex?" she asked in a whisper that only his ears could catch.

Alex smiled, but not too much. After all he had the role of his brother, and Sebastian did not readily smile. "You are very good at telling us apart. I thought perhaps dressed like him…"

"Oh, stop the act. You are as different as…why are you doing this? Acting the Duke, that is?"

"It was necessary, I assure you. My brother is caring for our mother, who had a fall."

Hallie gasped. Her worried eyes sought his for an explanation.

"Do not worry. She is fine. He will be here eventually with her. She would not miss this, you know. You have captured her heart. My brother did not want to alarm people and so asked me to act his part. Do the switch, so to speak." He grinned at her, a moment of true Alex before he caught himself and reverted back to his role.

"Well, you do seem to have fooled most of the guests. My father and uncle were certainly bought in to your deception."

"Admit it. You are the only one I could not fool. It is bloody boring playing the part of my brother. Staying serious and solemn is difficult for me, you know. It was my mother's idea."

"What?"

"Us doing the switch was her idea. She so hates to be the center of attention. She reminded us that it is your day, not hers. She thought it a good solution to buy time and keep the guests comfortable."

"She is quite special, I must say."

"I must agree with you on that."

He danced beautifully, just like Sebastian. She caught the admiring stares from guests and smiled her satisfaction at knowing she was part of a scheme once again. Another adventure.

"I have a favor to ask of you. I am certain Sebastian would approve and appreciate it too," she said, smiling coyly at her future brother. Her eyes sparkled with mischief.

"By all means."

"Ask my sisters to dance. They would be so pleased."

"Of course."

After their dance, Alex approached Violet.

Violet was acting the wallflower, standing behind the palms and looking at a book. Alex grinned at her. She was obviously hoping to appear invisible but was sadly failing, in his estimation. Her gown was conservative, but her curves and coloring denied her desire to be inconspicuous. Her strawberry blonde hair was pulled back for an artful arrangement in the back, but the wisps of stray curling hair surrounding her pretty face created a halo-like effect. Her lips were moving, as if saying the words aloud. She wore wire-rimmed glasses that did not distract from her beauty.

She obviously was trying to hide herself from the guests and enjoy a good book, but Alex had his marching orders. He approached her quietly so as not to startle her.

"Miss Martin."

Violet jumped even with his efforts to speak quietly. She quickly removed her glasses and slipped them, along with her book, into a pocket in her gown. He smiled at her efforts. How clever she was.

"Your Grace. I…"

"Please call me Sebastian. You are to become my sister."

She nodded. "Sebastian."

"I have come to ask you for a dance. No excuses, now." He held out his hand for hers. She took it reluctantly and was swept onto the dance floor before she could think of an objection.

Violet did not doubt her dancing ability with this partner. He was good. She took a look into his face and found him smiling at her.

"What were you reading, may I ask?"

"Oh, I am not supposed to read. It must be our secret. Besides, it was a Jane Austin book. One that requires all my attention. I should not have brought it here."

"Your secret is safe with me. I am many times bored by these events myself."

"Except for this one, of course. Your engagement is to be announced."

He laughed. "Except for this one."

"I have a favor to ask of you Your Gr…Sebastian."

"I am your servant."

"I asked Hallie this…and she was to talk to you. I only felt it fair to ask this of you personally." Her face was very serious, and Alex wondered what the favor entailed.

"You need only ask and if it is within my power to grant you your favor, of course I will do so."

"I wish to live with you and Hallie instead of going back to Ohio when my family leaves." Violet asked so quietly that Alex had to strain to hear her words. She obviously was nervous about this favor she was asking.

"Do you have a special reason for staying here in London? Do you mean to accompany us on our wedding trip?" he asked with a smile.

Violet blushed. "Oh, no. Of course not. My family will be here at least two more months. I just want to stay here and continue writing my stories."

"I see. You are a writer. Do your parents not approve?"

"Well, let us just say my mother has other recreations planned for me that do not include writing for enjoyment. My parents do not approve of my obsessive reading habit and would have me looking for a husband instead."

"What did Hallie say about your living here in London?"

"She wanted to help me with your approval."

Alex grinned. "Then you have mine too. I should love to have a sister underfoot. I am used to brothers, you know. And your reading habit is something I too enjoy…so we share that trait."

Alex suddenly wondered what he had got Sebastian into. Well, soon it will be Sebastian's problem, not his. He smiled at the thought of what he had just promised Violet. She suddenly seemed happier, as if that one issue had lightened the air she breathed. There was even more energy in her step.

He had slipped and shared his own love of reading, although he was certain Sebastian, too, loved to read. Sebastian had little time for pleasure reading.

Poor Violet.

She was not appreciated as a woman. Men had the advantage to do what they pleased, but women were frowned upon for wanting an education. It was felt that they would not be appreciated by men if they were perhaps... intelligent.

He hoped his brother would not be too much longer. People were wondering where the Dowager Duchess was and where Alex was. Two important family members were missing. He was constantly making the excuses and changing the subject. Derrick, too, was late.

Iris, dressed appropriately for her twelve years, was allowed to attend the party since her sister was to announce her engagement to a Duke. She was nervous and out of place standing by her mama, watching the dancers with awe. Her hair was braided down her back, adorned in white bows matching her white, youthful gown. Her hands were hidden in the folds of her skirt. Alex felt sympathy for her. He decided to ask for a dance. Since this was a family affair, it seemed to demand it.

He approached Iris and her mother and bowed.

"May I dance with my soon-to-be sister? He asked Alice formally.

Alice nodded and smiled at him.

"How sweet and thoughtful you are, Your Grace."

"Sebastian, please," Alex responded.

Alice nodded and nearly giggled.

He reached for Iris's hand, and she looked up into his face with...fear? "Do not fret, Poppet. I can lead very well, and you will feel like a princess."

Iris took his hand and nervously smiled. As they took the dance floor, Iris frowned and confusion clouded her face. Her eyebrows were knit together in thoughtful concentration.

"You will wait for me to grow up, Mr. Stainton. And then we shall be married. I rather fancy you."

Alex barked out a laugh. "Do you always speak your mind? No. No. I forget. You are an American and a Martin. A dangerous combination, to be certain," he said with amusement. His eyes twinkled, and he actually winked at her.

"I think we have some magic."

"You do? How do you think your sister will feel about this when she finds out her youngest sister wants to marry her fiancé?"

"Alex Stainton. Why are you playing the part of your twin?"

Alex nearly stumbled over his own feet. He was able to overcome his shock and glide Iris around a difficult step with grace. He stared at her in surprise, trying not to break character. She was looking at him intently, her large blue eyes focused on his brown ones, daring him to lie to her.

"Why Iris Martin. You can tell us apart."

"Don't be ridiculous. Why the switch?" She was suddenly looking much older than twelve, and he was becoming uncomfortable. No one…except for his mother and now Hallie… could tell them apart. What did this mean, he wondred? "I am waiting," she said with confidence.

"All right…so you can tell us apart. You must keep the secret. It is for a good cause."

"Tell me the cause. I already told you that I can keep a secret. You can trust me. After all, I am your destined future wife."

He wanted to laugh, but seemed somehow too serious to laugh at, and he actually thought she might put a spell on him… ridiculous, but she was a little scary to his mind.

"Well, my mother had an unfortunate accident and sprained her ankle, and my brother had to wait for the physician to give her permission to come. My brother wanted me to cover so that the guests were comfortable. Does that make sense?"

Iris nodded her head. "I am not a complete idiot."

"Well, of course not. However, we have quite an age gap. I do not see this vision of yours happening. Flattered though I am…it just is not feasible. I am old enough to be your father, Poppet."

"Nonsense. I am a romantic Mr. Stainton."

"Obviously."

"And I know my mind. I am determined. Of course, my mother would not be happy I want to marry an actor…"

"What's wrong with an actor? I am good, you know."

"Oh, I know. It is my mother we are talking about."

"Why are we even talking about this? It is all a fabrication of your vivid imagination, Poppet."

"Just keep believing that Mr. Stainton. I am not worried. If it is meant to be, it will be."

When Alex delivered Iris back to her mother, he heaved a sigh of relief. She was only twelve he thought again. Blast it all. Well, he did have fans from the theatre he dealt with, but this was not quite the same and reeked of disaster…she was not out of the school room. He could see the potential she had; her budding beauty, but she was a child. Alex needed to forget this for now or it would drive him crazy.

After dancing with the delightful Poppy, he resumed his position beside Hallie and smiled as he watched the dancers.

"I have accomplished my task with great enjoyment, I might add," he said, staring into the crowd whirling by him.

Hallie smiled. "I do appreciate your efforts. When will you make the switch, and how will you accomplish the feat?" She, too, stared into the swirling, colorful figures dancing by them with amusement. Oh, how she loved even the smallest adventure.

A little deceit, secrecy, and opportunity to act a part. Great fun, she thought.

"I will get a message from my brother to disappear, and then I will find a room to change into the colorful actor that I am. It should not be too much longer. In the meantime, shall we dance again to appease the guests?" he asked.

They took the floor, making a handsome couple, with admirers watching on. Hallie smiled up at the face of her future brother-in-law. His dimples were showing, his smile displaying perfect white teeth.

"You are a fine actor, Alex."

Alex laughed. "I will take this opportunity to thank you Hallie. You have made my twin happy. He laughs and actually seems to enjoy himself more. You have done that…sister to be."

A footman caught Alex's eye, as he held a silver tray with a message.

"Ah. I see I have a message."

He danced Hallie to the side of the room where the footman waited. Still holding her hand in his, he scooped the message from the tray and nodded to the footman. He opened the missive and read its contents, with Hallie looking over his shoulder.

I am on my way with Mother. Have a chair and stool ready for her. I will bring her through the servants' entrance. She wants to avoid attention to her condition.

"I will leave to find a room to change, and you may arrange for the chair and stool in a prominent position for my mother to see all the drama." He disappeared with a simple smile before Hallie could say another word, but she went to find her aunt to arrange for the chair for the Dowager Duchess.

After the chair was placed in a position of honor, she walked over to the doors leading to the balcony for a breath of air. There were couples walking the garden outside. Lanterns cast a romantic glow on them. Hallie looked across the room and saw the Dowager Duchess in the chair, surrounded by well-wishers. She smiled. Sebastian took good care of his family. He was protective.

She suddenly smelled spices and sandalwood. It created goose bumps. He was here and close. Before she turned from the balcony doors, an arm slipped around her waist and dragged her close to a solid hard body.

"Ah. Sebastian," she whispered under her breath.

"You missed me?" He breathed close to her ear.

She nodded her head and gazed into his dark eyes with longing. "I missed you, although your brother did a fine job with the switch. No one is the wiser."

Sebastian smiled as he grazed his lips over her cheek. "I was counting on him."

He did not care that kissing her in public was bad form. The only problem was it did not satisfy his need of her. His lust of her. He gazed at her with admiration. How did she do it? He never felt anything like this for another woman. How could one woman have it all? She was smart, beautiful, rebellious, and caring about her family. The family. He was of the same mind.

She was grinning at him now.

"What are you thinking, Your Grace? There are wheels turning as if…"

"The wheels turning are thoughts about you and what I would do to you if we were alone."

"Ah. Perhaps we can rendezvous later," she whispered in a throaty voice that nearly sent him over the edge.

"You are quite naughty, Red."

It seemed to take nearly nothing to…like her throaty whisper to overcome him with lust and a lack of focus. He took a deep breath and tried to control the urge to kiss her senseless. All the control that he had perfected, requisite for titles, was worthless when she set her wiles to work on him.

Sebastian heard a commotion at the entrance to the ballroom and glanced up to see Garrett, Derrick, and Alex laughing and sharing stories. They were offered champagne, and each took a glass and saluted him from across the room. Sebastian tapped his finger to his forehead in his own well-known salute and smiled.

Alex had changed his clothing. As Sebastian, he had worn black, as his brother had instructed him to do. But now, he wore a pale gray frockcoat with a slim fit, accentuating his fine, tall frame, with pin-striped trousers in darker grays. The frockcoat was the latest style, falling to mid-thigh. His cravat was striking in white. His hair was no longer slicked back as Sebastian, but in a casual, combed style that was more boyish and artistic, as Alex liked to say.

Garrett was a strong contrast to his friends, who all resembled each other in their dark good looks. Garrett was blond, with blue eyes, a stark indication that he was a friend, and not one of the brothers. His quick smile, tall frame, and close proximity, however, reinforced the fraternity.

Derrick was dressed more formally than his usual street clothing. He made an effort to look the gentleman with his dark frockcoat and gray waistcoat. There was no taming his wild hair, which seemed to have missed a combing. Most women found him attractive with his youthful appearance.

The trio made their way to his side. Hallie smiled her greeting as they approached. Young single and married women never failed to admire the four handsome men. Women's eyes followed these attractive well-dressed men, who seemed oblivious to their attraction.

"I am so happy that you were able to join us, brother. I have made a great many ducal decisions on your behalf that I expect your thanks for...," Alex announced with some amusement.

That did create a frown of concern from Sebastian. "Do tell what you have done, Alexander."

"For one, I have agreed to allow your beautiful sister in law to be to live with you." He grinned showing perfect white teeth and much admired dimples. "Violet was ever so persuasive that I had to give in to her very sweet request."

"I see. That should be no problem. Am I right Hallie?" Sebastian looked over to Hallie to see if he could read her reaction to this news.

Hallie nodded. "I was going to ask you..."

"Not a problem. It seems Alexander has taken care of ducal business all on his own and with confidence."

Derrick grinned at his brothers. Garrett took a gulp of his champagne and watched with interest. Garrett had always been a vital part of these three brothers' lives and considered himself part of their family. He had been in short pants with them, fighting battles by their sides, and slapping backs when there were occasions to be celebrated. He was one of the four. They had their first bloody noses together, their first sexual experiences with women, and their first fist fights, not to mention the bonding that tied them together. They supported one another without question and shared the same principals in life. There was honor and trust they all understood and, of course, loyalty.

Garrett looked at Hallie with appreciation. "You are to be congratulated, Miss Martin. Sebastian was a sworn bachelor, and he seems quite happy to have won you as his duchess. Although, I must say he seems a bit tame for you…er…boring and all that." He smiled, holding back a laugh.

Hallie looked at Garrett with some surprise and amusement. "Why Viscount Montjoy. For shame. His Grace has promised me adventure." She looked coyly at Sebastian, who raised an eyebrow at that.

"Adventure is it?" He laughed. "I can give you adventure, you little minx."

The men raised their champagne glasses in a silent toast.

"None of that yet," Benjamin Martin proclaimed as he approached the group. "I have been looking for you, Your Grace. We are ready to make the announcement, if that is to your liking." Benjamin looked for approval from Sebastian.

"Of course…and no 'Your Grace' between us now that we are to be relatives," Sebastian said, smiling.

Benjamin Martin was very happy tonight. His daughter Hyacinth was to marry a title and a Duke at that. He wanted this and felt somewhat responsible, although there was not much scheming on his part. But it seemed to be a love match, which pleased him even more. This visit to London had come to be successful for his family after all.

Benjamin stood in front of the small musical ensemble and cleared his throat. Several people clinked their glasses. Another said, "Here, here..."

Benjamin gave a gracious speech that brought tears to Hallie's eyes. She stood beside Sebastian as her father told the audience of close friends and family about his love for his bou quet and his wife and then how proud he was tonight. There was more, but Hallie found herself woolgathering and missed the rest. Her eyes caught Sebastian's, and he smiled as if he read her thoughts.

The guests could not help but see the attraction between Hallie and Sebastian. There was magic in their gazes and love in their hearts for each other. Everyone raised their glasses in a universal toast.

Sebastian leaned down to whisper in Hallie's ear. "Meet me in the garden in half an hour for a little adventure."

Hallie laughed. "Of course, Your Grace. Adventure is my middle name. Would this adventure have anything to do with passion?"

"It has everything to do with passion." Sebastian had hunger blazing in his eyes as he intently stared at her with longing.

"There's a gazebo just in back of the roses...it is said to be very private," she uttered in a deep whisper for his ears only. "It is said to be romantic."

"Indeed."

She could feel the heat radiating from his body. The night was cool, but no doubt she would not feel the cold once outside. She craved his touch. It had been too long since she felt his bare skin against hers. It had been miserable during the sleepless nights where she relived their union, and her mind dwelled on the passion that made her body quake with unspent sexual energy. Would it always be like this between them?

His hand found hers between the folds of her gown and he squeezed her gloved fingers. There was strength in his grasp, and she felt the affection surrounding his embrace of her hand in such an innocent action. It was a promise of sorts, and she sighed a soft smile of satisfaction.

Chapter 23

*H*allie stood in the shadows cast by the full moon and the lanterns. Her silver threaded silk gown glowed. The night air was brisk, but she dared not have gotten her wrap for fear of getting trapped by well-wishers.

She heard his steady footsteps coming her way. They were deliberate. Not a casual stroll in the garden. She knew the character of his stride. Then she smelled his beloved scent.

"Sebastian."

He stepped up onto the gazebo floor and took her into his strong arms in a much-needed embrace. It was warm and protective. She never wanted him to stop holding her. She felt safe and loved. Protected.

"You must be cold. No wrap...and this gown. Not much warmth, Love." He started to remove his coat when she shook her head in denial.

"All I need are your arms around me."

He smiled a wolfish grin. "I wish we were not among one hundred guests in the chilly night air."

He cradled the back of her head with his right hand and gently tipped her chin up with his left hand and then slowly bent down and brushed his lips over hers.

She closed her eyes and breathed in his scent. So familiar, so perfect.

"Sebastian. You are such a gentleman. You have honor, as you English like to admit."

She looked into his warm eyes. His hair was slicked back. So formal. He was perfectly groomed. Her hand reached up and grabbed a lock of his hair and pulled it forward until in hung down his forehead. She smiled, satisfied. That lock hanging on his forehead made him look younger, boyish…and rakish. Not so perfect.

He looked at her with confusion. One eyebrow quirked up.

"I want to muss you. Create some imperfection. I want you skin to skin. But that is not ladylike, is it? You challenge me to break your gentleman's mold."

His eyes widened just a moment at the shock of her words. But then, why be surprised by anything she did? She was American, and that said it all, did it not? Not to mention, Martins had their own code of behavior.

"Did I succeed in shocking you, my almost husband?"

Now he laughed. Really laughed. She waited. She was patient, and she did want his reaction.

"You want me to take you here and now? I have grown accustomed to your brazen ways, Red. Are you not satisfied that I have already taken your virginity? That hardly makes me a gentleman. We are to be married in several weeks. Is that not to your liking?"

"You did not 'take' my virginity. I threw it in your face. You would have been a villain to deny me," she shot back with a breathy voice. "And yes, I am happy to marry you soon, although it is not soon enough," she argued, her chin coming up a notch.

"You are all fire and attitude. Just the way I like you. You are very tempting, you minx."

"Are you always so under control? Do you not feel the urge to just do what comes naturally...just once? Can I not rattle your cool demeanor?" She set her hands on his chest and looked into his eyes with questions and determination. Her eyes scanned his face for any indication of his passion showing through.

He drew her against his hard body dislodging her hands. She draped her arms over his shoulders with a wry smile. She felt his hard body and the warmth of his body heat. He was all steel and strength. Not a soft part of him anywhere.

"Ahh. There it is. That's what I want, Sebastian."

"I am not a stranger to debauchery. You are a spunky handful." His lips found hers and their passion turned fierce with need. Her knees buckled, but he held firm against his body not allowing her to slip from his grasp.

Tongues dueled and arms wrapped tightly around each other, incapable of getting any closer. He traced his lips from her mouth to her ear and nibbled on her lobe, licking where his teeth had been.

Her sex clenched. She could feel his hard erection against her body and his warmth ignited a fire deep in her soul. Her breath hitched. She wanted to feel his bare skin. The scorching heat of their bodies nearly demanded she remove clothing. Hunger. Hot waves of pleasure.

Sebastian pulled away with a tortured sigh. His fingers dug into her shoulders as he gave her a measured glance.

"You will be the end of me yet. If not for a room full of guests...I would..."

Her lips twitched with humor. "I guess I will have to be satisfied with waiting for our wedding. A governess' words seem to haunt me. When I was very young, she told me that passion was a sin. Ladies hide their emotions. Of course, I did not listen to her. I am somewhat of a rebel, as you well know." Her hands caressed his chest as she gazed into his eyes, darkened with desire.

"She was an idiot. I hope your father fired her."

"Wait until you have a daughter and see how protective you become, "she whispered under her breath.

He gave a seductive chuckle. "Yes. I am certain I will have a few challenges married to you, Red. Convention will fly out the window, and we will create our own."

"I think it strange that here I am ready to marry a Duke... determined all my life to avoid marriage and find adventure. But I would have it no other way. You have promised me everything I want in life. I am truly happy."

He bent over her and placed a soft gentle kiss on her lips. "We are perfectly suited. I will find my life interesting and rich with you in it, I dare say. Adventure here we come."

And then he wrapped his arms around her and kissed her with passion. Yes, passion.

Epilogue

*T*he church was crowded beyond capacity. There were people lining the exterior yard eager for a peek of the bride and groom. A carriage, baring the crest of the Duke of Ashford, stood awaiting the newly married couple. It was decorated with flowers and ribbons, with four matched horses prancing in place. A footman stood awaiting the handsome couple. Four little girls with brightly colored gowns and straw bonnets waited at the bottom of the steps holding baskets filled with rose petals, waiting for the opportunity to throw them in the path of the bride and groom. Anticipation and excitement stirred the air.

Inside, the guests were quiet as they listened to the vows. Alexander stood beside his brother as witness. The bride wore a pale honey colored silk gown covered with seed pearls. Her veil was the finest lace. Violet stood witness beside the bride. The vows were delivered with a solemn sincerity.

Hallie paused on the "obey her husband" line until she saw a twitch of the lips on Sebastian's face. And then it was time to kiss the bride. He eased the veil up over her head and smiled at the beautiful face that was now his. He bent his head down to hers and brushed a soft kiss on her lips. The couple turned and smiled at their guests.

Sebastian took Hallie's hand and marched her proudly down the aisle as guests stood and offered congratulations. The crowded church guests began to exit, following the bride and groom, excitement in their voices as they all started to discuss the service.

Sebastian and Hallie descended the stairs as rose petals flew in their path. Hallie smiled at the little flower girls, and the crowd outside the church cheered their approval. The happy couple stood a moment in place nodding at their well-wishers and waving their greetings.

Then, suddenly, Sebastian picked up his surprised bride into his arms and rushed through the crowd.

A plain black unmarked coach pulled in front of the church, and a footman opened the door. Sebastian scooted in with his bride on his lap, and the coach took off at a break-neck speed. The crowd gasped. Alice and Harriet both screeched. The family looked at one another for explanation. There was confusion and chaos.

Alex ran through the confused and alarmed crowd to center himself in front of them. He held up his hands to beg attention and waited. It was a drama, after all. He was in his element. Even his mother looked alarmed. When the crowd grew quiet, he spoke to them in his most theatrical voice.

"Please do not be alarmed. You did just witness a beautiful wedding. The bride, my new sister, begged her groom for adventure and so he has granted her wish." Alex laughed. The guests looked at one another with frowns and questions. Everyone began to murmer at once.

"There is still a wedding breakfast hosted by the Martins, and we all shall gather there for a wonderful feast and to toast the bride and groom." Alex took a long theatrical breath and continued. "The bride and groom are off to visit foreign lands and seek…adventure. It is their happy ending and rest assured that they are, indeed, happy."

The crowd dispersed, everyone talking as they went. The wedding breakfast was the event of the season. There was much to discuss. It was not every day that the bride and groom missed their own wedding celebration. But they all knew that the bride and groom were, indeed, celebrating in their own way.

Read a passage from
Marriage by Proxy
By Cathy Duke

On sale now on Amazon
in Kindle and paper back format

A peek at "Marriage by Proxy"

Brightmore Manor, 1830

*B*efore putting out the candles in his bedroom, he would put on his silk robe and open the adjourning door to his wife's bedroom and watch her sleep for a moment. He loved to see her with her cloud of silky hair billowing out around her peaceful face. With the shadows of light her hair appeared white, much like he imagined an angel's might be. She didn't braid it like so many women did at night, and he liked it free and tussled. He wanted to run his hands through her lovely hair and feel the texture, but soon enough he would. She preferred sleeping on her side with one hand tucked beneath her chin. Her mouth would be slightly open with just a breath of air coming out. The first time he came into her room to check on her seemed like what you might and should do with a child just to make certain they were all right. But then he discovered he liked to gaze on her and he would imagine holding her in her sleep. Invariably his thoughts would cause problems for him in trying to sleep for himself later when he went to bed. But he would do it again and again without thought of that. It was such a pleasant and magical sight. It felt right having her in this room.

Tonight he had read in bed until he couldn't focus anymore and got up to check on his wife as usual. He opened the door and as the light from his room spilled into her darkened room he noticed her bed was empty, the covers pulled back as if she had been in bed. His eyes scanned the room looking for some sign of her, but she was not there. He looked to the side table by the bed and noticed the candle was gone. Where had she gone at this hour? Was something wrong?

Perhaps she went to the kitchen for something...or maybe the library for a book was more likely. He closed her door and took a candle from his room to start down the stairs in search of her. He passed the stern faced portraits of his ancestors which was a reminder to him how opposite he found himself to them and their beliefs. He sometimes actually felt their disapproval of him. He liked to smile and shake his head in denial of any harm they could do him now.

The library door was ajar and light spilled out. He didn't want to startle her so he walked softly through the doorway and looked around the room until he found what he sought. His mouth dropped open in surprise...and perhaps shock too.

Amy was draped across a chair facing his desk. She was unconscious...perhaps asleep, but better inspection gained him another suspicion. One of his crystal glasses lay on the floor, her finger tips stretched just above the glass as if the glass had rolled from her fingers. Her head lay against the back of the chair, her hair in disarray with a lock landing dead center down the front of her face. Her mouth was slightly open in a sensual pose that was kissable. But it was the book opened on her lap that drew his attention. It was that scandalous little book he had fun with as a young boy. He broke into a smile as he noted the page she had open. The little minx. She was foxed.

Arden took a quick glance at his decanter and saw that she must have had enough to fox her senseless. He carefully removed the book from her lap and shook his head in memory. He noted the page that had caught her interest. He chuckled to himself. That book had been adventurous to Bradley and himself. Not only had they studied the illustrations, but had actually taken it to a brothel and challenged some of the prostitutes to matching some of the positions with some live entertainment. He set the book back in its place and glazed at his wife. She looked properly mussed like she had been well loved. Quite arousing to say the least. At this moment he regretted his promise of a wedding and more importantly waiting to sate his sexual appetite.

He picked up the crystal glass and returned it to the tray that held the decanter of his best brandy and laughed to himself. This wife was quite the amusement. It would not be boring with her in his life. How beautiful she was. How unpretentious. That in itself made her appealing to him.

He scooped her up against his chest and threw her easily over his shoulder. He blew out the candles and picked up his and made his way up the stairs. She was light even when totally unconscious. He began to wonder what she thought of the little book. If perhaps it was shocking to her or interesting. That was something to think about. He had a broad smile on his face as he made his way to her room. Shaking his head and chuckling the entire way, he had not had anything that tempted him to laugh outright in quite some time. He lowered her to the bed and removed her silk wrap. He tucked her feet into the covers and drew the quilts up to her chin. He leaned down and kissed her sweet mouth ever so softly. Ah, she was such a seductive morsel. It was taxing on his control that was certain.

"Sleep well, my love," he whispered. Before turning to leave, he ran his fingers though her thick silky angel hair and drew it away from her face. She smelled of lavender and soap. He inhaled the scent that was Amy. Yes she would do, perfectly.

Coming Soon
Violet's story
The Flower of Modesty
Book two of the bouquet series

Cathy Duke

Cathy lives in Southern California with her husband and five rescued cats. Her daughter and son have left the nest leaving Cathy to her writing. She received her BA in Theatre and her MA in Film. For 25 years she was the CEO and founder of the independent San Diego Film Commission and wrote a monthly column for the San Diego Business Journal. In retirement, she loves writing, dating her husband of 47 years, spending time with her five grandchildren, and spoiling her fur babies.

Made in the USA
San Bernardino, CA
12 June 2018